
★

She was not aware of the overtaking car until it was level with her and she heard the roar of its engine. She glanced to her right in surprise, which turned quickly to horror as she realized that the car was not simply overtaking but was cutting in on her and forcing her over to the pavement on her near side and toward the wall and the sheer drop beyond. A glancing sideways blow on the off-side wing was enough. The smaller car mounted the pavement, demolished a section of wall and somersaulted into the park below. Kate heard her own despairing scream with a sort of detachment as she realized that she was about to die.

★

"Alex and Kate...establish themselves as a pair readers will root for and hope to see again."
—*Publishers Weekly*

PATRICIA HALL

THE POISON POOL

WORLDWIDE.

TORONTO • NEW YORK • LONDON
AMSTERDAM • PARIS • SYDNEY • HAMBURG
STOCKHOLM • ATHENS • TOKYO • MILAN
MADRID • WARSAW • BUDAPEST • AUCKLAND

THE POISON POOL

A Worldwide Mystery/April 1996

First published by St. Martin's Press, Incorporated.

ISBN 0-373-26198-5

Printed in U.S.A.

THE
POISON
POOL

ONE

KATE WESTON SLAMMED her filing cabinet drawer shut with more force than she intended and half turned as Ada Turner gave an audible start.

'It's not my fault I lost it,' the elderly woman sitting in the office's single dilapidated visitor's chair said testily. 'I were that flustered after last night. Gave me a turn, it did, finding Tom dead like that.'

Kate sighed. She knew Ada was not really there to discuss her mislaid electricity bill at all. She had something else entirely on her mind, and this time something much grimmer. Not for the first time, Kate decided that the advice centre paid her as much to listen as to advise.

'So what time did all this happen, Ada?' she asked, trying to ignore the sparkle the question brought to the old woman's creased features. Ada Turner licked her dry lips eagerly and settled herself more comfortably into the hand-me-down easy chair the centre provided for its clients.

'It were gone half past ten,' Ada said happily, sure at last that she had an attentive audience. 'Only just gone, mind. I came out to give Sandy his run just after t'news on ITV. Right after, mind, I told that inspector, because I were putting my coat on while they were reading t'football results. I don't teck much notice of football, myself, though our Fred were keen when he were alive.' She stopped for a moment, her pale watery eyes vacant as she remembered long dead Fred.

'And Sandy found the body?' Kate prompted her, thinking that if Ada spun out her tale too long she would not be free in time to meet Sam from school and they would miss the chance to go into the town centre to buy his new football boots.

'Aye, it were t'dog that found him,' Ada said. 'I'm not right keen to go up that ginnel at the back o't'flats at night, am I? There's no street lights up there, you know. But Sandy ran up and started barking. And then t'other dog—Tom Carter's dog—started up, too, and they both came running back down together, carrying on like nobody's business. You've never heard such a racket.'

'So you went up to have a look?'

'Aye, well, not straight away, but I thought it were right peculiar for Tom's terrier to be running around with his lead dangling like that. Tom were always so careful with that dog. Thought the sun shone out of its backside, he did. So I caught hold of it, and put my Sandy on his lead too, and I went up slowly with both of them. Pitch dark, it were. Black as t'ace o' spades. If t'dogs hadn't started snuffling about and whining I'd have fallen clean over him.'

Ada stopped for a moment and opened her capacious and battered brown handbag and took out a paper tissue. She blew her nose with dramatic relish and half rose to put the tissue in Kate's waste-paper basket before settling herself even more comfortably in her chair.

'Perhaps they'll listen to me now,' she said with a touch of asperity in her voice. 'I've always said that ginnel weren't safe at night. Petition after petition we've had asking for a street light at t'top. You know that,' she concluded accusingly, giving Kate a slightly bleary glare, as if holding her personally responsible for all the short-comings of the local council.

'Yes, well, I expect they'll do something about it now,' Kate said placatingly. She was used to being blamed for all the short-comings of all the various bureaucracies which controlled and circumscribed lives like Ada's.

'Closing t'stable door, as per usual,' Ada snapped. 'Any road, it won't help poor old Tom, will it? It's too late for him.'

Kate nodded sympathetically. Ada, she knew, had known the dead man since they had gone to elementary school together in a building which stood, abandoned and boarded up, at the bottom of the bleak modern estate where they had both found themselves in old age, waiting unsentimentally, as was the local custom, for an end which had come unexpectedly brutally for Tom.

'Aye, well, it gave me a turn, I can tell you, dogs or no dogs,' Ada went on. 'I could feel t'blood, all sticky on his head. So I didn't stop. The murderer could have been lurking up there in t'dark, couldn't he? So I nipped round to old Mr Streeter's on t'corner, and got him to come up with me then and have a good look at Tom with his torch. But it were too late, of course. He'd gone, had Tom. Not a spark o' life in him. Snuffed out by some little hooligan, I shouldn't wonder. They should hang them, I've always said so. Poor old bugger, out for a walk with his dog. You're not safe anywhere these days.'

'Have the police finished with you now, then?' Kate asked, knowing that Ada had spent most of the morning down at the central police headquarters making a statement. 'You won't have to go down to town again?' Most of the elderly people on the Highcliffe estate disliked the fifteen-minute downhill bus ride into the town centre.

'Aye, I've told them all I can. It's up to them now, isn't it? Though I doubt they'll catch anyone. They never do. We could all be murdered in our beds for all the police care these days, swanning around in their flash cars with orange stripes playing at Husky and Starch. You got a better service from t'bobbies when they came around on bikes and gave the kids a cuff on t'earhole if they were cheeky. That soon sorted t'lads out. They get away with murder these days.'

'Yes, well, I hope they don't in this case,' Kate said drily. She suspected the irony would be lost on Ada. 'Anyway, I'm glad you've got it all sorted out down there. If I were you, I'd get home now and have a nice cup of tea. You must be exhausted after all the excitement. It must have been a dreadful experience for you.' Kate hated the patronizing note which crept into her voice but she guessed that Ada had been patronized for so long and so consistently over a lifetime that she would no more notice it now than she had ever resented it. Kate had learned from experience that Ada's generation survived on a humorous stoicism. They left defiance to younger generations.

'Aye, well, you don't expect your neighbours to be murdered, do you?' Ada said more tremulously now, almost as if the shock of the night's events had only just reached her. She drew her thin coat around herself protectively and shivered. She was dressed in several layers of woollen garments and had a knitted hat of a nondescript brown colour pulled down over her ears, leaving only a few wisps of straggling grey hair to hang over her coat collar. She appeared to jerk herself back with difficulty again from her own bleak thoughts and looked around Kate's cluttered office vaguely for a moment as though unsure of where she was.

'Do you think it's one of them psychopaths?' she asked.

'Whoever it was, I'm sure the police will catch him very quickly,' Kate reassured her, coming round the desk and picking up her coat from the hook on the back of the office door. 'I really do have to go now, because I promised I'd meet my little boy after school and take him shopping,' she said, struggling into the blue anorak in the confined space. Ada pulled herself to her feet, lips pursed.

'Lads,' she said darkly. 'You want to be thankful he's still little, love. They're nobbut trouble later.'

'Pop in again, Ada, if the electricity board contact you,' Kate said, harking back to the reason why Ada had ostensibly come into the advice centre to see her an hour ago. 'I'll have a word with them if you want me to. The bill seems excessive to me.'

She ushered Mrs Turner out of the room into the equally cluttered outer office where the centre's manager, Derek Stevenson, was talking to a tall, balding stranger, with a thin face and sharp grey eyes which flicked her up and down with unnerving swiftness in the time it took to close the door of her office behind her. Derek looked up briefly as she passed.

'We've hit the headlines at last,' he said. 'This is Gordon Rangely from the *Echo*. Looking for background about the murder.' There was nothing anyone could have taken offence to in what Stevenson said, but his guest picked up the hint of a sneer in Stevenson's tone and flushed slightly. Rangely turned to Kate with a half smile of inquiry, though the eyes, behind thick glasses, were calculatingly neutral.

'Did you know this old boy as well?'

'Not really,' Kate said. She glanced at Ada Turner who had stopped and half turned in the doorway, her eyes full of eagerness and curiosity again.

'Mrs Turner here knew him, though,' Kate said, wondering whether she was doing the reporter or Ada the greater favour in making the introduction.

'Did you, love?' Rangely asked. 'An old friend, was he?'

Just for a moment Kate thought that Ada Turner looked slightly skittish at the question, before she remembered the solemnity that her acquaintance with Tom Carter now required.

'Aye,' she said. 'I knew him. I've known him since he were a lad.' Rangely pushed in front of Kate and put his arm around the old woman.

'Come and tell me all about it, then,' he said. 'Perhaps we could have a nice cup of tea . . .'

As soon as the two of them had gone, Derek Stevenson laughed, the bitter laugh that Kate had still not got used to after working with him for more than two years.

'She'll keep herself in cups of tea and buttered teacakes for weeks on the strength of this,' he said.

'She's lonely,' Kate said quietly.

'Aren't we all, love?' Derek turned back to the display of advice leaflets he had been rearranging. 'Are you off, then?'

'Yes, I told you I needed to be away early this afternoon to take Sam into town.' There was no particular reason why she had to justify her departure to Derek. Her contract with the centre allowed some flexibility over hours, and she more than made up for time off during the day by working evening sessions, but as usual Derek Stevenson made her feel as though she was in the wrong.

'Yes, well, I'll just get on with the bloody paperwork, then,' he said. 'I can do without murders up the back alleys, personally. They get in the way of the smooth running of this great enterprise. If you want to give me a hand later I'll be here till late ...'

'See you tomorrow,' Kate said flatly, and went out into the narrow tarmacked yard where her elderly Citroën CV4 was parked. But even as she hunted in her handbag for her keys, she became aware of two new visitors coming in through the double gates. Alex Sinclair was the detective-inspector who dealt with most of the serious crime which cropped up on the Highcliffe estate. She knew him well, as their paths crossed professionally from time to time. Her clients were also occasionally and generally unhappily his. Unusually, he was arriving at the centre on foot, and accompanied by another plain clothes officer she did not recognize.

'Kate', he called across the yard, raising an arm as an indication that she should not drive off. Kate sighed. Life was conspiring against her this afternoon, she thought, as she dropped her handbag on to the front seat and turned to greet the two approaching policemen. Normally she would have been happy enough to spend time talking to Alex Sinclair: she liked the man. In fact, she sometimes thought that perhaps she liked him with rather greater warmth than was strictly professional. But she shied away from analyzing that unwelcome thought.

'Go ahead, and talk to Stevenson,' Sinclair said to his companion and came across the yard to Kate alone. He smiled slightly. He was about her own age, and not much taller than she was, a broad, stocky figure in plain clothes and a dark mac, in spite of the warmth of the day. His unusually dark curly hair and blue eyes, which Kate occasionally admitted to herself she found attractive, were inherited from a Scottish father, although he had been born and bred a couple of miles from where they stood, in one of the terraced streets at the Victorian heart of the town. Acres of those streets had been demolished and their communities 'decanted' into the brick and concrete estate where Kate now worked and lived.

'Just formalities,' he said. 'We're talking to anyone who might have known Tom Carter.'

'I've been trying to think,' Kate said. 'I don't believe I've ever met him, although we see a lot of the old folk in here. They're always getting into a panic about their poll tax, or their electricity bills, or health problems. But I really can't recall Tom Carter. Perhaps Derek knows him.'

'Yes, well, perhaps he does. Sergeant Wilson can ask, anyway. We need to know about his background, whether he had any enemies.' Sinclair stood for a moment with his arm on the roof of her little car, as if reluctant to let her go. She hesitated, her hands in the pockets of her jacket and the fresh wind blowing her brown hair away from her face and giving it a healthy glow. She was, Sinclair thought, the picture of clean-scrubbed do-gooding womanhood and attractive with it in spite of the faint lines around her good-humoured eyes and the sadness which occasionally shadowed them.

'Surely it was a random attack, wasn't it?' she asked, surprised at the idea of the murdered man having had enemies.

'Oh, I expect so, these things usually are,' he said. 'Random, and mindless and messy. There'll no doubt be some young yobbo at the end of the day just waiting for us to pick him up.'

'Was he robbed?'

'Yes, his wallet was missing, although his wife says there wasn't much in it. Today's pension day, so not more than a couple of quid, she thinks.'

'Is she all right? Has she got someone with her?'

'There's a daughter lives locally, and neighbours have been in and out. I don't think she needs your ministrations,' Sinclair said.

Kate looked at him sharply. He was a man she respected as well as liked, and today he looked tired, with signs of tension around the eyes and mouth which were not usually there.

'What a waste,' she said.

'Oh, come on, Kate,' Sinclair said, shrugging irritably. 'We've both known worse. He was an old man.' Kate looked away, shocked. 'We'll catch the little bastard who did it and put him away for twenty years, and that might be even more of a waste. You know that.'

'You sound as if you've had a bad day,' she said.

'And a bad night,' he said. 'And now I'd better go through the usual procedures. You're certain you didn't know Tom Carter, are you?'

'Quite certain, Inspector,' she said, matching his own sudden formality.

At that moment she was aware that they were no longer alone. Her son Sam had come up quietly behind them and was standing silently watching on the other side of the car. Her heart leapt, as it always did when she saw her only child unexpectedly, and she took in his unbuttoned anorak, his unfastened school-bag and his stormy expression at a glance.

'Mum! You said you'd meet me, Mum,' the boy said angrily. 'We'll be too late now.'

'I'm sorry, Sam, it was my fault, I kept your mother talking,' Sinclair said quickly. The boy looked at him coldly for a moment and then his curiosity got the better of him.

'Have you caught the murderer yet?' he asked.

'Not yet,' the policeman said. 'But I don't think it will take long.'

'Did he get shot?' Sam asked. Sinclair looked quickly at Kate, a question in his eyes. She shook her head imperceptibly.

'No,' she said to Sam. 'Mr Carter wasn't shot. Come on now, if we don't get down to town the shops really will be closed.' She hustled Sam into the back seat of the car and got in herself, opening the window.

'If there's anything else I can do,' she said. Inspector Sinclair looked at her for a moment and then nodded.

'I'll be in touch,' he said, and watched thoughtfully as Kate Weston manoeuvred out of the centre's narrow gateway into the steep main road which led to the town centre.

'Mum, why do you help the pigs?' Sam said suddenly as she drove off. The question shook Kate and her lips tightened.

'Who taught you to call the police that?' she asked sharply. There was no reply from the back seat.

'Come on,' she said more angrily.

'It's what everyone calls them at school,' the boy said eventually, and she caught his sullen expression in her rearview mirror.

'Everyone?' she persisted.

'Well, nearly everyone.'

Kate sighed. She was sure that Sam was telling the truth but that made the answer no more palatable.

'Where do you think we'd be without the police?' she asked wearily. She knew from experience that her values, at least in the short term, were no match for the street wisdom of Sam's school friends. 'Who'd catch bad people like the person who murdered old Tom Carter?' There was no reply from her son and she half turned to catch a glimpse of him glued to the rear window of the car.

'What is it?' she asked.

'More police cars, up by our place.' Sam's reply was muffled as he twisted further round in his seat. Kate glanced quickly in her mirror and could just catch a glimpse of a patrol car, light flashing, close to the block where she and Sam occupied a top-floor flat, courtesy of the local council and the national charity which jointly funded the estate advice bureau where she worked.

'They'll just be asking questions about old Tom,' she said. 'How was school today? You never told me.'

'All right,' Sam conceded. He was in his last term at the local primary school, more than ready, both mentally and physically, for the move to the comprehensive after the summer holidays. He was at a stage when he grew out of his clothes at what seemed to be monthly intervals, and was heartily bored by primary school horizons. Kate sighed and wondered what his dead father would have made of this gangling, sulky child, half boy, already half man, who promised to be his physical and she suspected his intellectual equal.

She bit her lip. Even after all this time, she thought, she desperately missed Richard, and never more so than when she was concerned about Sam's future. She longed for someone to talk to about his development, about her worries, about the sudden joy he often gave her as, with all the fits and starts of childhood, he still grew and blossomed. She tried so hard to keep in touch both with his roaming mind and his lurching emotions, but then worried all the more that perhaps she was making him too dependent upon her as a friend as well as mother. She hated, she admitted, being a single parent.

ALMOST BEFORE Kate Weston had left Highcliffe, Detective-Inspector Sinclair had made the arrest he had been half expecting all day. He had gone through the motions of investigating Tom Carter's background, but his instincts told him that this was an opportunistic crime and that whoever had struck old Tom a shattering blow on the back of the skull—a blow, the pathologist had told him that morning, which would have killed the old man instantly—would turn up not very far away.

At half past four that afternoon the car radio told him and his sergeant that an anonymous call to headquarters in the town had informed CID that a youth had been seen on the estate with what looked like Tom Carter's wallet.

'Let's go,' he said to Sergeant Wilson, who had just joined him after questioning the advice centre director, Derek Stevenson, just as unproductively as Sinclair had questioned Kate Weston. Two blocks further down the main road they pulled into a slip road in front of the estate's single row of shops: a jumbled, overcrowded grocer's with its boxes of cheap offers spilling out on to the pavement, a betting shop with windows covered by a thick iron grille, a greengrocer's with a cheap line in browning bananas which incorporated a post-office counter in its inner recesses, and a steamy launderette. More than half the row was boarded up for lack of custom or as a result of the persistent vandalism which plagued the whole estate. A group of teenaged boys were sitting on the wall in front of the launderette, laughing, kicking their legs, and occasionally throwing an empty Coke can at a ginger cat which lay sunning itself outside Patel's grocery and general store.

There was a relatively subdued chorus of abuse as the two men got out of their unmarked car and approached the youths. Sinclair was relieved to see that none of the group was black. Relations with the town's black youngsters had been tense for months, and he knew that the slightest false step might spark off trouble in that community. But this group were all white, wearing the local uniform of jeans and leather jackets and half-smoked cigarettes, and apparently watching the approach of the police in a relatively subdued frame of mind.

'Now then, lads,' Wilson said, by way of greeting. 'Have any of you seen Joey Macready?'

'Joey who?'

'You mean Joey the clown.'

'What's it to you, punk?'

The answers and the giggles came thick and fast but Sinclair thought they lacked the sort of determined bravado that he would normally have expected from these boys in this place. He looked slowly down the line of faces, the pale, the spotty, the flushed with recent laughter, and one by one their eyes dropped. They knew, he thought, whom he wanted, and he was pretty sure they also knew why. He wondered if one of them had made the anonymous call to HQ fingering the boy Joey Macready.

'He's over on t'reck, mister,' said one of the group at last, pointing in the direction of the estate's recreation ground further down the hill where the ground flattened out

slightly before making its final dramatic drop down to the
town centre which could be clearly seen from almost anywhere in Highcliffe, a grey blur of tall buildings and dis-
used factories by day, a sparkling constellation of lights the
width of the valley by night.

Almost as the two policemen turned to go another voice
caught their attention, almost inaudible against the la-
bouring engine of a double-decker bus which was grinding
its way up the hill to its terminus at the top of the estate.

'And 'e's got t'wallet,' one of the boys said. ' 'E bought
us all packets of gum with t'money.'

'Thanks, lads,' Wilson said as they turned away again.
Sinclair could not bring himself to speak. The idea that an
old man had died for the price of a few packets of chewing
gum rose in his throat and almost choked him. He had, he
thought, so far remained as dispassionate as he could have
wished during the last frantic hours of his first murder investigation. He had supervised the murder team, which had
been hastily assembled late the previous night strictly by the
book, aware that he was being left alone because of staff
shortages at headquarters rather than any investment by his
superiors in his investigative skills. More than fifteen hours
since the first call had brought him straight to Highcliffe
from home he was desperately tired and the sheer pointless
waste of last night's killing suddenly sickened him. Sergeant Wilson glanced at him curiously.

'Right then, boss?' he asked.

'Let's have a look, shall we?' Sinclair agreed, his voice
strained with tiredness.

The 'reck' appeared deserted as they went in through the
iron gateway. It was an acre or so of roughly mown grass,
interspersed with patches of mud, dog mess and a couple
of netless football goals. In the farthest corner, where the
play equipment for the younger children stood protected
from wandering dogs by a dilapidated paling fence, they
could see two figures on the swings, one small and dressed
in bright red, the other taller, darker and, it appeared, far
too bulky for the low plastic seat of the swing.

'Shall I call for help?' Wilson asked quietly. 'There's another entrance over there. He could run.'

'Get a car to that gate, Dave, just in case,' Sinclair said, and the sergeant pulled out his radio. 'In the meantime let's just stroll over. He doesn't seem to have seen us yet.'

Very casually, as though out for a walk, the two men approached the swings, but neither of the two figures stopped their rhythmic movement, even as they came within speaking distance. Out of the corner of his eye Sinclair saw a patrol car pull up across the far gate to the recreation field. Now they were closer, they could see that a tall youth was swinging in time with a much smaller girl in red. They did not seem to be talking to each other, or even taking any notice of each other, simply swinging in time, the older boy lifting his feet with each arc of the seat so as to avoid dragging them on the floor.

'Joey Macready?' Sinclair called at last, attracting the boy's attention, and realizing for the first time that big as the boy was, all of six four in height, he guessed, and as broad as many men, the mind that looked out of those wide blue eyes was a whole lot younger than that. Joey seemed unalarmed by their presence and smiled a warm and trusting smile in response to his name.

'We need to talk to you, Joey,' Sinclair said. 'Can you come with us and find your mother?'

'She's out,' Joey said amiably, without interrupting the rhythm of his swing. Sinclair glanced at Wilson, who grimaced.

'He's only sixpence to t'shilling,' he said.

'In which case we'd better have a care,' Sinclair said quietly.

'What about your dad then, Joey?' Sinclair asked, but the boy just grinned again and went on swinging.

'He ain't got no dad, mister,' said the little girl on the second swing shrilly, bringing her feet to the ground suddenly in a sliding, braking movement which threw up a cloud of grit and dust.

'Are you t'police?' she asked, and at that Joey too stopped swinging and looked with more concentration at Sinclair, a slight frown wrinkling his broad brow.

'We're looking for a wallet, Joey,' Sinclair said, approaching the boy more closely, while Wilson edged his way round the back of the swings so that he stood immediately behind him. 'Have you seen a wallet? A friend of yours said you might have.' The boy did not reply, but his expression became less sunny, and a look of doubt, or it could have been puzzlement, crept into his pale eyes.

'He's got it, mister,' shrilled the small girl eagerly. 'He showed me. And he bought me some sweets.'

'Is that right, Joey?' Wilson said from behind the boy, startling him so that he turned on the low swing seat and almost lost his balance. He took hold of both of the chains and pulled himself to his feet, a movement so threatening that Wilson took an involuntary step away from him and Sinclair moved forward in alarm, ready to grab him. But Joey merely regained his feet and stood, arms dangling, his bottom lip trembling now and his eyes swinging rapidly from the small girl in the red anorak to the two men. Sinclair was slightly shocked to realize that the boy was a couple of inches taller than he was himself.

'Found it,' he said at last. 'Found the purse. There were nowt in it, honest.'

'Have you still got it now, Joey?' Sinclair asked. The boy hesitated again, his eyes still swivelling from one to the other and then away to the park gate, where two uniformed officers were quite clearly to be seen standing by their patrol car.

'Threw it,' he said at last, emphatically. 'Over there, in t'bushes. Not mine, not Joey's wallet.' He waved vaguely to the far side of the field, near the now guarded gate.

'Let's go and find it, then, shall we, lad?' Wilson said, putting a hand very lightly on Joey's arm, but ready for any sudden reaction. 'And then we'll go for a little ride in a police car. You'd like that, wouldn't you?'

'Home for tea,' the boy said, suddenly on the verge of tears. 'Mustn't be late.'

'Don't worry about that, Joey,' Sinclair said. 'We'll tell your mum where you are and get her to come down to see you. Now let's just find that wallet, shall we?'

'I'll help, I'll help,' said the small girl, who could not have been more than seven years old, Sinclair thought, but who pretty obviously understood the implications of the conversation better than Joey did.

'Is there a reward, mister?' she asked, and before either Sinclair or Wilson could stop her she had darted away across the tussocky grass towards the further entrance to the field and began bustling around in the straggly bushes which followed the line of the boundary fence leading up to the gates.

'Get her out of there, Dave,' Sinclair said sharply. 'Go on, man, run. She'll destroy any evidence there is, the way she's going on.'

With a grimace of protest, Wilson broke into a run towards the entrance. He was a heavy man, a former police welterweight champion but running to fat now as he avoided exercise in middle age as religiously as he had once sought it in his youth. Sinclair turned back to the boy who was still standing by the swings, watching events with a slightly happier expression on his face.

'Car? Wi 't' blue light flashing?' he asked, as Sinclair took his arm and guided him across the field towards the police car. By the time they reached it, the little girl had retreated down the road, where she stood watching events from what she obviously thought was safe distance, and Wilson was standing with the two uniformed officers putting a dark brown leather wallet carefully into a plastic evidence bag.

'Was this the one, Joey?' he asked the boy, who nodded happily. He glanced for a moment at the girl in red who, seeing his look, turned abruptly on her heel and ran off round the next corner and out of sight. Sinclair looked at Joey's unperturbed expression and sighed. Ever since the incriminating phone call had named Joey Macready as the possessor of an unexplained brown wallet, he had had little doubt that this was the way it would end. As far as he was concerned, the only complication ahead lay in the careful and lawful questioning of a boy who clearly had difficulty in comprehending the seriousness of the situation in which he found himself.

'Where do you live, Joey?' he asked gently, and the boy pointed vaguely in the direction from which they had just come, across the recreation field and back towards the shops, the flats and the centre of the estate.

'In t'flats.'

'And where does your mother work, do you know?'

Joey looked puzzled and shook his head.

'How old are you, Joey?' Wilson asked, but the boy merely shook his head and looked puzzled again.

'Do you have any brothers and sisters, Joey?' Wilson persisted and this time the boy nodded.

'Sister Tracey,' he said, 'on t'swings.'

'Damn,' Sinclair said. 'If we'd known that we might have got more sense out of this. Take him down to town, Dave, and keep an eye on him until I get there. We don't want to walk him back past the shops. It's quieter this way. But no questions yet. I don't want any allegations that we questioned him without an adult with him. He's to be treated exactly as if he was under age. We'll argue about his exact mental state later. I'll see if I can find out where to contact his mother and follow you down to the other car. Give me an hour or so.'

He turned to the boy.

'You go in the car with Sergeant Wilson, Joey, and I'll come to have a chat with you when I've found your mum. OK?'

Joey Macready nodded happily enough and squeezed his bulk into the back seat of the police car. Wilson nodded a touch grimly.

'A Majesty's Pleasure job, by t'look of it,' he said.

Sinclair picked his way carefully back across the field and drove slowly the few hundred yards to the centre of the estate. He felt no elation at what looked like the rapid conclusion to his first murder investigation. What felt more like the onset of a deep depression seized him as he parked outside the advice centre and looked across at the row of shops where some of the teenagers were still congregated, kicking their Coke cans around among the greasy wrapping papers which had spilled from an overturned litter bin beside the mobile fish and chip van which had taken up its daily station outside the Fox, the estate's single pub.

Charging a backward boy with murder, as he had no doubt he would have to do before the night was out, filled him with no pleasure. He was only too aware of the anguish it would bring the boy's parents, to add to the anguish he had already witnessed that day at Tom Carter's neat bungalow, where his wife was still no doubt sitting in the numbed state of disbelief which afflicts the suddenly and shockingly bereaved. Joey Macready had a well-dressed and well-cared-for look, in spite of his disability, and Sinclair did not doubt that he was loved.

Gradually the estate was coming to life as the lull between the children scuffling their way home from school and the workers returning home from the town came to an end. Several women appeared with shopping-bags, heading either for Patel's grocery, which stayed open until eight, or the fish and chip van. A red double-decker bus pulled up at its terminus on the other side of the pub and a handful of people got off and dispersed into the flats or the streets of semi-detached houses which ran down the hill towards the centre of the town. Suddenly Sinclair spotted Tracey Macready, in her bright red anorak, skipping up and down the steps which led to the shops across a barren and much trampled patch of grass and stunted shrubs.

Sinclair got out of the car quickly and slammed and locked the door behind him. On this estate, even police vehicles had been known to be dismantled in the odd five minutes an officer's back was turned on official business.

He crossed the road at a half run and called to the child. She turned and looked at him and for a moment he thought she was going to run away again. But eventually she shrugged her thin shoulders and, feet trailing, began to walk towards him.

'Did yer find Joey, mister?' asked one of the boys as he passed. Sinclair ignored him and put a hand tightly on the girl's shoulder.

'I need to see your mother, Tracey,' he said. 'Can you take me to your house?'

'Our flat, you mean? And she ain't there yet, any road. She's at work,' the child said, wriggling out of his grasp with what seemed like practised skill. 'She doesn't get back till late on Tuesdays. Me and Joey gets us own tea. I've got t'door keys.' She pulled two Yale keys, worn round her neck on a piece of string, from inside her anorak and showed them to him with pride.

'Then we'd better go and see if any of your neighbours know where your mother is,' Sinclair said in a tone which allowed for no argument, taking Tracey's hand in a firm grip this time. 'Come on, love. Your Joey needs to see his mum right away.' Tracey looked up at him mutinously and tried to pull her hand from his grip with unexpected ferocity, but it was a very determined female voice from just behind him which made Sinclair actually loosen his hold on the child.

'Excuse me,' Kate Weston said sharply, putting a restraining hand on what she obviously thought was a stranger's arm. 'What's the trouble, Tracey?'

Sinclair turned and they recognized each other with embarrassed surprise.

'I'm sorry, Alex, I thought...', Kate began. Sinclair nodded, with a slightly rueful smile, guessing what she had thought.

'I'm glad to see you,' he said. 'You can probably help.'

'I don't believe it,' Kate said as soon as Sinclair had explained why he was anxious to find Mrs Macready so urgently. She had paled, Sinclair noticed, and looked shocked by his news. She pushed her hair out of her eyes tiredly.

'Joey is such a gentle boy. Dear God, he's played with Sam for years ... They live on the next flat to me. Are you sure you've got this right?'

'Of course we're not sure at this stage. But it's sufficient for us to question him, and for that I need his mother,' he said.

'Annie Macready works at Tatton's warehouse in town,' Kate said. 'I don't think her shift ends until eight on a Tuesday. You'll find her there, I expect. If she's going to be any later than that she usually asks me to pop in and keep an eye on the children ...'

'Perhaps you'd better keep an eye on Tracey tonight,' Sinclair suggested, glancing at the child who was now dancing attendance on the older boys who were eating chips from paper bags and feeding her the occasional scrap. 'I might need her mother for some time.'

'I'll do that,' Kate said. 'She can come and watch television with Sam. What about a solicitor for Joey? I can get the chap we use at the centre. He's very good at dealing with emergencies.'

'I'll get Mrs Macready to call you from the station when we see what's needed,' Sinclair said. Kate looked at him, still obviously troubled.

'What is it, Kate?' he asked, making an effort to keep the weariness from his voice.

'I don't really understand what happens with a boy like that, Alex. He's not normal. He was severely brain damaged at birth,' she said.

'Can he distinguish between right and wrong? That's what the court will want to know if he's charged,' Sinclair said. 'If he did it, he'll either go to gaol if they think he knew what he was doing or to a secure hospital if they think he didn't. It's a bleak future, either way.'

'I'm not sure what he understands, how far he has a moral sense at all,' Kate said. 'His language is very limited. It's hard to know. He's always seemed happy, and lovable, and completely harmless . . .'

'He had the wallet, Kate. I have to find out where he got it. It's quite possible he did just find it, but we have to question him, if only to clear him. You know that.'

Kate nodded bleakly.

'You'd better find Annie,' she said. 'But watch out. She idolizes that boy. She'll defend him to her last breath. Her husband's left her, and Tracey's never come anywhere in her reckoning, I don't know why. She lives and breathes Joey. He's still her baby, though he's a foot taller than she is, now.'

'I'll bear it in mind,' Sinclair said.

'Keep me in touch,' Kate said. 'She may need help from the centre . . .'

'If we don't contact you tonight, I'll get the beat man to come round in the morning and tell you what's happening,' Sinclair promised. 'If I'm not back up here myself looking for someone else.'

'I hope you are,' Kate said. 'I truly do.' She turned away and threaded her way past the queue now waiting for fish and chips, and let herself into the front door of her block of flats with a key. Three flights of steep steps above the entrance hall she opened her own front door, one of two facing each other across the bleak landing. Sam was curled in his favourite armchair watching television, his new football boots and their long unthreaded laces lying on the floor with their box and wrapping paper carelessly strewn about. He hardly glanced up as she came into the living-room, but to her surprise, Sam was not alone. As she entered the room, Derek Stevenson turned away from the uncurtained living-room window, from which he had been watching the scene below.

'Trouble, Kate?' he asked, with unconcealed eagerness in his voice. 'They haven't been daft enough to arrest Joey Macready, have they, love? Surely the pigs haven't been that stupid?'

TWO

THE TOWN HALL CLOCK was striking nine by the time Detective-Inspector Alex Sinclair walked wearily back into the main police headquarters, a rectangular modern block which rubbed uneasy shoulders with the Victorian Gothic town hall next door. He was tired, and frustrated, and alone, having failed to locate Annie Macready at the mail order warehouse where she worked.

He made his way up the stairs without taking them two at a time, as he usually did. He was tired but not yet tired enough to take the lift. In the almost deserted main CID office he was surprised to find Dave Wilson at his desk, filling in a report form at his usual deliberate one-fingered typing speed and with a look of more than usually determined obstinacy on his face.

'You didn't stay with the lad, then?' Sinclair asked sharply.

'Wasn't asked to,' Wilson replied, not looking up. 'The boss took over.'

'What?' Sinclair snapped in disbelief. 'What do you mean, took over?'

'I mean decided to question t'lad,' Wilson said flatly, leaning back in his chair as if to challenge the detective-inspector to contradict him. 'Took DC Jones with him, and said he'd do the interrogation himself. Period.'

Sinclair flushed slightly and turned away from the sergeant's impassive gaze. It was always difficult to tell what Dave Wilson was thinking behind that heavy brow, but this evening impossible. They came from two different traditions of policing, the older man who had pounded the beat for ten years before joining the CID now junior to the younger university educated inspector, one of the force's high flyers. Wilson would, at forty-five, be lucky ever to make inspector now. Sinclair regarded the rank as a pretty lowly staging-post on the way to higher things.

They had started working together in unspoken suspicion which had changed only slowly to mutual respect, but there were still many things Sinclair, for all his sharpness, did not understand about his more intuitive sergeant, and still occasions when Dave Wilson's experience was more than a match for his inspector's rationality.

Tonight Sinclair admitted that he was at a loss. He sat down at the desk next to Wilson's and drew a deep breath. He hardly dared ask the next question for fear of what the answer might be.

'I couldn't find his mother. But she turned up here, then, did she, Dave?'

'Not as I know of,' Wilson said, finishing a section of his report as he spoke with a savage stabbing of the keyboard in front of him.

'Someone else who knew Joey Macready, then? Or a social worker?

'Not as I know of.'

'Where's the boy now?' Sinclair asked, trying to hide the anger in his voice without much success. Wilson pulled his report from the typewriter and handed the top copy to the detective-inspector.

'I don't know, boss. The super asked me to fill him in on what happened up at Highcliffe, and then sent me up here to write it up. I've not heard a word since. So—there's my report—sir.' The deliberate pause before the 'sir' told Sinclair that the taciturn Wilson was no happier than he was himself at the turn events had taken.

He glanced at Wilson's report.

'Get yourself off home,' he said. 'That's more than enough for one day, and you'll be sending the overtime account into the red again. I'll see the super and sort it out.' Wilson did not need any second telling. He picked up his coat from where he had dropped it on a chair and shrugged himself into it.

'I told the missus to expect me when she saw me, but her sister's at our place tonight and there'll be sour looks if I don't get back in time to see her at all,' he said. Sinclair smiled faintly.

'I know the feeling,' he said. 'It's three days since I saw my girls for long enough to speak to.'

'Coppers' kids should be used to that,' Wilson said.

'Kids, yes, but wives not always.'

'Aye, well,' was all Wilson vouchsafed to that before he left. Sinclair sat on at the desk he had appropriated and stared with unseeing eyes at Wilson's report. He did not doubt that it was the model of accuracy and concision that Wilson habitually produced. What worried him was not what had happened at Highcliffe over the past day and half the previous night, but what had gone on at police headquarters over the last two hours.

Detective-Superintendent Eddie Greaves was quite within his rights to take over the questioning of a murder suspect, if that is what he wished to do. Sinclair knew that his rank was abnormally junior to allow him to retain control of a case as serious as this one. But as the force's acknowledged 'high flyer' he had, he admitted to himself, got used to being allowed an unusually free run on his patch, which consisted essentially of the Highcliffe estate and a couple of the semi-rural villages beyond the escarpment upon which the outlying estate had been built.

But it was not just injured pride which caused him to sit in the empty CID room, breathing in the day's stale fug of cigarette smoke and centrally heated air, only half aware of a persistently ringing telephone in another office further along the corridor. The vague sense of unease which had assailed him ever since he had seen the amiable vacancy of Joey Macready's look as he faced them for the first time from his swing had blossomed now into genuine anxiety about the case.

As far as he could understand it, Detective-Superintendent Eddie Greaves had broken every unwritten rule in the book that night, and possibly some written ones as well. As the investigating officer for last night's murder, he would have to try to find out why, preferably without provoking a man who ran his department with an autocratic grip which was notorious throughout the county force. It was not a task he relished at the end of a long day which had followed a night when he reckoned he had had at most three hours' sleep.

He walked thoughtfully across the room, where desks were piled high with files as usual and into his own small office, hardly more than a partitioned-off corner of the main room. As he took off his coat and hung it up the phone rang. It was Greaves.

'Come in, will you?' the superintendent said. The peremptory summons was not unusual.

Greaves was at his desk in shirtsleeves when Sinclair knocked on his door and went in. And that was an unusual sight. By day, Greaves presented an immaculately dressed figure to the world, buying his suits, so it was said, in London on yearly trips made expressly for that purpose. He was not a tall man, but broad, and invariably well turned out, the ties and matching handkerchiefs carefully chosen to complement the discreet pinstripes and plain shirts he favoured, the thinning hair carefully trimmed and arranged to conceal the incipient baldness. He was a local man, but one of those who had meticulously ironed the northern intonation from his voice. It was folklore among the canteen gossips that Eddie Greaves had had ambitions to leave Yorkshire and move south, but they had come to nothing.

Greaves was studying some papers when Sinclair entered, and kept the inspector waiting for a long moment before looking up.

'Well, that was very well done, Alex. In record time, too, I'd think,' he said at last, waving Sinclair into a chair.

'Sir?' Sinclair said quietly, sitting down and arranging Wilson's report on the edge of the superintendent's desk in front of him, the knot of anxiety in his stomach growing tighter.

'Congratulations, lad, on bringing Macready in so promptly,' Greaves said with unexpected bonhomie. 'And it's particularly gratifying to wrap a case up in less than twenty-four hours, when it's not a domestic. The chief will be delighted.'

'You regard it as wrapped up, then, sir?'

'You didn't know that I'd charged him?' Greaves said, in a tone of pained surprise. 'I'm so sorry, Alex, I asked DC Jones to report to you as soon as you came in...'

'I haven't seen DC Jones, sir. I've been in the office ten minutes or so...'

'My dear boy,' Greaves interrupted him smoothly. 'I do apologize. It was your case, after all. But in the event, when I went to have a chat with Macready, there was no contest. He broke down and admitted everything. It was all over in fifteen minutes. I recorded it, of course. No doubt you would like to hear the tape?' The question was asked with a chilly formality that would have alerted Sinclair had he not been so shaken by what he had just heard.

'He confessed?' he asked. 'I rather got the impression that he wouldn't even understand a charge, sir.'

'Oh, I think that boy is not as stupid as he likes to make out, Alex. He understood all right. The defence may go for unfit to plead, but I'm not at all sure they'll get away with it. And with the circumstantial evidence of the wallet, plus the confession, I don't think we'll go far wrong, do you?'

'I believe there's brain damage, sir. Was he questioned with a friend present? I couldn't contact his mother.'

'No? Well, don't worry about that, Inspector. The lad's over age, you know. He's not a juvenile. Anyway, she's been located at home now and I've sent someone round to tell her what's what. She can see the lad and get hold of a brief before court in the morning.'

'I understood that when there was some question of mental incapacity, a suspect should not be questioned alone,' Sinclair persisted, although it was perfectly clear from Greaves's dismissive tone that this was not a remark he would wish to hear. 'That's why I was so anxious to find the mother.'

Greaves leaned back in his chair and slowly lit a cigarette and inhaled deeply before replying. His eyes were cold now and the voice had lost its slightly forced friendliness.

'Are you suggesting some irregularity in the way I handled Macready's interrogation, Inspector?' he asked.

Sinclair hesitated, and in that moment of hesitation knew that he had lost whatever initiative he might have briefly gained.

'I've no evidence for that, sir,' he admitted slowly.

'Indeed you have not,' Greaves replied. 'You'll find the transcript of the interview on your desk by now, I should imagine. The tape is locked in the safe until the morning, but then you are welcome to hear that too. I trust that those two items will satisfy your scrupulous conscience. In the meantime I suggest you take yourself home and get some rest. If there is anything further you want to say to me about Macready, I think it would be better kept until the morning by which time you'll have had the chance to sleep on it.'

'Sir,' Sinclair said quietly, getting to his feet with a sense of enormous weariness flooding through him. To his surprise, Greaves rose too and, coming round his desk, put an arm on his shoulder, his mood changing again as unexpectedly as before.

'What you seem to be forgetting, Alex,' he said, 'is that as the arresting officer you'll be the one getting the credit for this. And that won't do you any harm at all with the big promotion coming up. Oh, and by the way, have you and your wife made up your minds about that daughter of yours' schooling yet? Let me know if she's going to St Helen's, won't you? My youngest girl is still in the sixth form there, you know. A lovely school if you can afford it.'

'No, we've not decided yet,' Sinclair muttered, grudgingly.

'And there's that other matter I mentioned, too. It would do your career a lot of good to join.'

'I'll think about it, sir,' Sinclair said hastily, opening the door.

'Right, Greaves said with finality. 'Until the morning, then. I'll be in at eight-thirty if you need me. I've a meeting with the chief at ten.'

SINCLAIR MET KATE WESTON, accompanied by another woman he did not recognize and Derek Stevenson on the steps of the police headquarters just as he was leaving.

'Inspector,' Stevenson said angrily, barring his exit with an overtly aggressive arm. 'Inspector, you're just the person we need to see. I'm surprised you should be going home at a time like this.'

Sinclair bit back the hasty retort which sprang to his lips, and instead looked inquiringly at Kate. She too looked tense and angry and did not return his half smile. Her companion, a dumpy woman in an imitation fur coat, had clearly been crying, her eye make-up streaked and tear-marks running across the powder on her cheeks.

'This is Mrs Macready,' Kate said coldly. 'We've come to see Joey.' Sinclair sighed. Annie Macready looked at him for a moment without speaking. She was older than Sinclair had expected, her round face sagging into more than one chin, and her hair grey at the roots where the blonde dye was growing out. She said nothing but the look in her eyes disconcerted Sinclair with the passionate intensity of its dislike.

'I'll see what can be done,' he said quickly, turning on his heel and leading the trio through the revolving doors back into the reception area.

As they went in Kate Weston caught hold of his arm and drew him back from the other two and whispered fiercely, 'What on earth's going on, Alex? Annie says you've charged Joey. Is that right?'

'Superintendent Greaves has charged Joey with murder,' Sinclair said flatly. 'I'm sorry, Kate. It's out of my hands now.' She looked at him angrily, her face flushed and her eyes bright with tears.

'That's ridiculous,' she said.

'I'm sorry. There's nothing more I can do.'

Sinclair turned away to the desk sergeant who was already listening to Mrs Macready and Derek Stevenson's loud demands to be able to see Joey. He crossed to the desk and caught the sergeant's somewhat desperate eye.

'I'll authorize a visit in the circumstances,' Sinclair said. 'If you ask the custody officer to supervise.'

The sergeant still hesitated and looked at the three visitors and then back to Sinclair questioningly.

'It's highly irregular,' he began.

'I suspect the whole night's events have been highly irregular, Sergeant,' Derek Stevenson broke in aggressively. 'One more irregularity to comfort a mentally handicapped boy is going to be neither here nor there when this all comes out in the open. It might even stand you in good stead.'

'I'll authorize a visit, Sergeant,' Sinclair repeated firmly. 'Let Mrs Macready see her son for fifteen minutes, and let Mrs Weston go down with her. If there's any come-back tomorrow I'll handle it.'

Sinclair waited in the hallway while the sergeant took the two women through to the rear of the building. Stevenson stood with his hands deep in his pockets, reading notices on the board by the entrance and whistling softly between his teeth. At last he turned to Sinclair with an insolent stare.

'You bastards have really stuck your necks out this time, haven't you?'

'I don't know what you mean, Mr Stevenson,' Sinclair countered warily.

'Really,' Stevenson sneered. 'You amaze me, Inspector. I thought you were one of the new graduate coppers who were going to civilize the police force. I think we might be better off with the old brutality. At least then we knew where we stood. There was none of this hypocritical bleeding heart façade you put up, all this community policing rubbish, sucking up to Kate Weston and pretending some sort of shared social concern. Why don't you admit it?

You're just the same as all the others. A right bastard when it comes to the crunch.'

'You're entitled to your view, Mr Stevenson,' Sinclair said levelly.

'You think it's OK, then, do you, to lock up some half-witted kid for a crime he couldn't possibly have committed? I'm surprised you haven't thrown in a couple of rape charges as well to improve your clear-up rate. Joey isn't going to be able to argue about it one way or the other, is he?'

To Stevenson's evident surprise, Inspector Sinclair spun suddenly towards him and without actually touching him, pinned him against the notice-board, his face inches from his.

'I've never understood your motives, Stevenson,' he said in a fierce whisper, 'but I've never doubted that you were an evil-minded opportunist and trouble-maker. I can't stop you using the Macreadys for your own ends, but I warn you, if you drag me into this, and if you ever imply again that I might be corrupt, I'll see you downstairs in a cell. We'll start with wasting police time, and work our way up from there. That's a promise.'

Stevenson twisted away from Sinclair, and dropped into a chair on the other side of the hallway with a look of amused satisfaction on his face.

'Well, well,' he said. 'So there is a man under that immaculate exterior, after all, is there?'

Sinclair turned away again, a look of disgust on his face, although whether it was at Stevenson for provoking him, or himself for being provoked even he was not quite sure. They were saved from further exchanges by the two women who came back up the stairs behind the reception desk with the uniformed sergeant. Kate Weston had an arm around Annie Macready, who was sobbing on her shoulder.

'We'll organize a solicitor in the morning,' she said to the two men. 'I've no doubt that he'll be asking for immediate bail. As far as I can judge, far from having confessed, Joey hasn't the faintest idea what's going on.'

Stevenson took up a position on the other side of Annie Macready and between them they steered the weeping woman towards the exit. As they were about to push through the revolving doors, Annie Macready turned back to Sinclair with a look of such undisguised hatred that Sinclair flinched.

'You bastard,' she said, before Kate helped her, unresisting, out of the door.

Stevenson grinned back at Sinclair triumphantly.

'The end of a beautiful career, I shouldn't wonder,' he said. 'I think you've got it very wrong, Inspector, very wrong indeed.'

ALEX SINCLAIR WOKE the next morning with a foul taste in his mouth and a thumping head. He reached out to turn off the bedside alarm and took in the fact that it was seven-fifteen, and that his wife was sleeping with an elbow jabbing uncomfortably into his ribs. He turned over on to his back and groaned as the memory of last night's events flooded back. It had been gone ten o'clock when he had got home, and he had drunk several whiskies before persuading Margaret to switch off the television and come to bed with him. They had made love more, he knew, as a way of relieving his own unbearable tension than as an expression of tenderness.

He had rushed the whole proceedings in the almost savage urgency of his need, and although she had appeared to reach a climax of her own, with much moaning and sobbing, he wondered, not for the first time, if she was not dissembling. It was years, he thought, probably before seven-year-old Sally was born, since she had persuaded him into bed by word or touch or gesture. It was some time since he had admitted to himself that he no longer loved his wife, but he had no idea how she really felt about him. They had ceased discussing their feelings about each other years ago.

He touched her thigh and she moaned again, an unconscious reprise of the sounds she had made last night, and Sinclair turned away from her to the edge of the bed, ashamed. Margaret did not wake even then, and eventually he slipped out of bed, put on a dressing-gown and went out on to the landing.

The morning routine of the household fell, by his own choice, to him. Frequently coming home late, he cherished the hour or so before the children went to school in the morning as his only certain contact with them. He slipped into ten-year-old Jennifer's room first. She was a dreamy child, and needed time to wake. The room was still in semidarkness, the dark blue curtains filtering out most of the morning light, but Sinclair could see that she had tossed off her bedclothes in the night and lay curled up in a frilly nightdress in an almost fetal position, her arms around her knees. He picked the fallen quilt off the floor and covered her up again gently before shaking her shoulder.

'Come on, Jenny, wake up.' The child stirred and smiled sleepily at her father.

'I had such a nice dream,' she said. 'You took us to the seaside.'

'Well, perhaps I will, if that's what you'd like,' he said. 'It's not long to half term.' She smiled and shut her eyes again, so that Sinclair shook her, less gently this time.

'Do I have to get up, Daddy?'

'You'll be late if you don't,' he said, going out and leaving her door ajar.

Her sister, Sally, was already awake, her eyes full of mischief, more than ready to face the day. People always said how different children in the same family could be, Sinclair thought, but he had never believed them until he and Margaret had marvelled at the outgoing second baby who had succeeded their introverted first.

'And what are you doing today, miss?' Sinclair asked, his heart lifting at the sight of Sally's shining good humour.

'We're going to the museum with Class 3, silly, you've forgotten,' Sally said, scrambling out of bed and picking up several items of clothing which she had left strewn across the floor.

'You're an untidy imp,' Sinclair said.

'Can I have an egg for breakfast?'

'I expect so,' he said, 'unless the chickens have gone on strike.' He left her sitting on the floor struggling into her knickers, giggling.

Downstairs in Margaret's spotless kitchen, a Laura Ashley dream of pine shelves and sprigged wallpaper, he put the kettle on for tea and a pan of water for boiled eggs, before setting the table for three. Margaret seldom came down for breakfast. The children said goodbye to her in bed before they left at eight-thirty to walk the quarter of a mile to the local primary school. It was the fact that Jennifer was due to leave that school at the end of the summer term that had created a new crisis in Alex Sinclair's already strained relationship with his wife.

He had met Margaret Booth, the daughter of a local textile magnate, before he left his Milford comprehensive school to go to university. She had been a stunningly attractive seventeen-year-old when he went away, and they had maintained their relationship, in spite of her father's forthright objections, during Alex's student vacations. The Booths had little enthusiasm for his determination to join the police force when he graduated, even less for his persistent courtship of their only daughter, but when the young police constable and Margaret announced that she was pregnant and intended to get married as soon as it could be arranged, they swallowed their misgivings and pulled out all the stops.

Margaret had her white wedding in the local parish church, with all the trimmings, the honeymoon she had set her heart on in Venice, and the wedding present she most desired—and her father could well afford—a house in Broadley, the leafy suburb beyond Milford's ring road where many of her expensively educated schoolfriends were already settling down to a comfortable middle-class existence.

Ten years later, with Alex Sinclair now a detective-inspector and a further promotion imminent, Margaret could have felt her commitment to the man her parents had rejected on purely social grounds more than justified. Inspector Sinclair, it was widely agreed at Broadley coffee mornings, at lodge meetings and Conservative Club socials, had risen dramatically above his humble origins and would go far. Margaret Booth, it was now accepted, had shown some percipience in recognizing his potential when he was still an unsophisticated sixth-former with the broad vowels of the down-town neighbourhood where he had been brought up.

But Margaret Sinclair, ten years married and the mother of two, was not a contented woman. She had left her private school at seventeen and taken a series of short-lived secretarial and reception jobs, mainly with friends of her father's in the local business world. When she married she gave up work with relief, and now both the girls were at school spent her days at charitable coffee mornings in Broadley, and working for the local Conservative Party. On political issues she and her husband had always agreed to differ. He maintained at least a sentimental attachment to his Scottish father's fervent socialism.

With the children safely dispatched to school, Sinclair made her a cup of the China tea she liked and took it upstairs to the bedroom. Margaret was sitting up in bed, leaning against several pillows and her expression was one of some dissatisfaction.

'Do you have to go in today?' she asked. 'We really must get this school business settled. Jenny needs to know where she is, and so does Daddy if he's going to pay the bills.'

Sinclair put the cup and saucer down on the bedside table and turned to draw back the heavy floral curtains. He stood for a moment looking out at the broad tree-lined avenue, with its substantial four- and five-bedroomed houses on each side. Next door, their neighbours' two teenaged sons were leaving home in the distinctive uniform of Milford's independent boys' grammar school. His daughters, Margaret never tired of reminding him, were the only children in the road who did not attend fee-paying schools, and while she had acquiesced in what she called his 'socialist notions' while they were of primary school age, she was digging her heels in, with the active encouragement of her father who was willing to pay his granddaughter's fees, now that Jennifer was due to move to a secondary school.

'I've made another appointment to see the headmistress at St Helen's,' she said. 'You could come with me, if you like.'

Sinclair looked at her. She was wearing a pink satin nightdress through which her full breasts were clearly visible, the nipples prominent under the smooth material. She was no longer quite the beautiful young woman he had married: her fair skin and blonde hair had coarsened slightly already, and she was beginning to put on weight. But in spite of the state of almost continuous tension in which they now lived, her body still moved him frequently to almost unbearable desire. He groaned under his breath and shook his head angrily.

'There's a murder investigation on, remember?' he said. 'I can't possibly take time off.'

'Well, when are we supposed to talk, then?' she said. 'This is your daughter's future we're discussing—or rather, not discussing, because you're never here long enough to discuss anything. I simply can't understand what your objections are. Jenny wants to go to St Helen's, she did outstandingly well in the entrance exam, the headmistress says. It's not even going to cost you anything, thanks to my father's generosity. What's the problem? Just explain to me, please. I don't understand what the problem is.' She put her teacup down angrily on the bedside table and confronted him squarely, her blue eyes cold.

The fact that she did not understand what the problem was, was in itself a large part of the problem, Sinclair thought to himself.

'It's to do with belonging,' he said quietly. 'It's to do with the fact that your father and my father are hardly able to exchange a comprehensible word with each other although they've both lived and worked in this town for almost the whole of their lives.'

'That's just your ridiculous inverted snobbery,' she said bitterly. 'My father's always got on perfectly well with his workforce. They respect him. Anyway, all that's got nothing to do with the children. It's all old history, all that class nonsense.'

'That's easy to say from Broadley. You'd not get my father to agree, and I'm not sure I do either. What I am sure of is that I want my daughters to stay in contact with the world I was brought up in. At root, I suppose it's to do with identity, my identity, and the identity I'd like my children to have.' He stopped, realizing that his wife was looking at him with incomprehension bordering on disgust.

'If they were boys I suppose you'd want them to wear cloth caps, like your father, or go rampaging off to the Milford United match every Saturday afternoon with the rest of the hooligans from the Highcliffe estate. Well, they're girls, thank God, and they're my girls as well as yours, and I intend them to have the best education that money can buy. And I'll be eternally grateful to my father for offering to provide what we certainly can't afford ourselves on your salary.'

'I won't have it, Margaret. They'll come to no harm at the local school. It's not some inner city blackboard jungle we're talking about, it's a suburban comprehensive, for heaven's sake. Jenny'll do as well there as I did at my school, if not better.'

'Over my dead body,' she said, tears of frustration in her eyes. 'I swear to you, Alex, I'll leave you if this goes on. I'll take the children and go home.'

Sinclair looked at her, the face petulant now, her fists clenched like a child's on the quilt. This was the threat she had made at every crisis in their married life, and more often than not he had given in to her and she had stayed, taking their relationship one notch further up the scale of bitterness as she defeated him through his passion not for her but for his children. The thought of losing them clenched his inside with a physical pain which she understood and used, and he had never found the strength to withstand.

'This is crazy,' he said. 'Leave it until this evening. I'll get home early, I promise, and we'll settle it then. I've got to go now. There are problems at work.'

'There always are,' she said sourly, and flopping back on the pillows, closed her eyes against him and the daylight again.

THREE

KATE WESTON DROVE a distraught Annie Macready back to Highcliffe from the magistrates' court where Joey had been remanded in custody for a week. They had been allocated one of the duty solicitors who opined, having checked that no one was sure where Joey had been at the time of Tom Carter's attack, that there was no way he could prevent a remand at this stage. Joey had been led into the dock looking puzzled but otherwise none the worse for his ordeal in the cells, and after the brief hearing had gone back amiably enough with his escort without even a glance in the direction of his mother in the public gallery.

Kate drove straight into the yard at the advice centre, and pulled up with an unusually vicious squeal of the brakes. She helped Annie out of the car and into the main office where Derek Stevenson was waiting.

'Right,' he said as the two women walked in. 'What we need now is an action committee. I've rung Bill Bairstow and Father O'Leary from St Francis's. You're a Catholic, aren't you, Annie?'

Annie nodded and sat her considerable bulk down on one of the flimsy plastic chairs against the wall of the office. She was obviously still stunned by the speed of events but offered no objection as Stevenson went on to fill in the details of what he thought was needed. Kate too sat listening, her mind in a turmoil of anger and grief at the apparent helplessness of Joey's family and friends in the face of the juggernaut of the law. All her professional objectivity, she admitted, had been blown away by Annie's own emotion and the sight of Joey in the dock.

'First thing is to get you legal aid, Annie,' Derek went on. 'And if that won't get you the sort of representation you need then we'll organize some sort of appeal. Then we need to find out where Joey really was on Tuesday evening when old Tom was attacked. Someone must have seen him if he was out on the estate at that time of night. And then there's the irregularities in the police handling of the case last night. They'd no right to question him without a friend present.'

'They tried to find Annie,' Kate injected, but without her usual conviction. 'I know Alex Sinclair was looking for her.'

'Well, he didn't look hard enough, did he? Stevenson came back sharply. 'And they went ahead with the interview regardless. It's an absolute outrage, and they know damn well it is. And if we can raise a real head of steam on that, I shouldn't think the so-called confession will be worth the paper it's written on.'

'Tracey says he went out to get chips,' Annie said at last. She clasped her hands tightly on her lap, as if to let go would lead her to lose her grip on reality.

'Well, if that's right the fish and chip man should remember him,' Kate said.

'T'trouble is, neither of them is very good about time,' Annie said. 'Joey's never learned, and Tracey were asleep in t'chair when I got in from bingo, and Joey'd gone to bed. They'd had chips, all right, the papers were there, but there's no telling what time.'

'The police should be checking all this,' Kate said, angry again.

'Yes, well, I've no doubt they will do, if they think we'll put up a proper defence of the boy,' Stevenson said. 'They'll have thought it was open and shut last night, I dare say. A backward lad and a confession. No bloody contest.'

'Well, they've got another think coming,' Annie said fiercely. 'T'lad may be backward, but he wouldn't hurt a fly, our Joey wouldn't.' She was beginning to look more composed now, and a look of determination was taking over from the numbed grief through which she had faced the world since the police had knocked on her door the previous evening.

Kate put a hand on her arm briefly.

'We know that, Annie. I know it better than most. I've trusted Joey with Sam often enough.'

The centre door opened again to admit a tall, pale young man with long untidy brown hair. He wore dark trousers and a hairy grey sweater and if it had not been for the glimpse of a clerical collar beneath the crew-neck he could have been taken for a student rather than a priest. Annie half rose from her chair and the man embraced her briefly.

'I'm sorry I wasn't here last night, Annie,' he said. 'I'd gone to see my mother in Manchester and didn't come back till this morning. What's the situation with Joey now?'

'He's been remanded, Father,' Annie said. 'They say he's made a confession.'

'I find that difficult to believe,' Francis O'Leary said drily. 'I spent some time trying to get Joey to understand the nature of confession, without much success.'

'What worries me is that they've taken him to Bradford. That's no place for a boy like Joey,' Kate said. The priest nodded grimly.

'It's no place for anyone these days,' he said. 'It's grossly overcrowded. I'll ring the chaplain and get him to keep an eye out for Joey. He'll need it.'

The door opened again and a small, elderly man came into the centre, with a thick dark overcoat done up to the neck, overlaid by a woollen scarf which almost entirely concealed the lower half of his face, and topped off with a traditional cloth cap.

'Bill, I'm glad you're here,' Father O'Leary said warmly as the newcomer slowly unwrapped himself. Councillor Bill Bairstow, who represented Highcliffe for Labour on the Milford town council, was a small, tough-looking man, a former miner, who had been given early retirement from the pits on the grounds of ill-health and had worked for the trades unions and in local politics ever since. He slogged around the steep streets of the estate in all weathers visiting his constituents and acting as a one-man advice centre which, as Derek Stevenson had commented more than once, threatened to put the official centre out of business.

Bill hung up his coat and went over to Annie, gasping slightly for breath.

'What's all this, then, lass?' he asked, shaking her warmly by the hand. 'They've made a bit of a dog's dinner of it, haven't they?'

'Right, then,' Derek Stevenson broke in, officiously. 'Now we're all here, we can work out a plan of campaign. What did the solicitor say this morning, Kate?'

By the end of an hour's discussion they had drawn up their plans. Bill Bairstow would follow up what they all regarded as police irregularities in the handling of Joey's arrest and questioning the previous day, firstly informally and then, if necessary, through a formal complaint to the police and the police authority, whose chairman was a Labour colleague on the town council. Father O'Leary would launch a defence fund for Joey Macready after Mass on Sunday, persuading members of his congregation to organize house-to-house collections as it became clear how much might be needed to see Joey's innocence established. Derek and Kate would between them try to find witnesses who had seen Joey around the estate on the night of the murder, and liaise with the solicitor if they discovered anything useful for his defence.

'What about visiting Joey?' Kate asked Annie finally.

'The solicitor chap said he'd take me over there tomorrow because he wants to see Joey himself.'

'I'll take you the day after,' Father O'Leary volunteered. 'You'll be wanting to go every day, won't you?'

'Well, there's mi work,' Annie said doubtfully. 'I can't afford to teck time off. I'll have to see if I can do more late shifts and teck time in the day. And there's Tracey to see to...'

'I'll keep an eye on Tracey after school,' Kate volunteered. 'She can have her tea with Sam. That's no trouble.'

'Fine,' Derek Stevenson said determinedly. 'Let's get on with it, then. It's time those officious bastards down at police HQ learned where to draw the line.'

Bill Bairstow and Father O'Leary exchanged a slightly anxious glance at that, but did not argue.

THE WEATHER for the rest of that week turned unusually warm and the threat of thunder loomed over the High-cliffe estate, turning usually amiable clients at the advice centre cantankerous. Kate was just about to clear her desk and leave on the Friday afternoon, in time to give Sam and Tracey Macready tea and keep an eye on them until Annie returned from her daily trek to Bradford to see Joey, when her door opened and a woman she did not recognize slipped apologetically into the room.

'Have you got a minute?' she asked in a near whisper. She was a thin woman of middle age, dressed in cotton slacks and a white acrylic blouse which revealed the out-line of a darker coloured brassiere, her greying hair inex-pertly permed and a smear of lipstick her only concession to fashion. Kate stifled a sigh and waved her visitor into the visitor's chair.

'If I can help...' she said.

'It's my lad, Ken. He's disappeared.'

Ken was Doreen Leafield's only son, nineteen years of age, an apprentice plumber with the local building firm of Agarth and Bradfield and according to his mother's ac-count a steady, rather shy boy, a good worker, who pre-ferred fishing to girls, and a night in front of the telly to one at the pub.

'He were right upset on Monday when it came out about old Tom Carter being killed. Came home from work in a right state about it. And then on Tuesday morning when I went to wake him up, he'd gone. Packed his rucksack and gone without a word. Taken his post office book an' all. We never heard a sound, he'd crept out that quietly.' Mrs Lea-field rubbed her pale chapped hands together in silent anguish. 'Police say there's nowt they can do. He's old enough to go where he likes . . .'

'That's right,' Kate said. 'If he's of age, they'll just put him down as a missing person and not do much more about it. If he packed a bag and took money he obviously intended to go off.'

'But why?' Mrs Leafield broke in angrily. 'He's a good boy, never been a moment's trouble, not like some. Why should he run off?'

'Why was he so upset about Tom Carter? Did he know him?'

'Aye, they used to go fishing together when Ken were a lad. Not so much lately, though they did have a day on t'river a couple of weeks ago. But Ken seemed to be losing interest. Said there were dead fish in t'river and it wasn't worth bothering any more. I were quite glad really—it didn't seem natural to be spending so much time with an old boy like that. I wanted him to get out more with lads of his own age—and lasses.'

'But he'd still regard old Tom as a friend? He would be upset then, wouldn't he?'

'I suppose so, but not upset enough to run off. Why should he? It's not as if Tom Carter were family. He were a awkward old bugger, if you want my opinion.'

'Well, there is one obvious reason Ken might run away, Mrs Leafield,' Kate said slowly. 'Do you think he knew something about the murder?'

The old woman stiffened and looked away from Kate anxiously, her hands twisting in even greater agitation in her lap.

'He were at home with me and his dad all evening, the night it happened, I mean. We were all watching t'telly. He never went out. Anyway, they know who did it, don't they. They've taken that Macready lad away.'

'Did the police ask you about that night, though? Who did you see at the police station? Was it Inspector Sinclair?' Kate asked.

'No, it were just a sergeant. He didn't seem a scrap bothered. Said Ken'd be in touch if he wanted to be, and there were nowt the police could do unless there was evidence of something criminal behind it.'

'They weren't interested in Ken's connection with Tom Carter?'

'They weren't interested at all,' Mrs Leafield said bitterly.

'The only other people I know of who could help you trace Ken are the Salvation Army,' Kate said. 'You could try them. I'll find the address in town for you, if you like. And the local radio might broadcast an appeal for you, if you think he may still be staying somewhere locally. Don't you have any idea where he might have gone?'

'I don't. And I don't want everyone knowing our business,' Mrs Leafield said doubtfully.

'Are there no friends or relatives he could have gone to stay with?'

'All our family lives local. He'd not have gone to his aunties without me knowing.'

'No friends?' Kate persisted, glancing surreptitiously at her watch. She was, she thought, unreasonably perturbed by Mrs Leafield's story, although she could, like the police, pinpoint no reason to connect Ken Leafield's disappearance with the murder and Joey Macready.

'There were a lad from London he met in a fishing competition one time... But he couldn't have gone to London. He didn't have enough money to live down there.'

'Do you know where that friend lived?'

'I'm not sure. I might be able to find his address. He used to write to Ken now and then to tell him about competitions he'd been in. Sent a cutting from an angling paper one time.'

'Look,' Kate said. 'You see what you can find, and go down to the Sally Army and have a word with them. And I'll have another word with the police and see if there's really nothing they can do. Will that help?'

'Aye, it'll have to, I suppose,' Mrs Leafield said heavily. 'He's a good lad, our Ken. It's not like him to do anything so—so sudden. And there's his job. He'll lose that if he's not careful. We'll have to tell them summat if he doesn't turn up for work soon.'

'YOU'RE BEING over-emotional, Kate,' Alex Sinclair said sharply, turning away from his office window to face his visitor. He was in his shirtsleeves, with a desk piled with files, and was not bothering to conceal the fact that he thought Kate Weston was wasting his time.

'You're clutching at straws.'

'Don't you think it's odd, this boy disappearing immediately after the murder?' Kate persisted.

'Odd, yes. Suspicious, not particularly, if he was a friend of the old boy's. He'd naturally be upset and people do odd things when they're upset. You know that. There's absolutely no evidence that he had anything to do with the killing.'

'You've checked?'

'I've seen the desk sergeant's report. His mother says he was in all night with them watching television. We've absolutely no reason to disbelieve that. If she had anything at all to hide about his behaviour that night she wouldn't be rushing around the town broadcasting the fact that he'd run off, now would she? She wouldn't have been down here telling us the news, for a start.'

Kate shrugged helplessly.

'So there's nothing you can do?'

Sinclair sat down heavily in his chair and leaned across the desk, his chin on his hands, looking at Kate silently for a moment. She looked hot and harassed, her summer dress creased and her hair slightly damp at the forehead from the day's humid heat. There was anxiety in her eyes and Sinclair wondered if she ever found time to think about herself rather than her child, her clients and every other lame duck who crossed her path. He sighed.

'There's very little I can do,' he said. 'As far as we're concerned, the Carter murder case is closed, we have a confession, a remand in custody, absolutely no reason to look any further.' His own misgivings about Joey Macready he left unsaid.

'But Joey...' she broke in.

'I know you don't believe Joey Macready is guilty, but the magistrates have decided there's a case to answer and it's out of my hands now. It's not my job to prepare his defence. That's down to his solicitor, his family and that rabble of a defence committee Derek Stevenson seems to be assembling up in Highcliffe,' Sinclair said. He wished immediately that he had chosen his words more carefully, but it was too late.

'That's not fair,' Kate Weston objected, getting up from her chair angrily. 'You know that boy was improperly questioned. It's no wonder people are angry.'

'Are they really angry?' Sinclair asked. 'Or is Stevenson making sure they are?'

'I'm sorry I came,' Kate said. 'I thought you might be able to help Mrs Leafield, but if that's impossible, I'll see what I can do myself. I'm sorry I've wasted your time.' She turned away, her disappointment clearly visible.

'Kate!' Sinclair said sharply, and she turned, one hand on the door handle.

'I'll ask Sergeant Wilson to make some inquiries at the railway station and the bus station,' Sinclair conceded wearily. 'Someone there might have seen the lad if he left very early. But believe me, I'll have difficulty in justifying even that if I'm pressed. There are no suspicious circumstances to justify the use of police time on a missing person.'

He was rewarded by a tired smile as Kate brushed her damp hair away from her eyes. God damn you, woman, Sinclair thought to himself. What are you getting me into?

'Thanks, Alex,' Kate said. 'I knew you'd help.'

FOUR

DETECTIVE-SUPERINTENDENT Eddie Greaves was in an expansive mood as he tangoed around the Masonic ballroom with his arms around a very pretty woman who was not his wife. If Margaret Sinclair was affronted by the fact that his fingers were sliding across the small of her back with just a little more pressure on the royal blue silk of her evening dress than was actually necessary to steer her through the other dancers she gave no sign of it. If she had thought about it at all she would have put it down as the price to be paid for dancing with her husband's boss and thereby doing his career some good.

'You think he'll put his name forward this time, then,' Greaves asked, as he spun Margaret beneath the uniformed 'big band' which bi-annually played at the lodge's Ladies Night and steered her expertly the length of the ballroom again. 'You've persuaded him?' Opportunities for a more modern style of dancing were strictly limited at Ladies Nights and only really welcomed by the lodge's younger members, of whom there were surprisingly few these days. Most of the brethren were far happier to foxtrot and tango the night away in the time-honoured way.

'Well, I'm not sure I've persuaded him. But I think my father has,' Margaret said.

'Ah yes, your father.' Greaves nodded. 'He's here tonight, is he?'

'We're with him and my mother,' Margaret said, trying not to dwell on the fierce resistance Alex had put up to her parents' regular invitation this time. The struggle to persuade him to accept seemed to get harder as each six months passed and she knew that her reassurance to Superintendent Greaves over Alex's long postponed application to join the lodge was so much wishful thinking. It was an application she had come to realize with some chagrin that he would never make.

'And what about your girl? Jenny, isn't it? Alex tells me she may be going to St Helen's in September?'

'Yes, that's right,' Margaret said firmly, conscious again of that roving hand sliding perilously close to her rather small buttocks under the clinging silk. She leaned away from Greaves so that he had to move his hand up her back to support her more firmly. 'Yes, she's starting at St Helen's next term. That's all settled.'

'With Grandad's help, no doubt?' Greaves surmised. 'But you'll not regret it, you know. Our Clare's been very happy there. A lovely atmosphere. None of the rougher elements you get at the comprehensives.'

The tango ended with a flourish and the dancers applauded politely before beginning to drift back to their tables. Greaves put a proprietorial hand under Margaret Sinclair's elbow, aware that her naturally blonde good looks and her slim figure in what he guessed was a designer dress were as usual drawing admiring glances. He guided her back to the table where her parents and her husband were sitting. Alex Sinclair stood up and pulled a chair out for his wife, who sat down without acknowledgement.

'Can I get you a drink, sir?' he asked Greaves.

'Thanks Alex, yes. A double Scotch, please. Ice. No soda.' Greaves settled down comfortably beside Ted and Mary Booth, who waved away Sinclair's offer of refilled glasses.

Sinclair shouldered his way through the crowd to the bar, aware of attracting the attention of more than one of the women he passed on his way. His dinner suit fitted well and looked good on him, and he knew that he and Margaret were commonly referred to as 'that good-looking couple', the assumption being that two young people so uniquely blessed in a town like Milford could not avoid also being uniquely happy. If only it were that simple, he thought. Tonight his mood was one of distinct unease in this place and this company as he came under pressure from his wife's family and his colleagues to put aside his scruples and join the lodge at which he was such a regular guest of his father-in-law.

He bought himself a Scotch and drank it quickly at the bar before carrying Greaves's drink back to the table. The superintendent took the glass with a nod.

'I was just saying to Margaret how happy I thought your Jenny would be at St Helen's,' Greaves said, with a half glance at Ted Booth, who was sitting on the other side of the table, a large brandy and soda to hand and a Churchillian cigar between his lips. Booth nodded expansively.

'Quite right,' he said. Sinclair glanced at his wife, who seemed to be holding her breath waiting for his reply. The blue dress suited her fair, brittle beauty to perfection and alcohol and excitement had given her eyes a sparkle which was never there these days when they were alone. He could, he knew, ruin her evening at this point with a word and probably upset his father-in-law as well, although Ted Booth's unperturbability after a few brandies was legend. He was, Sinclair admitted with an affection which had grown over the years almost in spite of himself, a wealthy man who genuinely enjoyed spending his money.

'Well, you know the school, sir, so I'm sure you're right,' Sinclair said carefully.

Margaret glanced at him sharply, but said nothing.

'It's settled, then, is it?' Ted Booth asked.

'Oh, I think so,' Sinclair said levelly, still avoiding Margaret's eye.

'I'll talk to my accountant on Monday, then,' Booth said easily. 'And now, Mother, it's time we tripped the light fantastic, isn't it? If I'm not mistaken, this is a waltz.'

Eddie Greaves made his excuses too as the Booths took to the dance-floor with Mrs Booth, a woman as essentially kindly as she looked motherly, resembling nothing more, Sinclair thought, than a galleon in full sail in her full-skirted cream taffeta dress cut wide and low to reveal her fleshy shoulders.

'Do you mean that?' Margaret asked sharply as soon as they were alone. 'She can go?'

'It seems to be what Jennifer wants,' Sinclair said.

'Of course, it doesn't matter what I want, naturally.'

Sinclair looked around at the neighbouring tables to make sure that they could not be overheard.

'One day,' he said, speaking in a fierce whisper, 'you'll face me with a choice between my children and what I believe in which will tear me apart, and the family as well for all I know. When that happens, I'll never forgive you, and nor, quite possibly, will the girls. But this school business isn't the issue. Jenny's old enough to understand the arguments and she wants to go to St Helen's with her friends, so let's let it rest there, shall we? Just thank your lucky stars you've got away with it again.'

He picked up his empty glass and without another glance at his wife, who remained tight-lipped and pale alone at the table, he shouldered his way back to the bar with a lack of courtesy which brought him more than one angry and puzzled glance from fellow revellers. He ordered another double Scotch and took a deep sip. His hand, he noticed, was trembling as he put the glass down on the counter and lit a cigarette. Not for the first time he wondered how much longer he could tolerate a marriage which had turned into a form of war.

Sinclair was so lost in his own thoughts that Ted Booth had to clap him on the shoulder before his son-in-law became aware of his presence at his elbow.

'Now then, lad,' he said. 'You're knocking it back a bit this evening, aren't you?'

Sinclair raised his glass to the older man ironically.

'My father always says we Scots have this stuff running in our veins.'

'I don't want you to feel beholden, you know, over the school fees,' Booth said, gazing determinedly into his own glass. 'And if it comes between you and Margaret . . .' He hesitated, embarrassed.

'It hasn't,' Sinclair said truthfully. Whatever came between himself and Margaret went a lot deeper than a quarrel over Jenny's education. It was the difference between symptom and disease. But both he and Margaret had tacitly agreed to keep their disagreements from their parents, although Sinclair suspected that his own father and Ted Booth both had a shrewd idea that all was not well with the marriage.

'So what about this promotion, then?' Booth asked, obviously glad to escape from potentially deep waters. 'Any news yet?'

'Not yet,' Sinclair said. 'It looks as if it could be another six months or so.'

'Aye, well, not to worry. Word is you've got it in the bag.'

Sinclair raised a sceptical eyebrow at that but said nothing. His father-in-law's contacts were wide-ranging and on the whole he preferred not to know with whom Ted had been discussing his career prospects.

'And this murder case can't have done you much harm— a quick arrest, wasn't it?'

'Pretty quick, yes,' Sinclair admitted.

'But some political rumblings, I hear, up in Highcliffe? What's that about, then? A bit of pinko agitation?'

'There's some concern about the way the lad was questioned. He's not normal,' Sinclair said carefully.

'Did you question him, then?' Booth asked sharply.

Sinclair shook his head and his father-in-law nodded, satisfied.

'You're all right, then, aren't you? In the clear?' he concluded, lighting another cigar with a show of his usual satisfaction. He offered Sinclair his leather case but the younger man shook his head.

'So, come and meet a friend of mine who wants to make your acquaintance. Says he's heard a lot about you. James Agarth of Agarth and Bradfield. Calls himself MD, but there's no competition there, now. Old Bill Bradfield's long gone, so Jim IS Agarth and Bradfield. Used to be a regular here but he's moved on to higher things, provincial grand something-or-other, so we don't see so much of him these days.'

Booth put a proprietorial hand on his son-in-law's arm and guided him out of the main ballroom into a side room where the cigar smoke was almost thick enough to cut, and the company was exclusively male, and contentedly well over middle-age, middle-weight and middle-income. Ted Booth was at home here, waving a friendly cigar to friends and acquaintances as he led Alex Sinclair towards a group of men at a corner table well supplied with its own heavily depleted bottles of spirits, overflowing ashtrays and used supper plates.

At the centre of the group, Sinclair noticed, was one man who did not share the animation of the rest. He was tall, thin-faced, almost ascetic-looking, and the eyes which met first Ted Booth's and then Sinclair's own were a cold grey which did not change even when his lips offered a half smile of greeting to Booth.

'My son-in-law, Alex Sinclair, a likely lad in the county police force.' Booth made the introduction expansively. 'James Agarth, lad. Made his brass building police stations for the likes of you, you know, and that estate up at Highcliffe, aren't I right, Jim?' Agarth winced slightly at the diminutive but nodded.

'You've just had some success, I hear, Inspector,' Agarth said. 'Tom Carter was one of my pensioners, you know. A dreadful incident. I'm only glad it was cleared up so quickly. Mrs Carter must be comforted by that, at least.'

'Oh, I'm sure,' Sinclair said, with palpable lack of conviction. He felt, rather than saw, his father-in-law's quick sideways glance.

'Let me get you a drink, Inspector,' Agarth went on smoothly, raising a finger to a hovering waitress. 'Scotch? Ice or soda?'

Hospitality accepted, Sinclair had no choice but to sit for ten minutes between the two older men as Booth warmly, and not for the first time, and Agarth coldly, and with motives which Sinclair could not begin to fathom, tried to persuade him to join the lodge where he was so frequently a guest. It was, he decided, a very deliberate and premeditated attempt to bring him to the decision he had so long evaded, and the longer it went on the more silently angry he felt and the more convinced he became that he should not give way.

'Of course, the Roman Catholic Church has conscientious objections to the brotherhood. Your family are Scottish but they are not Catholics, are they?' Agarth asked at last, in obvious response to Sinclair's lack of enthusiasm. Sinclair shook his head.

'The only religion my father ever professed was socialism, and he can't find a political party these days which does anything like justice to his views, so he's pretty well given up politics and religion altogether,' he said, knowing his answer would embarrass Booth by its frankness. Sinclair's background was not a topic which his father-in-law ever mentioned in public, and Agarth too looked irritated by his reply.

'So you have no conscientious objection?'

'Only the objection that police officers should not, in principle, belong to secret societies,' Sinclair said at last, firmly enough to draw curious glances from some of the other drinkers around the table.

'Not a view shared by your chief constable, I know,' Agarth said coldly. 'Or by Superintendent Greaves.'

'Nor by some of my subordinates,' Sinclair agreed, nodding in the direction of Detective-Sergeant Wilson, who happened to be passing, a pint glass in hand. 'But that's my view, for what it's worth.'

'Ah, someone else I don't know,' said Agarth, watching the sergeant make his way through the crowd. 'Also a guest here tonight, I think, but a member of another lodge, perhaps?'

Sinclair merely nodded in response, feeling no obligation to fill in any details on Wilson for his interrogator.

'Well, perhaps we should be getting back to the ladies,' Ted Booth broke in, clearly embarrassed by the turn the discussion had taken. 'They'll be wondering where we are...' Agarth nodded, giving Sinclair a thoughtful look before reaching out to refill his own glass with brandy. He did not offer the bottle any further.

'Don't keep the ladies waiting, Ted,' he said, the slightest hint of mockery in his voice. 'And give them my regards, do. Your wife, and Margaret too.'

'We must get together soon,' Ted Booth floundered. 'A little dinner-party, perhaps, so you can get to know Alex better, have a longer talk.'

With some irritation, Alex Sinclair turned on his heel and pushed his way back into the ballroom. He would not, he determined, give in to Margaret's pleading next time one of these functions came around. The price was becoming too high.

FIVE

KATE WESTON TOOK a pew at the back of the tiny crematorium chapel, although there was no shortage of seats
nearer the front and the congregation for Tom Carter's funeral was sparse. She recognized Mrs Carter in the front
pew, bundled up in a heavy winter coat although the
weather was still unseasonably warm. She was flanked by
two middle-aged women of similar stocky build, one in a
black headscarf, the other bare-headed. In the pew behind, a gangling teenaged boy sat between two younger
girls, making occasional futile efforts to prevent them from
whispering to each other across him. The children, like the
adults in the pew in front, were obviously dressed in their
best clothes, and the boy kept running a finger between his
scrawny neck and its unaccustomed collar and tie to re-
lieve the discomfort. One of the little girls looked round
with bright, inquisitive eyes as Kate took her seat and she
recognized one of Sam's school contemporaries. She had
not realized that the child called Rosie was old Tom's
granddaughter.

Behind the children she recognized the tall hunched figure of Gordon Rangely, the local reporter who had been
covering the murder in the *Echo* since the day Tom's body
had been found. He sat half sideways in his pew, a notebook ostentatiously on his knee and a pencil in his hand, as
if to distance himself from the obsequies going on around
him. He glanced at Kate as she sat down and raised an eyebrow. She gave him less than half a nod of acknowledgement, irritated by his pose of amused detachment.

The coffin on its purple-draped dais at the front of the
chapel, flanked by large urns of white and gold chrysan-
themums which looked as though they were reaching the
end of their useful life, looked surprisingly small, Kate

thought. One of the family wreaths still on top of the coffin, she realized with a sense of surprise, had been woven into the shape of a large fish in a curious perversion of the florist's art.

She picked up the order of service and recognized a shortened version of the standard Church of England Book of Common Prayer rubric in which she had been brought up by her churchgoing parents and which had not on this occasion been translated from the glory of Elizabethan English into the banality of more modern prose. She gazed for a moment at the once familiar words and tried to compose herself for the service. There was no particular reason why she should have come to Tom Carter's funeral, no obligation, only a vague sense that someone in some sort of official position on the estate should be there to mark his brutal passing.

Even as the officiating clergyman came in at the front of the chapel and the congregation rose, she was aware of a gust of fresh air as the door at the rear of the chapel opened and more mourners came in. She glanced sideways and smiled faintly in acknowledgement as Doreen Leafield took a seat beside her. She was more surprised to see Inspector Alex Sinclair pass down the aisle without looking in her direction and take a seat a couple of pews in front, directly behind the reporter, Rangely.

The service was brief and without music and, Kate thought, unbearably bleak. There was no oration and as the officiating clergyman ended with the familiar blessing the old man's coffin slid from sight between the pale mauve curtains at the back of the chapel to the tinny strains of the Twenty-third Psalm which suddenly erupted at too high a volume from a hidden loudspeaker. Kate closed her order of service with tears pricking the back of her eyes. She could not hear the familiar Prayer Book words without being taken back with cruel clarity to the day six years ago when Richard's coffin had similarly vanished from sight and she had led her son, wide-eyed and silent, out of the crematorium to face life without him.

Kate bit her lip as the congregation stood while the women and children of the Carter family took that same solemn walk, grim-faced, with even Rosie reduced to a sort of awed submission by what she had witnessed. When they had gone Kate turned to Mrs Leafield.

'Is there any news of your son?' she asked as they made their way out of the chapel into the bright sunlight together.

'Aye, I had a postcard,' Doreen Leafield admitted, almost reluctantly, Kate thought. 'He's with his friend in London, which is what we thought. But he doesn't bother to say where that is, so we're none the wiser really. His father's right furious with him. Says if that's all he thinks about us he can stop where he is and good riddance.' Mrs Leafield took off the dark scarf she had been wearing in the chapel and twisted the silky material fiercely between her fingers, a look of raw pain disfiguring her features for a moment. 'He were such a good lad...' she said, her voice trailing away into silence.

The two women stood together for a moment looking at the dozen or so wreaths and bouquets which were laid out for inspection outside the chapel door. The fish was there, an intricate creation of white and yellow flowers with a bright gold and red everlasting bloom for an eye, which stared malevolently at the mourners. It was, it appeared from the attached card, a tribute from Tom's three grandchildren, Rosie, Karen and Steve.

Already the hearse and accompanying cars for the next cremation were drawing slowly up the cemetery path towards the chapel porch and the Carter family were being bundled into their undertaker's limousine for the half-mile journey home. The entire funeral had taken little more than a quarter of an hour.

'Would you like a lift back?' Kate asked, indicating her own car parked a little way down the driveway.

'That's kind,' Mrs Leafield said but as they moved towards the Citroën Alex Sinclair's voice made Kate turn back.

'Can I have a word?' he asked.

Kate looked at the policeman warily.

'It was kind of you to come, Inspector,' she said non-committally. Her anger at Joey Macready's imprisonment had not dimmed as his week's remand drew to a close. He was due to appear at the magistrates' court again in two days' time.

'I thought someone should,' Sinclair said. Kate relaxed and smiled faintly.

'Me too,' she said.

'Can we talk somewhere more private—unofficially?' Sinclair asked quietly. Kate glanced at her watch and then at Mrs Leafield, who was standing next to the green CV2, still twining her scarf anxiously between her fingers.

'I've got to get back in time for the children coming out of school,' she said. 'And I promised Mrs Leafield a lift. Why don't you follow me down to the estate and come and have a cup of tea? Derek will regard it as consorting with the enemy, but sod Derek.'

'At the centre or at your place?' Sinclair asked, amused by her vehemence.

'Oh, at my place. Why not?'

AT DOREEN LEAFIELD's insistence, Kate went with her into her terraced former council house, its glossy hardwood front door the infallible sign of a home which had been bought by its former tenants. Such houses were relatively rare in Highcliffe, where unemployment and low wages put even the attractive terms available to potential buyers out of the reach of many. The Leafields, though, with both parents and an adult son in work, were among the estate's most privileged residents and like so many before them had lavished every penny they could afford on their home. Kate stepped through the front door on to new fitted carpets and was ushered into the living-room where Mr Leafield was to be found watching horse-racing on a large-screen television set. He looked up in surprise as the two women came in and nodded to Kate without, she thought, too much enthusiasm.

'Mrs Weston wants to help us trace Ken,' Doreen Leafield explained to her husband apologetically. 'You know Mrs Weston from t'advice centre. He's on t'late shift today,' she said by way of explanation of his presence in the middle of the afternoon, nodding at her husband's unresponsive back. 'He likes the horses.' Eventually the race ended and Mr Leafield turned away from the television and grunted non-committally, although Kate found it impossible to tell whether this was in acknowledgement of her offer of help or a reaction to the result of the steeplechase.

'Tooting,' he said. 'Tooting was where that lad lived. I remember now.' His wife went over to the imitation mahogany mantelshelf over the fitted gas fire and handed Kate a postcard which had been propped next to the brass carriage clock. It was a familiar enough card, showing the Houses of Parliament and Big Ben, under an unbelievably blue sky, and on the back was scrawled the briefest message in a still childish hand. *Staying with Dave,*' it said. *'Don't worry, I'm fine. Plenty of work down here.'* It was signed simply Ken and there was no address.

'After all we've done for that lad,' the lad's father said angrily as he watched Kate read the message. She looked at the postmark and deciphered SW but could not make out the number which followed.

'SW something would be right for Tooting, I think,' she said. 'But you don't know the friend's name or address? London's an awfully big place.'

'I think he were called Dave Raider or Rider. There were a letter from him but I expect he's taken that with him if that's where he's gone,' Doreen Leafield said helplessly.

'But a cutting from a magazine? You said he won something. What magazine was it in, can you remember? We might be able to trace that.'

'It were in t'*Angling Times*,' said Mr Leafield. 'Ken gets it himself sometimes, but he hadn't seen this competition t'other lad won. He were right chuffed about it. He's never won owt himself.'

Kate looked round at the Leafields' gleaming living-room. On top of the television a photograph of a teenaged boy in a gold frame took pride of place. Ken was a tall, fair youth with a shy smile, short-haired and neat, wearing a green angler's anorak and a bright red scarf.

'We only ever had the one,' his mother said, her voice choked with emotion as she followed Kate's gaze. 'That's what makes it so hard.' Her husband looked away, his jaw tightening, back to the television where the horses were parading for the next race.

'It should be possible to trace this boy Dave through the *Angling Times,*' Kate said slowly. 'You could go down to London to see Ken then . . .'

Both the Leafields looked at her blankly and she realized that what she was suggesting seemed as remote to them as a visit to the moon.

'We've never been in London,' Doreen admitted. 'We flew to Majorca from Manchester that time . . . Just the once. We didn't really like it. All those discos, you know? Too noisy for us . . .' She trailed off, embarrassed, and glanced at her husband for a moment before turning back to Kate with a renewed look of appeal. 'Could you go for us? We could pay your fare, whatever it cost. We couldn't cope with London, and all those undergrounds and crowds. Could you go for us, please?'

DETECTIVE-INSPECTOR Alex Sinclair was sitting in an un-marked car outside the flats when Kate Weston returned home ten minutes later. She parked her car behind his and locked it. He followed her into the block and up the steep stone steps without speaking.

'Unofficially?' she said, a note of scepticism in her voice as she waved him into a chair in the living-room and went into the kitchen to put the kettle on. 'Talking unofficially? What does that mean?'

Sinclair shrugged as Kate came back to the kitchen door and stood looking at him curiously.

'I'm not really sure,' he said. 'Officially the case of Tom Carter is closed, out of our hands, gone to the Crown Prosecution Service for processing. We'll ask for a longer remand when Joey Macready comes back to court next week and the committal hearing will be in three or four weeks, I should think. I've no further information which could lead me to interfere with that process.'

He realized that he was speaking unusually hesitantly and that she must recognize his diffidence too. He had made the decision to talk to Kate Weston on the spur of the moment as he came out of Tom Carter's funeral, and was now having difficulty in finding a specific reason for his approach. It was born, he admitted to himself, only partly from his unease over the Carter case, and partly from his personal wish to mend fences with Kate.

Kate said nothing in response to his hesitant rationalizations and turned back to her kettle, and he heard the clatter of crockery and the sound of water pouring as she made tea.

He looked around the living-room of her flat curiously. It was the first time she had ever invited him in. It was a rectangular box of a room, small for its combined function of sitting—and dining-room. It would fit twice into his own spacious sitting-room in Broadley, he thought wryly. And there was no sign here of the *Homes and Gardens* attempts at stylish living which Margaret lavished on what was, as she often reminded him, essentially her house.

Even so, Kate Weston's living-room had a cheerful, lived-in look which Sinclair liked: the Indian rugs and cushions and the few prints on the walls, although inexpensive, had been carefully chosen for colour and style; the walls were lined with shelves of books and ornaments and a few of what were obviously Sam's most prized possessions—a model Porsche, a Hornby engine which must be almost a collector's item, and some sea-shells. Pride of place on the mantelshelf over the electric fire went to two framed school photographs of Sam, one taken around the age of five, the little boy's face cheerful and unformed, the second a more recent portrait of the thoughtful and slightly suspicious eleven-year-old he had met.

There was another photograph too, of a man he did not recognize but guessed must be Kate's husband Richard. It was a very young man who stared out at him, about twenty-five he would have guessed if he had been attempting a description, and one whom he recognized women would find attractive, the hair curly and brown and unfashionably long, a thin, slightly ascetic face, a mock-serious look for the camera and smiling eyes which uncannily reflected those of his son. For a moment Sinclair had a strong sense that Richard Weston was watching him with a less than totally benign interest.

'And yet?' Kate asked suddenly, breaking the spell her dead husband had cast and making Sinclair start almost guiltily. She came back into the room with a tray of tea-things and picked up the hesitation she had detected in his last remark. 'And yet you're not happy with the due process of the law, are you? Why's that, then?'

For a moment their eyes met and she recognized an unhappiness in his which she guessed was not entirely professional, and not for the first time she wished that she had met Alex Sinclair in different circumstances. While he, for his part, wondered for a moment if he dare confide all his doubts about the case to this sympathetic listener. But that would be madness, he concluded, his jaw tightening. He looked away.

'I know you blame me for what's happened to Joey,' he said.

'I blame the police,' Kate said. 'I think they behaved disgracefully. But that doesn't mean I blame you personally. You said it was out of your hands.'

'So it was—and is,' he said quickly. 'But that doesn't mean I'm happy about it. In fact I'm getting less happy by the minute.' He stopped while she poured two cups of tea. A calm, sensible woman, he thought, who juggled the conflicting demands of job and child with skill; not beautiful, but with a gentle smile and bright, intelligent eyes with only the faintest lines of strain around them. Kate glanced at her watch.

'Sam will be home with Tracey Macready in ten minutes,' she said warningly. 'We haven't much time.'

'OK,' Sinclair said briskly. 'So, I was unhappy enough about the case to do some listening around the estate over the last couple of days. It's not my job to demolish the case against Joey Macready, which in spite of all my misgivings, looks solid enough if you listen to the tape-recording of his interview with Superintendent Greaves. Joey quite clearly admitted the charge. But I know you and this defence committee of yours are looking for anything which will clear Joey, and that's fair enough if you believe he's innocent, that his confession is invalid.'

'What you're saying is that we can get on with it and you wish us well but you won't help us, is that right?' Kate asked coolly.

Sinclair looked angry for a moment, and then nodded slowly with a slightly shamefaced smile.

'If you like,' he said. 'Not officially, anyway.'

'And unofficially? That word again?'

'Unofficially, I was in the Fox the other night keeping my ears open with Sergeant Wilson, which is what we do as a regular routine. It wasn't something special for this case. And the word is that the villains are laughing at us over Joey Macready.'

'Laughing?' Kate asked incredulously.

'Laughing all the way to the bank, I was told, in one case,' Sinclair said grimly.

'But Tom had no money, only a couple of pounds, they said . . .'

'I know. It makes no sense. And I could get no names, just the rumour that, as your friend Derek Stevenson said the other night, we've got it very wrong.'

'And that's not enough for you to take some action? Come on, Alex. What are you there for if not to investigate that sort of rumour? This is an innocent boy we're talking about, and one that can hardly defend himself. And he's locked up in that appalling gaol. You know what it's like in there for a normal boy, never mind one who doesn't know what week it is.'

Sinclair shrugged almost imperceptibly and drank some more tea in order to escape Kate's outraged gaze.

'I have sixteen open cases on my desk, including an arson attack on a school, three cases of GBH, a rape, and what looks like the serious pollution of the river Maze, which could involve criminal investigations too. As far as my boss is concerned, Tom Carter's murder was a case that was mercifully open and shut within a day. I don't have the authority to overrule him on that—or, indeed, the time to try.'

'And then, as Derek says, there's your promotion coming up, so I don't suppose making too many waves is a good idea, is it?' Kate asked waspishly.

Sinclair put his teacup down with an angry clatter and got to his feet.

'That's not fair, Kate, and you know it isn't. If I get anything firm I'll pursue it. But I've got nothing firm, just rumour, just a hunch if you like, and Superintendent Greaves is not a great one for following up hunches. He prefers facts. All I'm saying to you is that in my view it is worth pursuing a defence for Joey. In spite of the tape-recording, I don't think you are wasting your time. I thought you'd like to know that.'

He went to the door without looking at her again, his eyes cold. Sam and Tracey were on the landing outside and pushed past him without speaking. Kate hurried out after him to the top of the stairs.

'I'm sorry,' she said. 'I didn't mean that. It's just with the funeral, and the murder, and Joey, and Annie never here, it's all such a bloody mess...'

'Forget it,' Sinclair said flatly, before heading down the stairs two at a time. Kate sighed in exasperation. She had not had a chance to tell him about her determination to go to London to look for Ken Leafield, she thought, as she watched him go. The street door slammed three storeys below, echoing up the bleak stairwell, and she thought that it was perhaps just as well she had kept her plans to herself.

SIX

THE JOEY MACREADY Defence Committee met at the Highcliffe Advice Centre that night. Annie was there, looking pale and drawn after almost a week of commuting in and out of Bradford with various sympathetic friends to see Joey. Derek Stevenson took the chair, as usual, with Kate on his left and Councillor Bairstow on his right. They were expecting Father O'Leary, who had driven Annie to Bradford that day and then been detained on parish business at the church at the other end of the estate. While they were waiting for the priest to arrive the conversation ebbed and flowed desultorily.

'He's getting more and more down,' Annie said, not for the first time. 'It's not like our Joey. It's making him right depressed, that place. I've asked them to take him out of t'cell he's in. There's three of them in there and I think they're bloody teasing him. It's not right to have a lad like that in there, cooped up God knows how many hours a day. I told the officer today. He can't cope with it. And visiting's only fifteen minutes. All that way for a quarter of an hour. Poor kid doesn't know what's hit him.'

'Well, there doesn't seem much chance of getting bail, the solicitor says. Not on a charge as serious as this. It's a bloody disgrace,' Derek Stevenson said with barely suppressed fury. 'It's the system that's all wrong, you know. There should be proper facilities for kids like Joey.'

'I don't want bloody facilities for him,' Annie Macready broke in. 'I want him back home where he belongs. He no more murdered anyone than our Tracey did. There's not a scrap of harm in him.'

At that moment Father O'Leary came bustling through the door, apologizing for his late arrival and depositing a large tin cashbox on the table with a clatter.

'That's what we've got so far,' he said. 'I've not even had time to count it yet but there's a lot there. People are amazingly generous.'

'Let's start the meeting, then, and get on,' said Derek Stevenson impatiently. There was little love lost between him and the priest, whose faith and institution Stevenson despised equally, though he accepted grudgingly that in this particular enterprise the support of Annie Macready's church was invaluable to his cause.

'The most urgent item on the agenda is what we can offer the solicitor for the remand on Wednesday—any new information which would help us get the case thrown out at this stage so we can concentrate on the real issues—improper questioning, wrongful arrest and compensation, even. That's what we need to know.'

'How far did you get asking questions around the estate?' Kate asked. 'What about the fish and chip man?'

'Damn-all there,' Stevenson said. 'He remembered Joey and Tracey buying chips but he can't be sure of the time to the nearest half-hour or more. It was after *EastEnders* finished on the television, he says, because he always gets a rush then, but before the rush when the pub closes. That's all he's prepared to say. And that's what he's told the police, apparently. He may be called as a witness, he thinks.'

'Well, I've not got much further either,' Kate said gloomily. 'I asked around among the mothers at school and anyone else I've bumped into this week but no one can remember seeing them that evening. No one at the flats seems to have heard them go in or out. But then that's not impossible if people had their televisions on. The front door doesn't make much noise unless you slam it hard, and the two tenants on the ground floor are elderly and a bit deaf anyway. They wouldn't have noticed anything less than the fire brigade trying to get in, and probably not even that.'

'So they'll bloody well send him back to Bradford for another week,' Annie broke in angrily, her face flushed with emotion and close to tears. Francis O'Leary put a hand on her arm.

'It could be much longer than a week next time, Annie. I think you ought to be prepared for that. But I did think that if it came to another remand I'd see if the solicitor could ask for Joey to be sent to a secure ward in a hospital instead of to prison. I'll raise it with them tomorrow.'

'He's not effing mad,' Annie replied furiously and then, realizing what she had said, she put an embarrassed hand across her mouth. 'I'm sorry, Father, I don't know whether I'm coming or going—or even what I'm saying half the time—I'm that worried about him.'

'I know,' the priest said. 'Don't worry.'

'That's something else we can put in the press release I'm going to do ready for the court hearing,' Derek broke in. 'The whole business of unsuitable accommodation for remand prisoners, especially disabled ones like Joey. I've got Gordon Rangely all lined up to give our little campaign a good spread on Monday in the *Echo* and I'll get hold of the Radio Milford people too, if I can. You don't mind being interviewed, do you, Annie?'

Annie shook her head, looking slightly dazed.

'I'll go to t'bloody moon if you think it'll help,' she said.

'There is just one possibility that is a bit more positive,' Kate broke in, and she told them about Ken Leafield's disappearance and the chance that they might be able to trace him to his friend's house in Tooting. 'Of course, we don't know if his disappearance had anything to do with the murder directly. He might just have got depressed and run off—boys of that age do that sort of thing. But it seems to me that it might be worth talking to him to find out.'

'Could you? Could you possibly go and see him?' Francis O'Leary asked hesitantly. Kate looked at the anxious faces round the table. Annie caught her eye for a moment with a look of such intensity that Kate caught her breath at the pain which was usually so carefully concealed, even from her.

'I'll give it a try,' she said.

KATE SWUNG HER CAR into Edgeway Road, Tooting, pulled over to the kerb and switched off the engine wearily. She was hot and exhausted after driving down the M1 and grinding slowly round the congested South Circular Road, and the long suburban street stretched ahead of her, lined with identical Victorian terraced houses, until it eventually turned a corner five hundred yards further on and disappeared from view. She glanced again at the street map on the passenger seat beside her. It had been obvious that Edgeway was a long road but the reality daunted her. Dave Rider, Mr Leafield had discovered from the *Angling Times,* which he had eventually turned up in his son's bedroom, lived here. But the brief news item on Rider's fishing triumph had not given a house number and the magazine had proved unhelpful when she contacted them by telephone. There was no record, they said, of any more detailed address and even if there had been they very much doubted if that was the sort of information they would give out over the telephone to anyone.

She could have gone to the police for help, Kate admitted to herself, but after their last encounter she was reluctant to approach Alex Sinclair again. She knew he would find it hard to forgive the particular insult she had flung at him in her anger about Joey. So she sat staring at the length of Edgeway Road, Tooting, wondering how long it would take to knock on every door and inquire about Dave Rider and his supposed visitor from the North.

She pulled a comb from her handbag and used the rearview mirror to tidy her hair. It was more than four hours since she had driven out of Milford on another hot, sultry morning with the threat of thunder apparent in the smoky clouds to the west. She had no doubt that even on a Saturday the drive home would take as long and, in her tiny car, be even more tiring. She must, she thought miserably, be mad to have come so far on what would probably turn out to be a fool's errand. It was only Annie Macready's increasing desperation which had driven her to take up Father O'Leary's suggestion and come to London.

She got out of the car and pulled her crumpled and sticky shirt away from her back and looked around her. The street was one of many in south London which had been undergoing a period of rapid change which had been abruptly halted in its tracks. Its three-storey terraced houses of yellow London brick, with square bay windows and stained glass porches, had been put up early in the century to house the city's burgeoning population of clerks. They had gone through a cycle of dilapidation, an elaborate and superficial tarting up by an influx of newcomers from overseas, and had then begun to be bought up by the serious renovators of the yuppie classes. But where skips had lined the kerb and scaffolding enfolded many of the houses as roofs were renewed, double glazing and burglar alarms installed and period features lovingly restored, now all was static. Estate agents' boards leaned at crazy angles outside many of the houses and one or two were boarded up. As for the rest, the gentrified rubbed uneasy shoulders with the still dilapidated, giving the street the air of a woman half-dressed for a party and unsure of her welcome.

Lads who win fishing competitions don't live in newly gentrified houses, Kate told herself determinedly, and decided to start by knocking only on the doors of houses which retained signs of their comfortable middle age. But her tenuous faith in her own pop sociology grew strained as she worked her way down the street, knocking only at doors which had not been stripped to the bare wood and using only bells and knockers which were not genuine brass.

At least half her calls went unanswered, the front doors remaining resolutely closed and the curtains unmoving in the sultry heat. Several of the houses she regarded as hopefuls were in fact empty and where there was a response she met only negative replies to her inquiries about Dave Rider, replies offered with the cool lack of curiosity of Londoners of every race in the affairs of their neighbours.

Half way down the long street, almost at the bend which took Edgeway Road off towards Streatham, she paused for a rest and looked back the way she had come. The street was empty, with not even a child in sight on the dusty pavement and even the small front gardens with their shrivelled daffodils and overblown tulips apparently dozing in the oppressive heat.

'This is crazy,' she said to herself and realized with embarrassment that she had actually spoken aloud.

'Come on, missus, it's the first sign of madness, tha knows,' said a voice behind her in the broad vowels of Milford. She spun round, startled and jubilant, knowing immediately that she had, after all, tracked down her quarry. And sure enough, coming out of the gate immediately behind her was the living original of the photograph on Doreen Leafield's mantelpiece, a tall, blond and unexpectedly smiling youth, Ken Leafield himself. Kate laughed.

'God, you made me jump,' she said.

'Sorry,' Ken said, and made to pass her and continue on his way up the street.'

'Wait a minute,' she said. 'I've come all the way from Milford looking for you. You are Ken, aren't you?'

The boy stopped in his tracks and his face shadowed.

'What of it?' he said sullenly. 'Are you t'police or what? I've done nowt wrong.'

'No, I'm not the police. Your mum asked me to come and find you. She's worried sick.'

Ken Leafield hesitated for a moment, apparently on the point of making off up the street without a further word. Kate wondered what she could do if he decided to go, when suddenly he gave a resigned shrug.

'There's a caff on the corner. You'd better come and have a cup of tea, seeing as you've come so far,' he said. 'I'm not coming home, mind. I'll tell you that for nowt.'

They sat at a red formica table up against the steamy window overlooking the Broadway. Outside the traffic swirled past a set of traffic lights on its way south to the leafier suburbs or north to the city, apparently without respite. But in the sultry heat of the afternoon the pavements were not crowded and they found themselves alone over milky cups of tea.

'How's Mum?' Ken Leafield asked shyly when they had settled in their seats.

'She's fine,' Kate said. 'But she's worried about you. You must have guessed she would be.'

The boy nodded glumly.

'Aye, well, I expect she'll get used to it. I sent her a post-card.' He avoided Kate's eyes determinedly and fiddled with the sugar spoon in an almost empty bowl for a long moment. She knew from long experience that she would not be able to push this conversation along any more quickly than the boy wanted to go. Pressure would be counter-productive.

'I couldn't stay, you see,' he offered at length. 'I had to get away.'

'Was it because of Tom?' Kate asked. The boy looked at her, his blue eyes puzzled rather than afraid, as if weighing her up carefully. Finally he nodded as if satisfied.

'You work at the advice centre, don't you?'

Kate nodded and he put down the sugar spoon and rested his chin on his folded hands as if to emphasize the serious-ness of what he had to say.

'Aye, well, you'll know about things, then, I reckon.'

'What things, Ken?'

'The way things are for people like us. How there's some things you can change and some you can't. You know,' he insisted. It was encouraging, Kate thought, that the boy at least believed that he could change some things. So many of his contemporaries on the Highcliffe estate were sunk into a permanent and debilitating apathy.

'And Tom couldn't change something? Is that it?' she hazarded.

'Aye, well, I think he knew summat that ought to be changed but he was too frightened to do owt about it for a long time.'

'What did he know about?' Kate asked quietly.

'He were right worried about the fish dying in t'river. We used to go fishing every weekend, been going since I were a little lad, and it were getting worse, the pollution. It got to the stage where you were lucky to get a bite some weekends, never mind catch owt. Other times it were OK, but then after a few weeks it were bad again: no fish. And then, in the end, we began to find dead fish and nowt else. That last weekend we went down to Mill Pool, it's a right deep reach, just above the weir at Town Lane. It's a favourite place of ours, Mill Pool. And we found a pike right on the edge, a right whopper it were, and stone dead...poisoned.'

The boy paused, remembered a scene which had obviously affected him deeply.

'But why should Tom feel he could do anything about it?' Kate asked, still puzzled. 'Everyone knew about it locally. There've been articles in the *Echo*. The river authorities are trying to find the source of the pollution—and even the police.'

'Aye, well, that's it. I think Tom knew the source o't'pollution. He never said owt, mind. At first he just seemed a bit frightened by it. Then one day he started talking about it coming from t'Beck.'

'You mean Highcliffe Beck? The stream that comes down through the park into the river? But there's no industry up there, is there? That valley goes right up behind the estate and up to Broadley Moor. Anyway, I'm sure they'll have tested the water in the Beck. The last thing I saw in the paper suggested that someone was dumping in the river at night, because the pollution seems to come and go. You've said yourself it's not there all the time, is it?'

Kate still could not understand why Ken Leafield had run away from home. Nothing he had said yet offered any coherent reason for his precipitate and secretive departure from Milford.

'Tom were never very clear. Any road, that's not all.' The boy hesitated again as if wanting to be sure that it was safe to go on.

'Last time we went out,' he continued slowly. 'That last weekend, we found three or four dead roach, and then down at the pool the dead pike—a lovely fish. Tom were right angry that day. It were raining and he sat under his umbrella and went on and on about it not being right. And then he said summat funny. He said he's warned them. And I didn't know what he was talking about. But then he just looked at me and tapped his nose and said I wasn't to worry, he'd fix it. And I laughed, and said, you know, Oh yeah, as if I didn't believe him or summat. And he got angrier then and he said I could laugh but he'd bloody well go and see t'boss and fix it. See if he didn't.'

'The boss?'

'Aye, that's what he said.'

'So who did he mean?'

'Old Agarth, I suppose, like in Agarth and Bradley, you know? I worked for them, and he did an' all before he retired. Worked for them for years. Agarth as in James Agarth, my bloody boss,' Ken said flatly. 'A right bastard he is.'

'So do you think that's what he did?' Kate asked slowly.

'I don't know,' Ken said. 'He were dead two days later, weren't he? And I remembered how frightened he'd been earlier on when t'fish first started dying, so I thought I'd come down here for a bit. I thought if Mr Agarth was involved and he found out I used to go fishing with Tom and Tom had crossed him I might not have a job much longer any road.'

'Are you suggesting that James Agarth might have had something to do with Tom's murder?' Kate asked incredulously.

'I don't know, do I?' the boy retorted angrily. 'How do I know? I were worried any road. I thought I'd lose my job.'

'The police think Tom was killed by a mugger, Ken. In fact they've already arrested a lad from the estate. There's no evidence that it was anything more sinister.'

'Who's that, then?'

'They've arrested Joey Macready. Do you know him?'

'Daft Joey?' the boy said scornfully. 'He wouldn't hurt a fly. He's a right soft bugger. He were in my class at primary school.'

'But James Agarth?'

The boy shrugged, dispirited by her reaction.

'Aye, well, perhaps you're right. All I know is that old Tom were right scared. But that last weekend down at Mill Pool he were angry too. He picked up that pike and he looked at it, and then he chucked it right out into t'centre o't'river, and it got carried over the weir almost as if it were alive. And he swore. I'd never heard him swear before. And he sat under his umbrella for ages muttering to himself. He were right mad. The next thing I knew he were dead. And then I got scared.'

Kate was silent for a long time as she tried to make sense of what the boy had told her. At last she looked at him, at the open face and the clear eyes and his obvious anxiety and she knew that she could not help but believe him.

'Would you tell the police all that?' she asked.

'No way,' Ken said flatly. 'Why do you think I came down here? I don't want to get involved wi't'police. No way.' Kate sighed. Even the most law-abiding youngsters on the estate apparently harboured this deep suspicion of the police.

'If it comes out they'll come looking for you,' she said.

'Then they'll not find me,' Ken said. 'Nor will you— again. I'll not be round here—you can bank on that.'

'INTERMITTENT POLLUTION usually means that someone is flushing waste into a waterway from an industrial site, or else dumping it,' said Dennis Wright, one of Milford's senior environmental health officers. 'If they were dumping from a truck or a car, you'd expect it to be at night, of course. Someone would notice in daylight in a built-up area like Milford. But we've questioned all the industrial sites up river and found no one who'll admit any illegal flushing activities. In any case, the chemicals involved don't make much sense for any of the firms we've questioned. We've detected mercury, lead and some wastes which could come from the manufacture of plastics in the dead fish. And we've not finished yet. It's a very bizarre cocktail. The profile doesn't fit any of the manufacturers around here. The trouble is, we've not got enough lab staff these days to do the tests quickly. They went in the 'eighty-six cuts, you know.'

If Wright was surprised to have a visit from Detective-Inspector Sinclair to inquire about the progress of his investigation into the pollution of the River Maze he had not shown it. His visitor was sitting uncomfortably on a hard wooden chair crammed into a corner of Wright's untidy City Hall office. Wright swung awkwardly in his own swivel chair to look at a large-scale map of Milford which was pinned to the wall behind him. He was a precise, grey-haired man of indeterminate middle age. His hair was thinning but he combed the wisps that remained to make the most of their ability to cover his scalp. But his vanity did not extend much further than that. He had the sort of blue shadow around his chin and cheeks that afflicts some dark men, and his suit, crumpled and with a distinct stain on the left lapel, was almost the same dusty shade of grey as his hair. A general air of decrepitude filled the tiny office and enveloped its occupant as well. Wright looked at Sinclair through a pair of slightly opaque horn-rimmed glasses with an air of mild suspicion to which he did not give voice. Sinclair for his part was becoming increasingly irritated with Wright's air of hopeless bafflement about the state of the river.

'The red marks indicate where the pollution starts and ends,' Wright went on. 'That's where we've found concentrations of poisoned fish and traces of chemicals in the water. The extent of the problem seems to vary with each incident but it extends roughly from Highcliffe here—' he pointed to the straggling outline of the estate, which followed the contours of the hillside '—where the Beck joins the Maze, down to the south side of the town, here, by the by-pass. Of course, the problem must move downstream with the current, although in a relatively slow-moving waterway you could get some movement against the prevailing current at a time of flood, such as we had in January, for instance.'

'Mill Pool, by the weir, seems to have been particularly badly affected, according to the fishermen who use it,' Sinclair said.

Wright looked at his map again and nodded.

'Yes, it might be. The water goes into the backwater and tends to become quite still there. You could get a build-up of pollution there, I suppose.'

'And what about the Beck itself?' Sinclair persisted, but Wright shook his head, relatively vehemently.

'We've tested it, of course, but it's been negative every time. Which isn't surprising. There's no industry to speak of up beyond the estate and it would be much less convenient to dump waste in a shallow stream like that than down on the banks of a deeper river. Much more private by the river, too, where it's heavily built up with factories and nicely screened from the road for most of the way. That river walk is quite deserted at night. The trouble is, we don't have the staff to mount any sort of surveillance. We're run off our feet as it is.'

'I thought there were old mine workings up on Broadley Moor, though. Couldn't that be your source?' Sinclair asked.

'There shouldn't be much up there but coal waste, as far as I know,' Wright said. 'Those workings were sealed up in the 'fifties when they were worked out—before the Highcliffe estate was built.'

'By Agarth and Bradley, wasn't it?' Sinclair asked.

Wright looked surprised. 'Yes, I think that's right. But of course there's not much contracting in this town they've not been concerned with one way or another. They built the Highcliffe estate itself, you know, so they must have been working up there for ten years or more, before it was finished. And they put up at least three of the secondary schools—including Alderman Jackson where I went. You weren't there, were you? No, I didn't think so,' he went on when Sinclair shook his head impatiently. 'And they built that sports centre out at Braybrook. They're a big firm, you know. Local, but big.'

He leaned across to take a box file from a shelf and drew out some yellowing papers.

'That's mostly either council land or common land up there at Highcliffe, you know, and what isn't has all been surveyed at some time or another for housing need, so we've got quite detailed plans.' He spread another map out on his desk and Sinclair drew his chair nearer so that he could look at it more closely. Wright drew a finger down an irregular line which bisected the page.

'This is a planning department map, of course, but I keep a copy for reference—waterways, and drains and that sort of thing, and industrial sites. This is Highcliffe Beck with the estate on the west side. It runs down from the moor right past the entrance to the old working here—see, it's marked: sealed mine shaft. In fact it's not a shaft as such at all. Those were driftworkings going into the hill at a very slight angle, upwards in some cases, I believe. The seams are very shallow and quite thin. That's why they were worked out so quickly. They were never nationalized in the 'forties, but the company running them packed up soon afterwards, I'm told. There was no money in it. All before my time, of course, and yours too, Inspector.' He gave Sinclair a thin smile.

'And Agarth and Bradley sealed them off?'

'Yes, that's right. But as I say, there's no waste of any significance in an abandoned drift mine. They were sealed just to prevent the local kids from scrambling about in there and getting themselves trapped in a landslide,' Wright said.

Sinclair smiled briefly to himself. He could clearly remember as a member of a gang of eleven-year-olds scrabbling around those same workings trying to find a way through the very solid wall of rock and concrete with which they had been blocked off. He doubted if any succeeding generation of inquisitive lads had had any greater success.

'Would police surveillance of the river help?' he asked. 'If you think whatever you're looking for is being dumped?'

Wright pursed his lips and looked uncertain.

'The trouble is, the problem is so intermittent,' he said. 'There was one incident in January, and then two the following month, and then nothing at all until a couple of weekends ago. If your men sat watching, or patrolling, or whatever they do, they might hang about for weeks and then still miss whatever it is that's going on.'

'Is there nothing to link the incidents? No common factor?'

'Well, the chemicals seem to be the same, so no doubt it's coming from a single source. But if it's being brought in drums it could be coming from anywhere in the county, or even further afield—up the motorway, say if I had an extremely unpleasant chemical cocktail to get rid of, I suppose I'd take it as far away from home as possible,' Wright concluded with a somewhat helpless shrug.

Sinclair leaned back in his chair again and looked at Wright with some irritation. The man's defeatism annoyed him, but no more than his own inability to pursue the questions which really interested him. As a police officer with no more than a watching brief over the pollution in the Maze he could not press much further into areas which were the concern of the City Hall authorities. Only when they came to him with *prima facie* evidence that a crime had been committed could he intervene more forcefully.

If he was honest with himself, he knew that he should not even have made this trip from police HQ to the neighbouring City Hall to talk to Wright. He was following not even a hunch, but a mere insinuation which Kate Weston had offered him in a hurried telephone call that morning. 'See if you can find a link between the pollution in the river, James Agarth and Tom Carter's death,' she had said tersely, and when he had pressed her for her reasons she had hung up on him.

Well, he had done his best, he thought to himself as he thanked Dennis Wright and made his way back out of the City Hall along highly polished corridors panelled in Victorian mahogany. In fact he had done more than that woman deserved, with her insulting suggestions and peremptory demands.

Behind him, Dennis Wright sat thoughtfully at his desk for a long moment after Sinclair had left, before getting up and shutting his office door firmly. He opened a drawer in his desk and pulled out a bottle of whisky from which he took a furtive swig. Wiping his mouth on a grubby handkerchief and taking a strong mint from a packet on his desk, he put the bottle away again, picked up his telephone and dialled a local number with hands that were trembling.

WHEN ALEX SINCLAIR got a lunch hour, which was not often, he liked to take the opportunity of calling on his father who still lived, alone now, in the stone terraced house where Alex and his sister had been brought up. This stood, in the perfectly understood hierarchy of a northern city, a significant step up from the lowest level of society. It was,

Alex thought with an affectionate smile as he parked his car, a street which had always belonged to the respectable working class, though that was a distinction his father would not have deigned to make. To Sinclair senior the working class was indivisible.

The street was broad enough to have made a handsome playground even in the early 'sixties when cars were becoming frequent enough not to bring the children running out to gawp admiringly at them any more. Some of the dark stone frontages had been scrubbed now the air was cleaner and they glowed a pale golden yellow in the sunshine. Each house boasted a narrow strip of front garden, some of them immaculate with late spring flowers, others overgrown with weeds, but still a clear indication, along with the stone-silled bay windows and the small vestibules between front door and narrow hallway, that these were homes to be clearly distinguished from the flat-fronted terraces of the unskilled, where street doors opened straight into living-rooms and outside privies had still been common when Alex was a boy. Most of those streets were just a memory now, pulled down to make way for the faceless semis and blocks of flats of Highcliffe and the other estates which had mushroomed as the 'sixties progressed and Alex worked his way happily and easily through everything his enthusiastic primary school teachers could throw at him.

But Warwick Street was not the same community it had been when Alex had lived there and played schoolboy cricket along its length. More than half the houses had been bought now by newcomers, still undoubtedly members of the respectable and hard-working class of his youth, but from a different Continent. They painted the woodwork more colourfully than their ageing indigenous neighbours and they had filled the street with wide-eyed and dark-haired children, dressed in bright silks and satins, diminutive groups of whom watched silently as Alex knocked on his father's front door.

The old man was slow in answering. He was getting stiff in the knees and his hearing was not as good as it had been, Alex knew. He knocked again more firmly and waited patiently, knowing that Sinclair would not be out at the time of day when his son was most likely to call. Eventually the door opened.

Andrew Sinclair was not the man he was. Alex had watched him with inner pain as he had seemed to shrink physically after the death of his beloved wife, Joyce, without whom he admitted he felt only half a man. The older Sinclairs had moved to Milford from Scotland as a young married couple looking for work, which Andrew had found with the freshly minted Coal Board. He had not minded the hardship of the mines, buoyed up by the hope that their nationalization had laid the foundation for a new sort of industry and a new sort of society. Both their children had been born here, first a girl and then unexpectedly, after a gap of almost ten years, Alex himself, the second child and longed-for son his parents had almost despaired of conceiving. They had been brought up frugally, on principle as much as from necessity, on a miner's wage and what Joyce could occasionally earn as a young mother intermittently employed in local shops and offices.

There had never been money to throw around in this house, with its gleaming paintwork and brightly polished but worn furniture, its chilly linoleumed bedrooms and threadbare carpets and the concessionary coal fires even now not replaced by central heating. What spare cash Andrew and Joyce had was spent on political causes and books, the two expenses over which they felt no guilt. But Alex remembered a warmth in the house which had not been dissipated until his mother died. Puritanical his parents may have been, but it had been a puritanism made gracious by love and laughter and conversation in abundance, and Alex grieved afresh each time he crossed the threshold for what was now missing.

Andrew's stocky figure was beginning to stoop. Grief and loneliness were destroying him physically in a way which the hard grind of the pit, from which he had been made redundant ten years previously, had never done. He had never worked since he took his redundancy settlement while Alex was still at university, and for four short years he and Joyce had revelled in their new freedom to take modest trips and holidays, or just to walk in the park, or share a new book together at their leisure. Cancer had killed her quickly and cruelly and Andrew had never really recovered. He went out little now, even forgetting more often than not the political meetings which had been his life-blood for so many years. It was as if the struggle he had lost over his wife had sapped his energy for any further battles.

'Come in, lad,' he said to Alex curtly. 'It's chilly out there. We don't want to let the heat out.' And he slammed the door on the warm spring sunshine outside.

Alex followed his father into the single living-room, where the remains of a meal of bread and cheese lay abandoned on the table. There was no cloth, but the plates and a buttery knife lay on top of the previous day's edition of the local paper, spread out and crumpled with much reading.

'How are you?' Alex asked automatically, although he knew that he would not get an honest answer.

'Nae so bad,' Andrew replied, although his cardigan hung loosely from his shoulders and his skin looked a sallow grey colour and his fingers were stained yellow with nicotine. His eyes remained sharp, though, in the obstinate, square-set face, eyes as blue as Alex's own and betraying the same warmth as father and son surveyed each other with less dispassion than either pretended.

'So how are those lassies of yours?' Andrew asked, settling himself down again in his favourite brown velour armchair by the coal fire and pushing his carpet-slippered feet out towards the warmth of the glowing coals. 'Ye've not had them down to see me for a while.'

'They're fine,' Alex said. 'Both fine. Margaret's fine.'

Andrew snorted quietly but said nothing. His opinion of his daughter-in-law had never been high, but he had long since abandoned that ground as an unfruitful one for discussion.

'Did ye decide on Jennifer's school, then?' he asked, returning to a subject upon which he had already made his views very clear to his son and on which he felt he could still exert some leverage. Alex sighed. He had avoided visiting his father for the last couple of weeks, far from unconsciously, he admitted to himself, because of his reluctance to tell the old man that he intended giving way to Margaret on the school issue.

'Ye'll let her have her own way once too often,' he said. 'And ye know the damage that'll do the bairns.' Alex took the seat across the fireplace from his father and shook his head wearily in response.

'As much damage as having us split up completely?' he asked. 'I thought you disapproved of divorce.'

'Aye, well, I canna say there's much to be said for it,' his father admitted. 'But there's nae much to be said for letting your wife walk all over you either, is there? There's a case for a man being master in his ain home. And there's mebbe a case for these modern marriages where it's all partnership and equality. I can see that, though your mother and I found little enough need for it. But I canna see much case for a man being a doormat in his ain house on any grounds at all . . .'

'Dad,' Alex broke in angrily. 'That's enough. It doesn't help and it's really none of your business.'

'No? Well, I suppose those grand-daughters of mine have never been any of my business, have they? They're Booth's bairns, not mine, though they have my name. When you moved up there you left more than me and your mother behind.'

Alex bit back another angry retort, shook his head and went over to the table. He cut himself a couple of slices of the loaf and made himself a cheese sandwich before coming back to the fireside and sitting down again. The argument was one of those interminable family disagreements which never ended and to which a solution would never be found. His father-in-law might have resented Alex's marriage to his daughter in the early days, although once the decision was made he never voiced his reservations to either Alex or Margaret. And as his son-in-law had progressed and made something of a success of his career, he had forgiven, or more likely simply forgotten, his modest background and made him welcome in his own strata of Milford's society. Ted's was not an aristocracy of birth, but essentially one of money and success, and although Sinclair would never make much of the former as a policeman, he had earned enough of the latter to become acceptable to Booth and his friends.

Andrew Sinclair, on the other hand, took a more austere view. He had always regarded Alex's marriage as a betrayal both of principle and of class, an unfashionable view to which he clung with dogged tenacity, and as such, it was a betrayal which could never be fully forgiven or forgotten. It was, indeed, a betrayal which was being constantly compounded by Alex's progress in the police force and by the crises of his family life. During the miners' strike of 1983, relations had been strained almost to breaking between father and son. Now the issue of Jennifer's education was driving another wedge of deeply felt ideology between them, made all the more bitter by Alex's own regret that he had let Margaret defeat him on the issue.

'It's decided, Dad,' Alex said. 'It's for the best.' The old man snorted again and shook the coals in the grate with an angry poker.

'Your mother would be saddened by it,' he said.

You bastard, Alex thought, his face as grim as his father's, but he said nothing. He sat silently for a minute or two eating his sandwich, finding it difficult to swallow through his anger, before changing the subject abruptly.

'Do you remember James Agarth from your time on the Trades Council?' he asked at last and was pleased to see a spark of interest, belligerence even, flash into the old man's eyes.

'Aye, he's not a man ye'd forget,' he said. 'Anti-union to his last breath, just like the other one who died—what was his name? Bradley, was it? Aye, Agarth and Bradley, Bradley and Agarth. Screwed their workforce into the ground and then hammered them home.'

'They've not changed from what I hear,' Alex said.

'But old James Agarth died,' his father said. 'Way back. This James Agarth who runs the firm now must be the son, same name, about forty, forty-five?'

'Yes, that would be about right,' Alex said.

'Went away to the university, as I remember. Came back to run the business when the old man died, fifteen, twenty years ago. Then Bradley went too, and there were no children there, so Agarth took over the lot. A ruthless bastard as far as I know. Like father, like son.'

'Aye,' Alex said, meeting his father's eyes with a flicker of amusement. The old man looked at his for a moment and allowed himself a brief smile.

'Your mother and I were lucky,' he said. 'We had more than thirty years of something which you don't seem to have found at all. Don't take too much notice of me, eh?'

'I don't, don't worry,' Alex conceded quietly. He finished his sandwich while his father gazed into the fire, his thoughts with his wife, as they often were.

'So what do you know about Agarth and Bradley?' Alex asked at last, breaking the spell. 'Is he just anti-union or is he crooked?'

Andrew looked at him sharply.

'Is that what ye think?' he asked. 'Well, I'd not be surprised, though I've no evidence for it. But he's as thick as thieves with anyone who's anyone in this town and has been for years. They're all freemasons, of course.'

Alex nodded wryly. He had not told his father how close he had come to joining that brotherhood.

'So is my father-in-law,' he protested mildly.

'Aye, well, that's his business, but ye're not telling me that the fact that Agarth and Bradley have won every important construction contract in this town since the war has nothing to do with their cronies at the lodge—councillors, council officials, the lot? Policemen too, as ye very well know. Agarth built Highcliffe estate. And Hillbrow on the other side. At least two schools, sports centres—they've never been hard up for work while I've lived here.'

'They're supposed to have filled in the old mine working on Broadley Moor, too.'

'Aye, that's right, I think they did. That had to be done before the estate could be started, I recall. It was soon after your mother and I moved here. I was looking for work but those drifts had just closed. It all had to be made safe and the drainage channelled into Highcliffe Beck before they could start building lower down.'

'Drainage?' Alex asked sharply.

'Aye, they were very wet, some of those drift mines. There was some channelling done up there, I think. The person who'd know is Bill Bairstow. Do ye know Bill? He's one of the Labour councillors up at Highcliffe. Right on your patch. Ye must have come across him. He had to come out of the pits because of his lungs and he was an official in the construction union after that. They always had a lot of trouble with Agarth and Bradley. There were a couple of attempts to get it unionized and a couple of strikes. Anything ye want to know about that gang of highwaymen, Bill should be able to put ye right.'

'Yes, I've met Councillor Bairstow,' Alex said.

'Oh, aye, I forgot ye were having trouble up there wi' this young lad ye've arrested,' his father said sharply. 'I read about it in the *Echo*. Hae ye made some sort of dreadful mistake there?'

Alex shook his head slowly. 'I honestly don't know,' he said.

'They're saying the lad was bullied into confessing.'

'Who's saying?'

'My people, lad. The Trades Council, the Labour councillors...'

'And the professional agitators?' Alex broke in sharply. 'Isn't there just as much of a freemasonry there? Plenty of people ready to jump at any opportunity to knock the police? Aren't there some good political reasons to stir it up over Joey Macready?'

'There was a time when ye'd not have asked a question like that, Alex,' the old man countered angrily. 'There was a time when ye knew whose side ye were on.'

'I may still know whose side I'm on, but I've lost a few knee-jerk reactions along the way,' Alex came back. 'There was a time when I believed everything you said was gospel. But you also told me never to put my faith in religion. So I didn't. What bothers you is that I gave up your religion along with the rest. If your friends can give me evidence that Joey Macready is innocent, I'll listen. If your comrades can convince me, I'll do anything in my power to get him released. But so far all I've heard is outrage and protestation, without a shred of factual evidence to back it up. That's not good enough for me as a policeman, and it won't be good enough for the judge and jury if it comes to that. And it shouldn't be good enough for you, if you're honest.'

Andrew Sinclair straightened himself up in his chair and sighed heavily. Time was when he would have continued the argument, seizing and enjoying the challenge Alex had thrown out. But now the fire which had flashed briefly in his blue eyes died quickly away again and they looked tired and grey.

'Mebbe you're right,' he mumbled.

Alex stood up abruptly, his verbal victory bringing him infinitely more pain than pleasure.

'I have to get back,' he said. 'I'll talk to Bill Bairstow. Don't get up. I'll see myself out.'

'Take care, lad,' the old man said.

'And you, Dad.'

EIGHT

SAM WAS LATE home from school. Kate had let herself into the flat soon after five and discovered it as empty as she had left it at lunch-time when she had come home briefly for a sandwich. She knocked on Annie Macready's door with no response before she remembered that Annie had decided to take Tracey with her to Bradford that day because Joey had asked to see his sister. They would not be back, Kate thought, for at least another hour.

She went back into her own flat slowly and closed the front door, wondering which of Sam's friends she could telephone to find out if he had gone to play there after school. She picked up the notebook in which she kept phone-numbers and flicked through it. As always when she was anxious about Sam, a cold lump of fear seemed to settle in her stomach and she felt slightly sick. It was more than six years since two policewomen had arrived at her front door to tell her that Richard had been killed in a car accident on the M1, but whenever Sam was unexpectedly late, as he was now, the deep and only semi-rational fears for his safety crowded in. She knew that it would be more than she could bear if she were to lose her son as well, and the very idea seized her with a paralysing panic.

She picked up the phone with a hand which was trembling slightly and dialled the advice centre's number. Derek Stevenson answered and she asked him if Sam had been to the office to look for her.

'Should he have?' Stevenson asked impatiently. She could hear other voices in the background.

'He's not home yet, and I thought if he had lost his key or something he might have gone to look for me. I did some shopping on the way back so I could have missed him.' She knew Stevenson would pick up the hesitation in her voice and despise her for her weakness.

'I should think he's just off playing with his friends, isn't he?' Stevenson suggested, reasonably enough. 'It's only five o'clock.'

'He usually comes straight home,' Kate said lamely. 'I always tell him to come straight home...'

'Well, I shouldn't worry. He'll turn up. Boys will be boys and all that,' Stevenson said dismissively and put the phone down.

Kate bit her lip and flicked the pages of her notebook. But before she could settle on which of Sam's friends to call, there was a ring at the door. She almost ran to the answer phone.

'Who is it?' She felt her voice tremble and despised herself for it.

'Police,' came the answer she most dreaded, and for a moment she went icily cold before she heard another voice more faintly on the intercom.

'It's me, Mum,' said Sam, and her heart lurched back to something approaching normality.

She watched him come up the stairs to the flat behind one uniformed policeman and followed by another. He looked incredibly small between the two burly men and even in the dim light of the stairwell she could see that he looked unusually pale and tense. She motioned the trio into the living-room in silence and looked at the leading police officer questioningly.

'This is your son, is it, Mrs Weston?' he asked, tucking his uniform cap under his arm and taking a notebook from his breast pocket. 'Samuel Richard Weston? Aged eleven?'

Kate nodded dumbly, unable to speak.

'I'll need to confirm a few details,' the officer went on unemotionally. 'I'm afraid we found him in Woolworths, engaged in a bit of shoplifting. They're likely to prosecute.'

Sam moved away from the second officer who had followed him into the flat and came to stand beside Kate, who
put a protective arm around his shoulder.

'Is this true, Sam?' she asked quietly. The boy shook his
head emphatically.

'I didn't,' he said. 'I didn't. We were just looking.'

'Come on now, lad,' the officer who seemed to be acting as spokesman said impatiently. He was a man of more
than middle age, old, Kate thought, to be still a constable,
but not an avuncular-looking man. No Dixon of Dock
Green, this, but an officer of uncompromising grimness
and cold, unsmiling eyes. He turned back to Kate.

'He and his friend were found with toy cars in their
schoolbags. The store detective had been watching them
and we searched their bags as soon as we arrived.'

'I didn't take them,' Sam said again, a tear creeping
down his cheek now. 'I really didn't, Mum. I wouldn't. You
know I wouldn't.'

'You won't mind if we take a look round the flat, will
you, Mrs Weston?' the police officer asked.

'I can't see any reason why you should,' Kate said, a
flicker of anger taking over from her anxiety now. 'What
exactly are you looking for?'

'These things go in waves, you know. There's been a lot
of it going on in the town centre lately, when the kids come
out of school. We'd just like to have a look in Sam's room.'

'He's not looking at my room,' said Sam angrily, pulling himself away from his mother's arm. 'I didn't steal
anything, and I never have, so there!' The boy rushed
across the room to the second policeman who had picked
up the Hornby locomotive from the shelves by the fireplace and seized the model from him.

'That's mine. It was my dad's. Leave it alone,' Sam
shouted, and ran into his bedroom, slamming the door behind him.

'That sort of behaviour isn't going to do him any good,
you know, Mrs Weston,' said the second officer, continuing to look curiously along the rows of books and orna-

ments on the shelves. 'He's over the age of criminal responsibility.'

'I think it would be better if you went now,' Kate said firmly. 'I'm quite sure that Sam has nothing here that doesn't belong to him. I would have noticed if he had. You'll just have to take my word for that now.'

'We can get a search warrant, madam,' the second officer said suddenly and curtly. Kate spun round to face him.

'I'm sure you can if you think this is sufficiently serious to justify one,' she said. 'But you know as well as I do that you'll have to convince a magistrate about that... And I wouldn't have thought that the alleged theft of a toy car is sufficient grounds. This is hardly Fagin's kitchen!'

'With boys of this age, the theft of a toy car can lead on to all sorts of other things,' the policeman responded sharply. 'You're a single parent, aren't you, Mrs Weston? Sam's father isn't here any more.' The question was offensive and clearly meant to be so.

'I'm a widow,' Kate said coldly, swallowing her anger.

'Ah.' The officer nodded, with a knowing look at his colleague. 'Does he often go into town on his own after school, then, your son? Normal, is it?'

'No, it isn't normal. It's highly unusual. Normally I'm here when he comes home from school.' Kate bitterly resented the defensiveness which was creeping into her answers now. She knew very well that they were pigeon-holing Sam as the latch-key child of a working mother, with all they thought that implied, and she hated her own vulnerability to their insinuations.

'The normal procedure now is to wait to make sure that the shop really does want to prosecute. After that, we'll want to interview him—you can be present, of course, at a formal interview. If he admits the theft, and I must say I'd advise you to persuade him to do that, then he'll probably get off with a caution at his age. They don't usually take a lad as young as that to court unless there's evidence of persistent delinquency or truancy. He's not been bunking off school has he, to your knowledge?'

Kate shook her head angrily.

'Of course not,' she said, tears pricking the back of her eyelids.

'Well, it's probably just a one off, then. He's just trying it on. Perhaps you haven't been giving him as much attention as you think you have recently. Perhaps he's feeling a bit neglected, is he, for some reason? You're involved in this Macready business up here, aren't you, Mrs Weston?'

The hostility inherent in the final question hung in the air between the three of them, and Kate felt an unexpected frisson of fear. Why, she wondered, would a police constable from the town centre be so acutely aware of her activities for the Joey Macready Defence Committee?

The two officers put on their caps then and went politely enough. As the front door closed behind them, Kate felt a wave of nausea sweep over her, and she rushed into the bathroom and bathed her face in cold water from the tap, fighting off the urge to retch. She felt, rather than heard, Sam creep up behind her and she reached out blindly for his hand.

'Are you all right, Mum?' he asked, his voice thick with tears. She turned around and hugged him to her roughly.

'Yes,' she said. 'I'm all right. How about you?'

'I didn't do it, Mum. I promise you, I didn't. I promise Dad.' She looked at the pale tear-stained face and the blazing blue eyes, and believed him. Sam seldom spoke of his father, although she knew he could remember him quite clearly. To have mentioned him in this context was proof enough of the sincerity of his denials.

'So what do you think happened? How did the toy get in your schoolbag?' she asked, picking up a towel and drying first her own wet face and then his cheeks which were still damp with tears.

'I think the pigs put it there,' Sam said, perfectly matter-of-factly.

'Policemen,' Kate corrected him automatically.

'It sounds silly but I can't think of anything else. The shop man stopped us and said we'd been stealing, and we said we hadn't, but he didn't have time to look in our bags, the police came so quickly. It was the policeman who looked and said the cars were there. One in my bag and one in Gary's. But we didn't put them there. Honest.'

'Gary? Gary Robinson?' Kate had to think hard before she could put a face to the name. 'The red-headed boy who plays football?'

'Yes, Gary. He wanted to go to Woolworths to see the price of football boots, so I said I'd go with him. Because we bought mine the other day. I knew you were going to be late tonight and I thought you wouldn't mind.'

'You must ask first, Sam,' Kate objected almost automatically. 'You mustn't go off anywhere without telling me. So where is Gary now?'

'They took him home first. I waited in the car with the fat one, while the other one took Gary in to his mum. The pig—sorry, the policeman said he thought his dad would give him a good hiding when he came back. Gary's dad hits him a lot. It's not fair. We didn't do anything.'

Kate sighed. How like her son, she thought, to be more worried about what might happen to his friend than about his own predicament. And how like Richard.

'Look,' she said decisively. 'Don't worry about it any more tonight. Tomorrow I'll have a talk with Inspector Sinclair and find out a bit more about what happened today and what we can do about it. If you are quite sure you did nothing wrong, then I'm sure we can sort it all out. In the meantime, shall we have fish and chips from the chippie for supper?'

Sam's eyes lit up, as she knew they would. Fish and chips from the van which parked outside the Fox were a treat for Sam which she used sparingly, but, she thought, on this occasion at least, to good effect. But while he was out buying them, she sat anxiously by the window watching him run the short distance to the mobile chip shop. Could she have imagined the note of menace which had crept into the policeman's voice as he questioned her about her status and her involvement with the action campaign? Could she really have been warned off in some way? She went over the conversation again in her mind. It could have been innocent, but she remained convinced that it was not.

THAT NIGHT AFTER Sam had finally gone reluctantly to bed, Kate sat gazing at the television but not really watching it. She was still thinking about Sam and the police, when a ring on the doorbell made her jump for the second time that evening. She went to the intercom and this time it was Alex Sinclair who identified himself. Her immediate assumption was that he had heard what had happened to Sam and had come round to reassure her. She smiled faintly as she listened to him climbing the stairs two at a time. But as he rounded the last bend, her half smile of greeting froze. Inspector Sinclair looked pale and in control, but as grim-faced as she had ever seen him.

'Did you come about Sam . . . ?' she began hesitantly as he came into the flat and closed the door behind him and leaned against it, looking as if he could not find the right words for what he had to say.

'Sam? No, what's happened to Sam?' he said at last uncomprehendingly.

She told him briefly, but he hardly let her finish, brushing off her only half-implied complaint that she was being harassed.

'Never mind that now, Kate,' he said harshly. 'Something much worse has happened.'

He took a deep breath before he went on, and Kate looked at him with growing anxiety clutching at her stomach.

'What . . . ?' she began.

'It's Joey Macready. He's killed himself in his cell. I have to break the news to his mother and I wondered if you would come with me . . .'

Inspector Sinclair stopped as if he could not bear to go on and Kate realized what an effort it must have taken to come to her for help in these circumstances. Then the full horror of what he had said hit her like a physical blow.

'Oh God,' she said, and reached out blindly for a moment to Sinclair for support.

'I'm sorry,' he said, leading her by the arm to the easy chair by the fire and helping her into it. 'That was clumsy. I've shocked you.'

Kate buried her face in her hands for a moment, trying to fight back her tears. Sinclair put one hand tentatively on her shoulder, wanting to take her in his arms, but not daring to. At last she looked up at him.

'You forget how well we knew Joey here,' she said, her voice strained almost to inaudibility. 'He was almost part of the family. Sam will be devastated. Whatever happened? Annie was there this afternoon with Tracey.'

'He hanged himself with a bedsheet,' Sinclair said flatly. 'It's not the first time, and I don't suppose it'll be the last. There've been more than enough complaints about remand prisoners in that place. There've been other suicides. The system...' He broke off and shrugged wearily, looking utterly defeated. 'What it comes down to is that the system doesn't work. It sickens me to think that by arresting someone quite legitimately, I may be condemning them to death in that hole...'

'Annie said he was being teased,' Kate said. 'They were going to try to get him moved when he came to court again this week.'

'The irony is that I'm told she was playing hell there again today when she visited and they'd actually moved him to a single cell. If he'd stayed with the rest of them he probably wouldn't have got away with it. It was only possible because he was on his own.'

'Poor Annie,' Kate began, her horror growing as the full implications of what had happened began to sink in. 'This will kill her. She's devoted her life to that boy.'

She sat quietly for a moment trying to order her scattered thoughts. But the more she thought about Joey's death the more she realized that this was like throwing a pebble into a lake: there was no telling where the ripples would end. Sinclair still had his hand on her shoulder. She shook it off and stood up to face him, the pain still there in her eyes but a more determined look replacing the first disintegration of shock.

'You do realize, don't you, that people are going to be very angry about this on the estate? No one really believes Joey murdered Tom Carter, you know, no one, that is, except the police.'

'I know,' Sinclair admitted. 'Do you think there'll be trouble?'

'Well, I shouldn't think it'll get to riots and petrol bombs, but yes, there'll be trouble. There are enough people out there who want trouble to capitalize on something like this and make sure it happens.'

'Your friend Stevenson?'

'Not only Derek,' Kate countered quickly. 'People like Derek can't manufacture trouble, they can only stir the existing brew.'

'This is my patch. I'm certain to be asked what I think may happen—what we can do to avoid a reaction,' Sinclair said. 'Do you have any suggestions?'

Kate looked at him coolly, composed again now.

'What sort of suggestions, Alex?' she asked. 'What do you want? A list of people most likely to throw rocks at your patrol cars? You can't be serious. You know what I think about the police handling of this case. On top of that I've had a personal dose of police bullying today.

'If it comes to the point, I'll do my best to keep things calm and legal, but if you think I'm not angry too, you overestimate my professional dispassion. Joey's death makes me bitterly resentful of the system, the police force, even, to some extent, you—though I want to believe you're an honest man, an honourable one, even, if that old-fashioned word has any meaning any more.'

She looked at him pleadingly as if willing him to confirm that belief in some way but he did not respond. She shrugged helplessly.

'But what's the point of that if the system itself is rotten and you won't help those who want to do something about it?' she asked. 'In those circumstances, you really can't complain if people get angry and throw the odd brick.'

Sinclair pushed his hair away from his brow wearily and turned away from Kate's angry gaze, refusing to rise to her challenge. At heart, he knew she was right and he felt as bitterly as she did about what had happened.

On the drive up to Highcliffe with Sergeant Wilson he had discussed his dissatisfaction with the Macready case at length with the older man. The sergeant had been noncommittal. Trying to re-open the case would be 'nobbut trouble,' he had suggested.

But the discussion had clarified Sinclair's mind, nevertheless. He was determined to pursue his inquiries about Tom Carter's death much further than the brief investigation so far had taken them. And if Superintendent Eddie Greaves demurred, he would take his request to the top, to the Chief Constable if necessary, to get permission.

He would like to have told Kate Weston all that. But she was an outsider, and a pretty hostile outsider at that, and some vestigial loyalty to the force he had up until then been proud to serve prevented him from confiding in her.

'At least, please help me to break the news to Annie,' he said at length. 'She's going to need you.'

'Of course,' Kate said, going with him to the door. 'Of course I'll come with you. It's the least I can do for Annie.'

IT TOOK TWO DAYS for the Highcliffe estate to stir itself out of its normal apathy and for the reaction to Joey's death to begin to break the surface. That morning slogans attacking the police were found daubed along a wall on the main road to the town centre. Every passenger on the way to work on every bus down to Milford must have been able to read the opinion that 'the pigs' killed Joey, and that Joey was innocent, before council workmen came up with buckets of black paint in the middle of the morning and obliterated the graffiti.

But swift action by the council could not quell the outrage which was gathering strength as people gossiped in the shops, and drank a lunch-time pint in the Fox. Even before Joey's body had been released by the coroner for burial—tentatively planned for the end of the week by Annie and Father O'Leary, who had been an almost permanent visitor at the flat since the news broke—he had effectively become a martyr to police incompetence and prison squalor.

Derek Stevenson had called a public meeting at the community centre for the following night and he and Kate made sure that posters and hand-bills were distributed as widely as possible around the neighbourhood. It might at least provide something of an escape valve for local emotions, Kate thought, and might just possibly help to convince the police that they should re-open their inquiries. In any case, she found that throwing herself into the task of organization did something to dull the pain of watching Annie's dreadful grief at close quarters.

By the evening of the meeting, Kate felt as though she had not slept for a week. Her eyes were gritty and her tongue furred as she and Annie, with Tracey and Sam following them closely, made their way to the prefabricated hall which adjoined the advice centre, in a dusk made lurid by a spectacularly red sunset over the distant Pennine hills.

Kate was glad to get out of the oppressive atmosphere of the Macreadys' flat, where she too had spent much of the two previous days, sitting with Annie and preparing and drinking endless cups of tea as sympathetic visitors came and went. But she still felt some faint misgivings about so public an airing of the issues surrounding Joey's death so soon after it had happened when she saw a steady stream of people making their way to the community centre, all uniformly grim-faced.

The hall was already packed when they arrived, and there was a murmur of sympathy from the crowd as Kate helped Annie down the centre aisle to her reserved seat on the front row. Annie had insisted on coming and had put on a dark dress, rather too tight round the hips and rather too short at the knees, and had done her best to disguise the puffiness around her eyes with a more than usually thick application of blue eye-shadow and mascara.

But the make-up had already begun to run slightly by the time she took her place as she wiped away an occasional tear. She held her head high as she sat down and did not turn around in response to the muted inquiries after her health that came from members of the crowd who knew her best. Tracey sat next to her, her face pale and her blue eyes bright with curiosity, but clutching her mother's hand tightly.

Kate knew that Annie's stability was a fragile thing. After the first stunned shock had worn off two nights previously, she had subsided into a tumultuously tearful grief that only the doctor's sedatives seemed able to assuage for a little while. She had insisted on coming to the meeting, although Kate had tried to persuade her otherwise, but now she was here, surrounded by a noisy and sympathetic crowd, Kate thought she detected the first faint flicker of her normal belligerence that she had glimpsed since she had gone with Alex Sinclair to break the news of Joey's death.

Kate settled the children in their seats and then glanced around the hall. The front rows were filled almost exclusively with people she knew, mainly neighbours from the flats and the houses closest to them on the estate. Ada Turner and a whole group of elderly women from the sheltered accommodation were sitting just behind them. Whole families were there, many of them with young children, sitting on knees or running around in the aisles between the collapsible plastic chairs. Babysitters were difficult to find on an estate like Highcliffe and most evening outings for two parents included all but the very youngest children, whether it was to the social clubs or the community centre. The single young people, black and white, mainly young men and boys but with a scattering of girls among them, had congregated at the back of the hall, either leaning against the walls smoking or sitting precariously on the backs of chairs so that they could see more clearly.

There were no uniformed police in evidence either outside or inside the hall and Kate was surprised to see Alex Sinclair and his sergeant standing to one side, slightly apart from the jostling crowd of young people. She caught his eye briefly but did not return his nod of acknowledgement. Sergeant Wilson, she noticed, was surveying the noisy youngsters with a look of some concern. She had no doubt that the two men were there to keep a watching brief on events.

Turning back, she caught the eye of Gordon Rangely, the reporter from the *Echo* who had been haunting the estate asking questions ever since the news of Joey's death had been released. He smiled a wolfish smile in her direction and waved his pen.

'Can I talk to Mrs Macready?' he mouthed, and she shook her head sharply at him. She had turned all Press inquiries away for the last two days, reckoning that Annie would probably only regret anything she said now when she saw it repeated coldly in print.

'The nationals are showing an interest,' Rangely insisted. 'Too many deaths in that dump.'

Kate nodded. She would have to talk to Derek Stevenson about the Press later, she thought. It was quite clear that the campaign for Joey's release was not going to die with him: it was becoming a campaign for all sorts of other things now.

A table had been placed at the front of the hall and Derek Stevenson had ostentatiously taken the most central chair behind it, with Councillor Bill Bairstow on his left and Father Francis O'Leary on his right. Once he was sure that Kate and Annie and the children were comfortably settled on the front row, Derek cleared his throat, tapped a pen against the jug of water in front of him, and brought the noise level down a few decibels so that he could be heard above the hubbub.

'Ladies and gentlemen,' he said loudly, doing some more tapping. 'Ladies and gentlemen, friends and comrades. Can we have a bit of quiet, please?' The noise subsided a little further, allowing him to continue in a more normal voice.

'First of all, can I say how pleased we are to see so many of you here tonight to discuss what has become a most serious issue: the treatment of young people on this estate by the police, the treatment of young Joey Macready in particular, and the disgraceful conditions at the prison which led to Joey's death.'

The audience applauded this introduction noisily and it took some time before Stevenson could make himself heard above the noise again.

'Secondly,' he went on at length. 'Secondly, we are here tonight to offer Annie Macready the sympathy of the whole estate in her grief, and to offer whatever help we can to get justice for Joey, even though, tragically, he is no longer here to benefit from the clearing of his name.'

The audience was relatively quiet now. You had to hand it to Derek, Kate thought, he was very good at this sort of thing. She had often wondered why he had not gone into politics himself, but had concluded that he must believe that he could wield more influence in the background, in the unique position his job at the centre offered to gather intelligence and influence opinion, without ever having to put his personality or his more extreme views to the test of the ballot box.

Derek had introduced Bill Bairstow to the meeting to discuss the formal complaints which had already been lodged about Joey's treatment, and how the inquest into his death would function.

'It'll be a bloody cover-up,' someone shouted from the back of the hall as Councillor Bairstow brought his monotonous exposition to an end and this outburst, waved down by Derek, still brought another frenzied outburst of applause. Father O'Leary leapt to his feet at that, and began to tell the meeting about the funeral arrangements that he had made for Joey a week ahead. This calmed the meeting again, and Kate felt Annie shudder as she tried to suppress a sob.

'We are, I would hope, all religious people here, some Moslems, some Christians, although I know you are not all of my own church, but I would hope that as a community we would find it in our hearts to forgive those who we believe have harmed Joey and his family, and to seek to find constructive ways ahead which will avoid this sort of tragedy ever being visited on our community again. I hope I will see all of you, of whatever faith, in church for the requiem mass for Joey.'

The priest sat down to a scatter of applause this time, and what sounded like a menacing murmur from the back of the hall where the young people were now packed three or four deep against the walls. Kate was aware that the tension as well as the temperature in the packed room was rising and she glanced round again to where Alex Sinclair had been standing just in time to see him whisper something to Sergeant Wilson and the sergeant push his way with some difficulty to the nearest exit and out of the hall.

Derek Stevenson was on his feet again by the time she turned round, and tapping on his water jug to make himself heard. He stood lightly behind the table swaying backwards and forwards slightly like a boxer on the balls of his feet. The movement was hypnotic, and so were his eyes, which had taken on a slight gleam in his sallow face. A nerve throbbed at his temple, and Kate noticed that his left hand, which he held at his side, was tightly clenched, the knuckles gleaming white. When the noise had subsided, he began to speak again, very quietly at first.

'Everyone in this room knew Joey Macready,' be began. 'Everyone in this room knew he was a gentle, harmless boy. Everyone in this room would have trusted him with their own child, with their grandchild, even with their grandmother. As many of you did. There was no harm in Joey. No harm at all.' The room murmured its assent to this.

'So what did Joey do wrong, you may ask,' Stevenson continued, speaking quietly still. 'What did he do to deserve being arrested, a big boy, but with the mental age of a little child, locked up without his mother, and forced to confess to something which we all know he couldn't have done, wasn't capable of doing, and for which there was absolutely no direct evidence that he did?'

The audience was very still now. Even the children had stopped shuffling in their chairs. But the silence was not an easy one. It was more like the moment of calm before a storm.

'I'll tell you what Joey did wrong,' Derek Stevenson went on. His voice was rising slightly now and his eyes had taken on an almost manic glitter. The audience had become rapt, hanging on his every word and Kate began to feel increasingly apprehensive. She felt Annie give another convulsive sob, which shook the seat beside her, and she reached for her hand and squeezed it gently.

'What Joey did wrong was to be born disabled in the first place. That's not a good thing to be in this society where the weakest go to the wall. The second thing he did wrong was to be born on this estate. We all know what that means in this town. Highcliffe is the pits, Highcliffe is a dump, Highcliffe gets the dirty end of the stick when life's comforts are being handed out.'

The audience murmured in approval, a little more emphatically this time.

'And there's a third thing Joey did wrong. That was simply to be out and about and unable to account for his movements at the moment the pigs needed a convenient scapegoat to lock up for Tom Carter's murder,' Stevenson declared.

'Tom Carter was stupid enough to live on this estate too. Tom Carter was of no more account than Joey Macready in this town's scheme of things. So what better solution for Tom Carter's murder than to pin it on Joey Macready, who couldn't have done it, but couldn't ever prove that he hadn't done it. Find a Highcliffe murderer for a Highcliffe murder and case closed. That's it. Very convenient. End of story.' There was a collective murmur of anger from the audience, but Stevenson had not quite finished. He held up his hand for silence.

'So Joey Macready's locked up. So Joey Macready's dead. So what? Who cares? No one does. Case closed, I tell you—unless, and it's a big unless—unless you, the people of Highcliffe, make them keep it open. In the end, my friends, comrades, it's up to you. No one else gives a damn. If it's action you want, you're the ones who have to take it. I know what I'd do.'

As Stevenson's delivery had become more staccato his voice had risen, but at the end it dropped again, almost to a whisper, as he challenged the audience directly to action. The climax was too much for several people in the hall. Councillor Bairstow actually seized Derek Stevenson's arm in protest before he came to a stop, only to have his intervention shrugged off impatiently. And even before he had finished, with the audience nodding in unison to each of his statements and the murmur at the back of the hall growing with each, it all became too much for Annie. Before Kate could stop her, she stood up and turned to face the hall.

'He were murdered,' she shrieked, tears running down her face. 'My Joey were innocent and he were murdered by t'pigs.'

The noise in the hall rose to a roar then, and from the back came a clear young voice.

'Kill the pigs!' it cried, and was taken up by a dozen more shouts as a door banged open at the back of the hall, chairs were overturned with a clatter, and a significant section of the audience spilled out into the night baying and shouting abuse.

Kate looked round the hall, where almost all the audience were now on their feet as parents panicked at the incipient violence in the air and scrambled to get their children home to safety. She grabbed Sam's hand firmly and turned for a moment to the top table where Stevenson was now involved in a furious argument with Father

O'Leary and Councillor Bairstow, both of whom were clearly berating him for his concluding remarks.

'Bill,' Kate called sharply. 'Will you please get Annie home?' Without waiting for an answer, she dragged Sam towards the side of the hall where she had last glimpsed Alex Sinclair. He was still there, pinned against the wall by an aggressive group of women one of whom was screaming abuse into his face, almost spitting in her fury. He caught Kate's eye through the crowd and she beckoned him towards her. Shouldering his tormentors away, he joined her just as the sound of splintering glass from the front of the building told them that the incipient riot had become a real one.

'Come with me,' Kate said. 'We can get out the side door and into the offices that way. I've got a key.' With Sam between them, they left the hall and stood for a moment breathlessly in the relative calm of the advice centre, which was lit only by the yellow glow of the street lights outside.

'Thanks,' Sinclair said curtly. 'That was getting nasty out there. I sent Wilson to call for reinforcements five minutes ago. The heavy mob should be here soon.'

'I'd no idea it was going to be like that,' Kate said.

'Stevenson laid himself open to a charge of incitement with that last little effort,' Sinclair said, glancing out of the window towards the front of the building. 'The man's a menace.'

Quite suddenly the light in the room turned from its street-light yellow to a flickering orange. 'Christ!' Sinclair said. 'They've turned a car over and set it on fire. I hope to God there was no one inside it.'

'Let me see, let me see,' shouted Sam, pushing his way in front of the inspector to get a better view. 'Great!' he said, at last. 'Kill the pigs!'

'Sam!' Kate shouted, outraged.

'You don't mean that, Sam, do you?' Sinclair asked quietly. The boy turned and looked at him for a moment before running over to Kate and flinging his arms round her and bursting into tears.

'They killed Joey,' he said over and over again between his sobs. 'The pigs killed Joey.' Kate looked across the distraught child in despair.

'What have we done?' she asked, but Sinclair turned away to the window again grim-faced and did not answer.

'We could get across the road to the flats without being seen,' Kate suggested at last. 'You can't go out on the street on your own.' Sinclair shook his head and crossed the room and picked up the phone.

'I'll get them to come and pick me up here,' he said. 'I blame myself for this. I should have seen it coming. I knew how angry people were about Joey. What I didn't bargain for was Stevenson screwing the youngsters up like that. I should have tried to do something to stop him in there.' He spoke briefly to his headquarters and asked them to pick him up discreetly at the back door to the advice centre.

'They'd have howled you down at the very least, if you'd tried to intervene,' Kate said.

'Or lynched me, you mean? I suppose it's all part of the job but that sort of venom comes as a shock even so. I wasn't expecting it.'

Within minutes the flashing blue lights of approaching police vans illuminated the room even more bizarrely than before. With the arrival of the police in some force the crowd of young people outside the community centre began to run in all directions, still shouting angrily, and throwing whatever missiles came to hand in the general direction of the police and occasionally against windows, adding the crash of breaking glass to the general cacophony. Since his outburst against the police, Sam had clung closely to his mother's side and avoided looking at Sinclair, who continued to watch the riot grim-faced. At last he turned away from the window.

'It'll be safe enough now. They've moved off down Carlton Road. Let me see you back to the flats.'

'Don't be silly,' Kate said. 'If any of those yobbos sees you alone they'll have you.' At that moment there was a gentle knock on the door and after checking who was there, Kate let Sergeant Wilson into the centre.

'Sorry, boss,' he said to Sinclair. 'I couldn't get back to you. By the time I got through to HQ it had all hit the fan. They didn't get me, but they got the car.'

'That was ours, was it?' Sinclair said grimly. 'Eddie Greaves is going to do his nut about that. Detectives aren't supposed to get their cars fire-bombed. That's the prerogative of the uniformed boys.'

'Yes, well, the plods are having their work cut out down Carlton Street and round the high school. I've got fresh transport outside if you're ready to move?' He opened the door again and peered out nervously before slipping out. They heard a car start up.

Sinclair paused for a moment by the door and looked back at Kate and Sam, obviously still anxious.

'We'll be fine,' she said. 'No one is after our blood.'

'Thanks for the use of your office,' he said drily, and closed the door quietly behind him.

NINE

ALEX SINCLAIR WATCHED his daughters walk side by side into Broadley primary school. Jennifer pushed open the swing gate into the playground to let a skipping Sally go in ahead of her, before waving to her father. Alex waved back with a slow smile. Gentle Jennifer, he thought, she would take all life's problems in her stride while Sally would rage and fight against the slings and arrows and exult over the joys in a perpetual turmoil. That morning the two of them had sat over their cornflakes, Jennifer quietly reading the uniform list which had arrived in the post from St Helen's, while Sally almost fell off her chair, hooting with laughter at the requirements for a grey hockey skirt, grey knee socks for day wear and red knee socks for sport.

'Knee socks, knee socks,' Sally had shrieked. 'Nutty nutty knee socks.' The joke had lasted all the way to school in the car, and would no doubt be repeated around the playground all day, to Jenny's chagrin, although she was by no means the only girl from the school who was going to St Helen's next term. In leafy Broadley, barely half the primary school leavers went on to the local comprehensive. Perhaps my Sally will refuse the privilege when it's her turn, Alex thought wryly and wondered what Margaret would make of that.

He sat for a moment watching a few late-comers hurrying up the road to the school gate. The girls had almost been among them this morning. He had slept so heavily that the alarm had not roused him and he had wakened both the girls a good twenty minutes later than usual and there had been a mad scramble around the bathroom and the breakfast table. He had had, he guessed, no more than three hours' sleep, creeping into bed in the small hours without disturbing Margaret.

Reporting back to headquarters after the worst of the previous night's mayhem had subsided, he had written a report on the night's events there and then, ready for the urgent debriefing which had been convened by the deputy chief constable at noon. He had left HQ at four in the morning and until his meeting he was ostensibly free. Free to sleep, he had thought longingly, although he had got out of bed, shaved and dressed formally for his meeting, determined to spend the hours between dropping the children off and his noon appointment conducting some independent inquiries of his own.

He started the car and drove thoughtfully towards the town centre for a mile, and then took the dual-carriageway ring road to the west. He tuned in to the local radio station to listen to the nine o'clock news bulletin, which led on what the police were describing officially as 'an affray' on the Highcliffe estate the previous night. Sixteen people had ultimately been arrested, it turned out, and would appear in court later in the day, most of them charged with public order offences. Two police cars, one of them his own, injudiciously parked he now realized right outside the community centre, had been burnt out.

The centre itself, the high school and Patel's grocery shop had been damaged, one police constable was in hospital with burns, and four more had been treated for minor injuries. The Joey Macready Action Committee had issued a statement saying that they deplore violence, the radio presenter said in that irritatingly light tone which never did justice to the gravity of much that the station had to report, but that they understood the deep feelings of anger in the local community as a result of Joey Macready's tragic death.

Sinclair turned the radio off angrily. The statement, he supposed, had come from Derek Stevenson, the man he held personally responsible for the night's violence, and the possibility of whose arrest on a charge of incitement he intended to raise at the deputy chief constable's meeting later that morning. He had framed his report the previous night with that very much in mind.

Sinclair swung the car off the dual-carriageway into the slip road which led to the steep hill to Highcliffe. The neighbourhood was quiet enough now, although uniformed police officers were much in evidence, patrolling in pairs. Sinclair skirted the centre of the estate, where the front of Patel's shop was already receiving the attention of the glaziers, and turned into a narrow residential road, pulling up outside a row of terraced houses, modern cottages, each with a neat pocket-handkerchief garden in front still colourful with wallflowers and tulips.

Mrs Carter was quick to answer his knock. She was a small, solidly built woman, her thinning grey hair permed to a frizz which still revealed a glimpse of her pink scalp. She had her sleeves rolled up and wore a traditional flowered pinafore over her dress and woollen cardigan. She nodded quickly in recognition when Sinclair offered her his warrant card but there was no warmth in her pale eyes as she motioned him into the house.

'I wondered when you'd come back,' she said, following him into the living-room where a duster and tin of polish lay on the wooden coffee table. She moved awkwardly, as if her knees were giving her trouble. A small brown terrier was lying on one of the armchairs and she shooed it off impatiently. 'Bobby,' she said by way of explanation. 'He were Tom's dog really, but I haven't the heart to get rid of him. You'd better sit down. I were just meckin' a cup of tea.'

'One sugar,' he said, recognizing, as he was meant to, her oblique hospitality. He glanced around the room. The last time he had been here it had been full of flowers and Mrs Carter's friends and relations on the day immediately following Tom Carter's death. His visit had been respectfully brief, almost perfunctory, he realized now, as he and Sergeant Wilson had gone through the routine questions about Tom Carter's movements on the last night of his life. He wished now he had spent a little more time with the old woman. It might have saved a great deal of subsequent trouble.

Mrs Carter came back into the room from the kitchen carrying a tray with two cups of tea in flowered china cups and a selection of biscuits neatly arranged on a plate with a white paper doily underneath. A biscuit selected and the tea tasted with suitable appreciation, Sinclair felt able to move from the social pleasantries to the business in hand. He glanced at the stuffed fish which held pride of place on the mantel over the gas fire.

'He was a great fisherman, wasn't he,' he said. Mrs Carter nodded grimly.

'Aye, and he had a right to expect a few more years of it an' all,' she said. Sinclair put his cup down, leaned back in his chair and looked at the old woman speculatively. She appeared unmarked by her recent bereavement, her plumpish face relatively unlined for her age which must be, he guessed, well over seventy. But her eyes were shrewd and her faculties, he knew, as sharp as many a younger person's. There was not much went on in the neighbourhood which passed Mrs Carter by.

'Do you think Joey Macready killed your husband, Mrs Carter?' he asked quietly at last.

She smoothed her pinafore down over her ample thighs for a moment before replying. But when she did she looked him straight in the eye, and there was anger there.

'I do not,' she said. 'It's a great pity you didn't ask me that before.'

'The boy confessed,' Sinclair said.

'Aye, and he wouldn't be the first to do that in a police station, would he? Or the last, I dare say. I knew young Joey. Everyone did. He wouldn't hurt a fly.' Mrs Carter pursed her lips angrily and put her cup down with a clatter. 'I suppose now he's dead you've realized you made a mistake?'

'Well, not quite,' Sinclair prevaricated. 'Not officially anyway, but I'd like to take the inquiry a bit further, if you don't mind answering a few questions.'

'Get on wi' it,' Mrs Carter said brusquely. 'Though I don't know what good it'll do you now. You've left it a bit late if you ask me.' Sinclair nodded in acknowledgement of that barb and finished his tea. He had not expected to find much of a welcome in Highcliffe this morning after the events of the previous night, but had not been quite prepared for this hostility from the wife of the murdered man. He drew a deep breath and started again.

'Was Tom worried about anything in the weeks before he died?'

'Aye,' she said. 'He were right worried about t'dead fish. He kept on and on about it every time he came back from t'river.'

'Did he have any idea what was causing the pollution?'

'I don't know. I'm not right sure. That last trip with young Kenny he came back angrier than I've seen him in a long while. He didn't say much, but then he weren't a great talker, weren't Tom. But he were doing a lot of thinking.'

'There's been a suggestion that the pollution could be coming from the old drift mines up on Broadley Moor. Did Tom mention that to you?'

'Tom helped to seal off those old drifts, way back, it must have been about nineteen fifty-three or 'fifty-four. I remember him working up there and coming home all covered with coal muck. It were when he were first working for Agarth and Bradley. Our Sandra were just a little lass...' The old woman fell silent for a moment, staring at a slightly faded black and white photograph on the mantelpiece of a young family group which Sinclair guessed was the Carters and their two daughters. She sighed heavily.

'It were around that time that Douggie Smith died. He were a right lad, were Douggie, Tom's best mate. I always had a soft spot for Douggie. And to go like that, so quick... Tom never really got that...'

Sinclair left the silence hanging for a moment before pressing her any further. She came back to the present with a little shudder, almost as if she had passed out of time to be with Douggie. She recovered quickly and looked hard at Sinclair again.

'Tom went down to see Mr Agarth last Monday,' she said. 'Summat about his pension, he said. Put his best suit on—and a tie.'

'Did he tell you what had happened afterwards?'

Mrs Carter shook her head grimly.

'He said nowt about it to me,' she said. 'But he were in a right funny mood that day, and t'next. That were the day he were killed.'

'He saw James Agarth the day before he died?' Sinclair asked sharply. The old woman nodded.

'You didn't tell me about all this. Why not?' Sinclair asked, his voice hardening. The old woman shrugged.

'I never thought it were important at t'time. Now I'm not so sure.' She looked past Sinclair again at the snapshot on the mantelpiece for a moment. He let her take her time, sensing there was more to come.

'He paid him a good pension, you know,' she said at last. 'Right generous, really.'

'Too generous, maybe?'

'Aye, maybe. And I'm to keep half of it now he's gone. He came round to tell me that himself.'

'James Agarth did?' Sinclair asked, surprised. He could not fit visiting the bereaved into his view of the managing director of Agarth and Bradley. 'When was that?'

'Jut before t'funeral, the Tuesday or Wednesday, I'm not right sure now. Had a cup of tea, he did, and stayed half an hour. I were on my own as it happened and we had a long chat about Tom and t'old days. It were in his father's time, of course, when he first worked for t'firm.'

'Can you remember what you talked about—exactly, I mean?' Sinclair prompted Mrs Carter.

'Oh, just the usual things—how long we'd lived in Highcliffe—we moved into this house when it were built, you know—and how long Tom had worked for t'firm, and what it were like bringing up kids on t'wages in them days. Just that, you know the way you do when someone's passed away.' Mrs Carter sat in silent thought again for a moment.

'He admired that fish an' all,' she said at last, nodding in the direction of the stuffed pike. 'Asked about Tom fishing and who he went with, all that sort of thing.'

'Did you tell him about Kenny Leafield's disappearance?'

'Disappeared, has he? I weren't sure. His mother's right close. Just said he'd gone away to work. But I thought it were ever so queer he never came near after Tom went. A nice lad, Kenny, quiet like and no harm in him. He must have been fishing with our Tom since he were six or seven years old. He's got no grandad of his own, you know, and that Leafield's not much use to a boy like that. Stuck in front of his telly most o' t'time watchin' t'horses, as far as I can meck out.'

'Did you tell Mr Agarth Ken had gone?' Sinclair persisted.

She hesitated for a moment and then shook her head.

'I'm not right sure, but I don't think so, no. I don't think I did.'

'Douggie Smith, the friend who died,' Sinclair began again slowly, and was aware that the name and the memory still had power to shock from the almost imperceptible look of pain which crossed the old woman's face. 'He worked with Tom at Agarth and Bradley?'

'Aye, they were on that mine job up on t'moor when Douggie were took ill.'

'Does he have family around here still?'

'His wife remarried. They'd only been wed six months when he went. I don't know where she is now, I'm sure,' Mrs Carter said. 'She may be dead for all I know. She weren't that much younger than me. Betty she were called, Betty Braithwaite before she were married, but I don't know her married name second time around.'

'Were there brothers, sisters, can you remember?'

'A brother I think she had. Fred, or Ned, summat like that. But it's all so long ago, lad. I can't really remember.

It were Douggie who were a friend o' Tom's. I hardly knew Betty. A right plain girl. I couldn't see what he saw in her.' Mrs Carter fell silent again and Sinclair had a clear impression for a moment that the grief he had resurrected for Douggie Smith, Tom's long dead friend, was not entirely sisterly. The old woman was still regretting a lost and probably never consummated love.

Inspector Sinclair stood up abruptly.

'You've been very patient,' he said. 'Thank you.'

'Aye, well, it's time you got a shift on and found out who really knocked Tom on t'head that night,' Mrs Carter said sharply. 'It were never Joey Macready, you can bank on that.' Sinclair nodded non-committally and took his leave. He would not have admitted it to Mrs Carter, but he was increasingly convinced she was right.

HE DROVE BACK to the centre of the estate and into the yard at the front of the community centre. Workmen were busy here too, sweeping up broken glass and boarding up a shattered window. The advice centre door stood open and Sinclair found Derek Stevenson inside, deep in conversation with Gordon Rangely from the *Echo*. Stevenson scowled when he saw the policeman.

'Can I have a word, Inspector?' Rangley asked quickly. 'About last night?'

'Not with me, Gordon, you know that,' Sinclair said. 'Talk to the Press office, would you?' Rangely shrugged his displeasure. Like most reporters, he found communicating through official channels frustrating and never gave up on attempts to extract additional information by other means. It was a game he never won with Sinclair but the question was still ritually put every time they met.

'I'm amazed you've got the gall to come up here today, Inspector,' Derek Stevenson broke in sharply.

'We'll be wanting a word with you later in the day, I expect, Mr Stevenson,' Sinclair said curtly. 'There'll be a great many statements to be taken. In the meantime, is Kate Weston available?'

Stevenson looked for a moment as if he would pursue his attack, but then he too shrugged and nodded towards the door of Kate's office.

'She's in there.'

Sinclair knocked and went in. Kate was sitting at her desk, which was covered in paperwork, looking tired and tense. She glanced up at Sinclair and her lips tightened.

'That was a dreadful mess last night,' she said. 'It should never have got out of hand like that. There were dozens of children in that hall, including Sam.'

Sinclair nodded.

'I know,' he said. 'We misjudged it completely. We should have had more men up here from the start. Your friend Derek has a dangerous line in rhetoric.' Kate cupped her chin on a hand and looked at Sinclair for a moment, before shaking her head and sighing. Her eyes were a very cool clear grey and Sinclair searched them in vain for some warmth.

'What a mess,' she said again. 'So what can I do for you now?'

'Two things. First I came to thank you for last night. You got me out of a nasty situation. I'm grateful.'

Kate nodded grimly, and looked down at her desk.

'We're not all barbarians up here, you know,' she said without looking up. 'Which doesn't mean I don't think all this couldn't have been avoided with more careful police work from the start. You fell for Joey as a convenient scapegoat . . .'

'Yes,' Sinclair interrupted sharply. 'That was the second reason I came in. I wanted to tell you that I'm going to make a formal request for the murder investigation to be reopened. I'm no longer satisfied with Joey's confession. I'd actually decided before Joey died, but his death makes it even more imperative to clear the case up properly because if we don't it will never come to court at all now. It will just be left to the inquests, and that's never very satisfactory.'

Kate looked at him for a moment without speaking. She got up from her desk and stood silently staring out of the grimy window with its view of the bleak rows of houses running in parallel down the hillside towards the town. She turned at last and Sinclair saw that there were tears in her eyes.

'It's a pity you didn't feel able to say all that before Joey died,' she said. 'Or even last night.'

Sinclair stood up and realized to his surprise that his first instinct was to put his arms round Kate and comfort her. He shook himself mentally and thrust his hands into his pockets instead.

'I'm sorry,' he said quietly. 'But I don't think anyone would have listened rationally to me last night. And there'll still have to be an official decision before I can go ahead. I can't start looking for Tom Carter's murderer again without the approval of my senior officers. But I promise you, I'll get that, and then you can help. I'm going to need to talk to young Ken Leafield, whatever he thinks about that, and I think you know where he is.'

Kate went back to her seat slowly and sat looking at her hands again for a long moment.

'I promised him I wouldn't tell anyone where he'd been staying. Indeed, I'm not even sure that he'll still be there. He said he might move on rather than talk to the police.'

'I can ask the Met to look for him,' Sinclair said. 'It would be quicker and easier if you told me. I'll have to find him.'

Kate nodded but still looked uncertain.

'Let me think about it,' she said. 'I may be able to contact him by phone...'

'Obstructing the police is an offence,' Sinclair said.

'I know that, Inspector,' Kate replied. They looked at each other warily for a moment until Sinclair relaxed and smiled faintly.

'I'm sorry,' he said. 'I don't even know yet whether I have any authority to pursue this inquiry. But believe me,

I'll go to the chief constable, if necessary, to get it. And then I'll need to talk to the boy. Then, I'll need your help.'

'You know I'll do anything I can to clear Joey's name. That's what Annie wants now, more than anything, and so do a lot of other people on the estate. You'll get the help you need if people believe there's going to be a proper investigation this time.'

Sinclair nodded, satisfied.

HIS FINAL CALL was at another house on the estate where he found Councillor Bill Bairstow just about to leave to take the bus into the town centre where he had a meeting at the City Hall.

'I'll give you a lift down if you can answer a few questions on the way,' Sinclair offered. Bairstow wrapped his maroon woolen scarf around his neck. He too looked tired out this morning and his skin was an unhealthy yellowish colour and his breathing harsh.

'I reckon it's you ought to be answering t'questions this morning,' he offered grimly. 'A right pig's ear you lot made of it last night.'

Sinclair nodded. It was clear that his painstakingly built up relationships on the estate had been shattered by the previous night's events.

'It'll be on t'agenda at public policy committee this afternoon,' Councillor Bairstow offered as he got into the car beside Sinclair. 'They'll not be happy.'

'I don't suppose they will,' Sinclair said. 'But your friend Derek Stevenson has a lot to answer for.'

Bairstow looked at him shrewdly.

'No friend of mine, lad,' he said. 'Incitement, do you reckon?'

'Possibly,' Sinclair conceded. 'It'll certainly be considered—but don't quote me on that.' Bairstow nodded with what looked to Sinclair like satisfaction and settled himself deeper into his seat.

'So what did you want to talk about, then, lad?' he asked. 'James Agarth, was it? I reckon it's not before time.'

'Who told you that?' Sinclair asked in surprise.

'Nay, lad, it were only your father,' the councillor said reassuringly. 'I bumped into him last night at t'Labour Club and he told me you might be in touch. Summat about Agarth and Bradley and those old drift mines, was it? A right mucky job that was: I remember it well. They brought in a gang of Irish navvies and were paying them about half what the local lads got. A fair bit of recruiting t'union did as a result of that.'

'What exactly did they do up there, then?'

'Well, before they could start on the estate lower down t'hill, they had to take all t'water draining out o' t'drifts and channel it into t'Beck. They had men up there for months that winter, 'fifty-four it must have been, first on the drainage and then on the actual sealing of the drifts. It were a long job.'

'Did they fill the old mines in completely, then?'

'No. Those tunnels went right back into t'hillside, half a mile or more. They just sealed off the entrances with waste and a lot o'concrete,' Councillor Bairstow said.

'So there are effectively still tunnels under the moor?'

'Aye, I suppose there are,' Bairstow said thoughtfully. 'And I suppose you're wondering if there could be owt there shouldn't be in those tunnels, aren't you?' He glanced sideways at Sinclair as he pulled up at traffic lights, but his companion's face remained impassive. 'I reckon the answer to that is that there could be, but you'd have a hell of a job getting in there to find out. They were very thoroughly sealed up. You'd not get in wi' your bucket and spade.'

'Do you remember anyone called Douggie Smith?' Sinclair asked. 'Worked on that job with Tom Carter, and died soon afterwards.'

'I worked months on a compensation case for Douggie Smith's widow,' Bairstow said sharply. 'Old Agarth were adamant his illness were nowt to do with him. Pneumonia was what went on t'death certificate, and in the end it were impossible to prove different. In the end Douggie's widow gave up. I think she got a couple of hundred quid *ex gratia*, and that were that. Betty Smith. Aye, I remember her well.'

'Do you know what happened to her afterwards? Where she might be now?'

'Not off-hand I don't,' the councillor said. 'But I dare say if I looked through t'union I might be able to turn summat up. We don't throw much away at Amalgamated. It's all down in t'cellar in cardboard boxes. There's a new young chap in t'office now who says he's going to put it all on computers, but he's only got back to nineteen eighty-five so far. It'll take him a lifetime at this rate.' And Bill Bairstow gave a satisfied chuckle as though his young colleague's experience had proved a point he had made many times before.

'I'd be glad if you'd do that, Bill,' Sinclair said. 'I'd like to talk to Betty Smith, if she's still alive. And there's something else. The pollution in the river. Have you seen the official reports on the water samples?'

'No, I've not. But I can get hold of them from Dennis Wright if you want me to.'

'It might help, although he says that all the reports on water from the Beck are negative, and if the pollution is coming down from the moors that can't be right.'

'I'll look into the monitoring,' Bairstow promised. 'Are you suggesting our own results are being tampered with?'

'I don't know,' Sinclair said gloomily. 'If they are, then this conspiracy runs right through this town.'

'If it runs as far as City Hall, I'll find out,' Bairstow said flatly. 'If Agarth's being protected there, or anyone else for that matter, I'll get it stopped, make no mistake about that. Some of these flashy young councillors think I'm old-fashioned, you know. Not market-oriented. All that nonsense. But there's nowt old-fashioned about running an honest council. I'm due to be Lord Mayor again next year, and I'll not have any corruption in Milford spoiling that.'

SUPERINTENDENT Eddie Greaves's summons was as peremptory as usual. Inspector Sinclair put down the phone and looked at Sergeant Wilson questioningly.

'The boss wants to see me,' he said. 'Perhaps this is the response to the memo.' The sergeant looked up from the file he was studying on the other side of Sinclair's desk.

'I should prepare for fireworks if it is,' he said. 'I get the distinct impression that the last thing the brass want is to re-open the Macready case.'

The previous day had been a gruelling one for Sinclair and Wilson. The two hours' debriefing on the Highcliffe riot had centred to a large extent on whether they, as the 'patch' detectives responsible for local intelligence, could or should have predicted the likelihood of violence that night, and whether they had reacted to the threat quickly enough by calling in uniformed reinforcements when it did emerge at the public meeting.

It was clear to them both that they had not fully convinced the deputy chief constable that they could not have safely arrested Stevenson when his speech became inflammatory. Their only satisfaction in a wholly unsatisfactory affair lay in the fact that their reports on Stevenson's behaviour were to go to the Crown Prosecution Service for consideration.

After that they had spent another couple of hours composing a memo to Superintendent Greaves summarizing Sinclair's reasons for wishing to re-open the inquiry into Tom Carter's death. It was Wilson's trenchantly expressed view that the case Sinclair made was not strong enough to convince their superiors that the can of worms should be reopened, with all the risks it entailed of inflaming passions in Highcliffe further. But the memo had gone in, and the

two men had ended the day discussing how they might set
about tracing not only Kenny Leafield in London but also
the widow of a long-dead labourer called Douggie Smith,
and anyone else who might have worked with Tom Carter
thirty years before.

'Stand by for squalls, then,' said Sinclair, pulling on his
jacket and tightening his tie and grinning wryly. He knew
he was sticking his neck out, and that the sergeant fully expected him to get his head chopped off. 'It'll be traffic duty
for us both if you're right.'

He was surprised to find that the superintendent was not
alone in his office, and slightly alarmed to see that Greaves
was as angry as he had ever seen him.

'I've asked Chief Superintendent Swallow from Ketley
division to sit in on this interview in view of its serious-
ness,' Greaves said.

'Sir?' Sinclair said, with a puzzled glance at the impeccably uniformed officer, who sat behind and slightly to one
side of Greaves, rigid on a straight-backed chair. Swallow
merely nodded slightly in acknowledgement, unsmiling.
This was not at all what Sinclair had expected and he felt a
faint stirring of anxiety.

'My memo, sir...' he began in the uncomfortable silence which followed, but Greaves did not let him continue.

'That's not why I asked you in, Detective-Inspector,' he
said. 'This is an entirely different matter. Different and very
much more serious.' He had not asked the more junior officer to sit down, and Sinclair felt himself automatically
stiffening to attention as the two men continued to look at
him grimly.

'Sir?' he asked again. Swallow seemed, at this point, to
take a sudden and unusually intense interest in the ceiling
while Greaves opened a buff folder on his desk with great
deliberation.

'Tell me, Detective-Inspector, where you have your bank
accounts,' he asked at length.

The question took Sinclair by surprise and he hesitated for a moment before answering.

'My account, sir,' he said at last. 'My bank account is at County in Broadley. There's just the one branch there.'

'And your salary is paid into that account?'

'Yes, sir, of course.'

'And any other income? Where do you bank that?'

Sinclair looked surprised again.

'I don't have any other income, sir,' he said, his anxiety increasing. 'Margaret—my wife—has her own account at the same branch. Her father still makes her an allowance...'

'You say you have no other income,' Greaves broke in, his voice dispassionate and controlled but his colour rising. Swallow continued to look anywhere but at the officer standing in front of him. 'So you don't have an account at the main County branch in Kirkgate in the town centre?'

'No, sir', Sinclair said flatly. He glanced with some foreboding at the buff file in front of Greaves where he could now see the familiar lay-out of a County Bank statement of account. Greaves stared at him for a moment in silence, drumming his fingers on the file, and then handed him the sheet of paper.

'How do you explain this, then, Inspector?' he said.

Sinclair took the statement with a hand which, he was irritated to see, was not quite steady. He glanced at the name and address at the top of the form and was not entirely surprised to see that it was his own. His eyes travelled down the columns of figures. The account was not well-used and the statement covered a period of more than six months, during which time regular monthly payments of £500 had been credited, and no withdrawals made. The balance stood at £5,500.

Sinclair found that his mouth had gone unaccountably dry. He cleared his throat and glanced at Greaves and Swallow, who were both waiting for him to speak in a distinctly unfriendly silence.

'Well, Detective-Inspector?' Swallow said at last, testily. Distaste showed clearly on his face, although whether it was for Sinclair himself, or the nature of the proceedings, or both, was impossible to gauge.

'I've never seen this before, sir,' Sinclair said quietly. 'I have no account at that branch.'

'Well, County Bank clearly think you have, lad,' Greaves responded, quickly this time, anger thickening his voice. 'Come on now, Alex, if you're trying to keep a bit of cash out of sight from your missus, you can tell us. That's no crime. Or is it your father-in-law giving you a sub for the school fees? I thought you told me he was going to do that? If there's a straightforward explanation, tell us now, we can check it out, and that's all there'll be to it . . .'

'That's not my account, sir,' Sinclair broke in angrily, handing the statement back to Greaves. 'I've never seen it before, and I don't know where that money is coming from. The bank must have a record of who opened it and when, surely. It certainly wasn't me, even though it's in my name.'

There was another long silence.

'That's not what the manager tells us, Inspector,' Greaves said at last. 'In the circumstances, I took the precaution of making preliminary inquiries. The bank says that it is your account, and the manager recalls you opening it just over a year ago. You signed the forms in his office.'

Sinclair's anxiety hardened then into a certainty that he was in deep trouble. Greaves's next question did not surprise though it sickened him.'

'I have to ask you formally for an explanation of these payments, Detective-Inspector Sinclair,' he said. 'You know this force's attitude to corruption. It won't be tolerated. We are completely within our rights to demand an explanation.'

'I'm sorry, sir,' he said, his voice sounding unreal to him now, almost disembodied. 'You have every right to demand an explanation, but I can't give you one. I can only tell you what I've told you already. I know nothing about that account, or about where the payments into it might have come from.'

'Are you saying this is some sort of forgery, lad?' Greaves suddenly exploded, banging his fist on the bank statement. Chief Superintendent Swallow intervened smoothly.

'Inspector Sinclair,' he said. 'You must realize that if you can't come up with any reasonable explanation for this account then we will have to institute disciplinary, and possibly criminal, inquiries. Are you quite sure that you have not, perhaps, forgotten—or overlooked—the account?'

The irony was heavy and Sinclair had to swallow his anger. He shook his head, unable to trust himself to speak for a moment. At last he regained control.

'I can't offer you any explanation, sir,' he said. 'I know nothing about the account.'

Greaves glanced briefly at Swallow, who nodded. The superintendent turned back to Sinclair and looked at him with undisguised hostility.

'I've no alternative but to suspend you from duty pending an inquiry into these unexplained payments,' he said. 'You know the procedures. I must say it grieves me personally to see a young officer of your ability straying down this road, but there it is. You'll leave your cases in the hands of Sergeant Wilson for the present. We'll let you know when we want to see you again in the course of our inquiries.'

'Sir,' Sinclair said quietly, and turned to go, the shock showing clearly on his face.

'Sinclair,' Swallow called as he opened the door. The inspector half turned.

'I should take legal advice, Sinclair. Get a brief. You'll need one.'

ALEX SINCLAIR DROVE HOME through the thickening rush-hour traffic. His mind was numbed by the speed of events. He had returned to his office, explained briefly to Wilson what had happened before being relieved of his warrant card by a stony-faced Detective-Superintendent Greaves,

and within ten minutes of his interview he had left the
building. Without even thinking about it, he headed the car
in the direction of Broadley, and eventually found himself
parked in front of his own house without any clear impression of how he had arrived there.

He switched off the engine and sat for a moment in silence, trying to take in the magnitude of what had happened. As far as he could see, his professional life lay in
ruins. Unless he could find some way of proving that he had
not opened the offending bank account, the very best that
could happen to him would be dismissal from the force to
which he had devoted himself without reservation for over
ten years; the worst, prosecution and quite possibly gaol.
The courts, quite rightly in his view, did not take kindly to
police corruption. The last officer he knew who had been
convicted of taking bribes had been sent down for four
years.

He glanced across the gravelled drive towards his own
front door. His most immediate anxiety was how to break
the news to Margaret, who he knew would take it badly. She
had made great efforts early in their marriage to overcome
her reservations about the nature of his work. She would
much rather have been able to chat to her friends about his
career as an accountant or a lawyer, or even in business like
her father, than about his rise through the ranks of the police force, rapid though that had been. Even now, he knew,
his rank was not sufficiently impressive for Margaret to find
her status comfortable when in the company of her
wealthier friends. He was, to that extent, already an embarrassment to her and she desperately cared about the de-
lay in his next crucial promotion. With him suspended from
duty for a possibly prolonged period, she would find it very
hard indeed to cope with the social repercussions among
her friends.

Sinclair picked up his coat and empty briefcase from the
passenger seat with a sigh, and let himself into the house.
It was not until he had closed the front door behind him
that he realized, from the profound silence and the clean

and tidy state of the hall, that Margaret and the children were not at home. He recalled then that they had all gone to the Booths' for tea and would not be back until Sally's bedtime.

Sinclair wandered into the kitchen and made himself a cup of tea which he topped up with whisky from the cocktail cabinet in the sitting-room. He sat at the stripped pine kitchen table with his hands cupped around his mug for a long time, deep in thought, before finally gulping down his drink and going quickly upstairs into the master bedroom. He packed a small suitcase with a selection of his casual clothes, and changed into slacks and a sweater. Back in the kitchen he sat at the table again and composed a note for Margaret.

IT WAS ALREADY DARK when Kate Weston and Sam returned home from the school's parents' evening. Kate opened the front door and was in the middle of telling Sam to go straight to his room and get ready for bed when she broke off with a gasp of surprise. Seated at the table by the living-room window, a figure was silhouetted against the grey of the sky. Kate grabbed Sam's coat and pulled him back towards the door and, with her heart thumping, switched on the living-room light. Alex Sinclair turned towards them, blinking in the unexpected brightness. He had a bottle of whisky and an ashtray brimming with half-smoked stubs on the table in front of him and a half-full glass in his hand.

'I'm sorry,' he said. 'I needed to see you.'

'You frightened the life out of me,' Kate exclaimed angrily. 'How the hell did you get in?'

'You learn these nefarious tricks in the police force,' Sinclair said. 'It's a good preparation for a life of crime.' It was not said quite lightly enough and Kate picked up the underlying bitterness at once.

'Sam, get ready for bed, please,' she said to the boy, who was staring at the policeman mutinously, his hands thrust belligerently into the pockets of his jeans.

'Oh, Mum,' he protested, but she pushed him firmly in the direction of his bedroom.

'I'll bring you some cocoa. You got a good report at school, so don't spoil it now.' The boy did not argue any further although he closed his bedroom door behind him with more force than it required, setting the thin cotton curtains billowing in the draught.

Kate did not go into the kitchen at once. She pulled the curtains across the window and sat down at the table opposite Sinclair.

'Something's gone wrong?' She searched his face, which was grey and drawn, anxiously.

'You could say that,' Sinclair said, his hand tightening around his glass. 'I'm sorry to break in on you like this, but I didn't know where to turn...' He took a long drink and a deep breath and slowly began to tell her what had happened. Kate listened, horrified. When he had finished he lit a cigarette, his hand shaking, and they sat in silence for a moment before Kate spoke.

'I can't believe it,' she said at last.

'What can't you believe? That I'm on the take? Or that I got caught?'

She shook her head quickly.

'I don't believe you're involved in corruption, Alex,' she said flatly. 'Not for a moment. But what's even more incredible is that someone should try to incriminate you— what do you call it? Set you up? Surely Superintendent Greaves doesn't believe it?'

Sinclair buried his face in his hands for a moment, and Kate fought back an urgent desire to reach out and put her arms around him.

'It doesn't really matter what Greaves believes,' he said at last. 'If there's *prima facie* evidence there, he has to follow the procedures, call in an outside officer...'

'And suspend you?'

'And suspend me. He's gone by the book. I can't complain about that.' Sinclair looked away from Kate and she waited patiently, knowing there was more he wanted to say but that it needed time. This is where being a good listener gets you, she thought wryly. You get to be a universal shoulder to cry on.

'I haven't told my wife,' he said at last. 'I can't. I don't know how. I just packed a bag and left a note saying I was going away for a few days. It's a miserable trick but the best I could think of . . .'

'Surely she'll find out.' It was a statement more than a question.

'Surely she will. It won't take long and it won't be from me, and that, I guess, will be the end of our marriage on top of the rest of it.'

'Is that what you want?' Kate asked quietly, trying to keep the emotion out of her voice by pretending that this was just another interview, just another dispassionate session at the advice centre, another client seeking a clear path through an emotional and legal maze. But she knew it was more than that. Sinclair looked at her and shook his head hopelessly and did not give her the answer she wanted.

'I don't know,' he said, his voice dull. 'I don't know what I want. I can't bear the thought of being without the girls. But I guess Margaret will take the decision now, anyway. She found it hard enough to cope with my job before. She's not the sort to stand by her man in this sort of mess. It'll go on for months, possibly years. I can't imagine her coming to visit me in gaol.'

He took a final draught of the whisky in his glass and reached out for the bottle. Kate got there before him and removed it from his grasp.

'I don't think that's a good idea,' she said.

For a moment she thought that the anger which was simmering under Sinclair's surface façade of calm was about to erupt and she drew back a little, half afraid that he might try to take the bottle from her by force. But he quickly regained control, with a dispirited shrug.

'Your son's calling you,' he said.

'Oh, the wretched cocoa,' she cried, and with the whisky bottle firmly in her hand she went into the kitchen.

Sinclair sat silently at the table while she was away, turning his empty glass around monotonously.

'I thought you were imagining things when you complained about the officers who brought Sam home that time,' he said when she came back. 'But now I think it's all of a piece. I think we've both been effectively warned off, in my case possibly for good.'

'But who by?' Kate asked angrily. 'Who can suborn bank managers into inventing bank accounts?'

'Oh, I think there are people who are big enough and powerful enough in this town to get away with that,' Sinclair said heavily. 'And James Agarth could be one of them. The question then is whether we are big enough and powerful enough to thwart them.'

'But we'll try?' Kate asked, putting a tentative hand over his. 'We can't let them get away with it.'

'We?' Sinclair asked, a note of doubt clearly in his voice. His eyes were fixed on her hand but he did not withdraw his own.

She did not answer him directly.

'Where were you going to stay tonight?' she asked.

'With my father, I thought. Though this business will kill him. It was bad enough my being a copper, but to be suspected of being a bent copper...' He shrugged, dispirited again.

'Stay here,' she said.

'Are you sure?'

'Of course I'm sure. You can sleep on the sofa. It's not very comfortable but you're welcome.' She kept her voice carefully neutral.

'Ah,' he said, glancing at the sofa with a wry expression.

She looked at him sharply, the faintest hint of amusement in her eyes. She let go of his hand and touched the side of his face lightly, conscious of the tension in him.

'Did you expect more?' she asked in a low voice. 'I've never been sure with you, and I don't go out of my way to take men away from their families.'

'That sounds very prim.'

'I live with a child who lost his father,' she said very quietly. 'I wouldn't inflict that on anyone else's children.'

'I'm sorry. I wasn't thinking,' he said. 'I've never been sure either,' he said. 'About you or myself. But it didn't need you to come between me and Margaret. We managed that all on our own a long time ago.'

Abruptly he got to his feet and pulled her towards him, pushing her hair from her face and kissing her, gently at first, and then with increasing fierceness, starting at her brow and working his way towards her mouth. She made a token effort to push him away, a tiny flare of panic making her gasp. But it did not last and as his lips met hers, she put her arms round him and pulled him closer, meeting him more than half way.

She could taste the whisky on his tongue and feel the urgency of his desire and she gasped for breath as she was swept up in a surge of passion such as she had not felt since Richard's death. She knew there would be no going back now. He pulled away at last and held her from him in silence, as if searching for something. The day's anxiety had drained away but his eyes were still questioning, as though he could not fully believe what was happening.

'Are you sure?' he said again at last. 'You're not just taking in another of your waifs and strays?'

She laughed aloud and he realized how rarely he had ever heard her laugh without inhibition. Her face lit up and he wondered why he had never thought she was beautiful.

'Some waif,' she said. 'What do you take me for? I've wanted to do that for a long time, though I hardly dared admit it to myself.'

'Shameless hussy,' he said, laughing too, and feeling his residual guilt about Margaret fall away. 'I never guessed,' he said. 'You're always so cool, so self-controlled.'

'I've learned to be that,' she said. 'Widows get lots of propositions but not much commitment, especially when there's a child around.'

'What about Sam?' Sinclair asked, kissing her again gently but achieving the same instant, uninhibited response.

'Sam's just like his father,' Kate said, and was surprised to find that she could say it without a tremor. 'Once he's asleep he sleeps like a log.'

KATE SAT IN HER dressing-gown alone at the kitchen table next morning, sipping coffee thoughtfully and trying to come to terms with the events of the previous day and night. She had lain in bed for a few extra minutes after the alarm had gone off an hour ago simply to enjoy the unaccustomed luxury of sharing her bed with another human being. She had woken to find Sinclair's arm around her, her breast cupped in his hand. She had slid away from him gently without waking him and closed the bedroom door quietly behind her, leaving him sound asleep, one arm already thrown carelessly across the space she had just left.

She had sent Sam off to school without telling him that their guest had stayed overnight. She knew that the boy would not have welcomed the news. He would have to be faced, just as Alex Sinclair would have to face his wife and family, sooner rather than later, but at this moment she was not prepared to take the edge off what had been for her a night of fierce delight by talking to the boy about what had happened.

Even so, her unease deepened steadily as the warm physical memory of Sinclair receded. She had looked at herself in the bathroom mirror for a long time. Was she behaving like a slut or a romantic schoolgirl? she asked herself fiercely. She had been attracted to Alex Sinclair for at least a year, she admitted to herself, but she had gone out of her way to avoid giving any hint of that as their paths had regularly crossed. And she knew that her resolve had as much to do with not wanting to upset Sam as to any puritanical belief that she should not get involved with a married man. Now, in a crisis, at the very first indication that Sinclair might share her feelings, she had fallen into bed with him like an infatuated seventeen-year-old, she thought, and all the consequences of that precipitate decision would have to be faced.

She sighed and got up to pour herself another coffee. She caught sight of her own reflection again in the mirror by the kitchen door and smiled at herself as people do, momentarily appreciative of her glossy hair, which she searched in her vainer moments for signs of grey, and skin which had an early morning glow about it. You can't be as old as all that, she thought to herself, smoothing her dressing-gown over her breasts and looking at the effect critically.

The moment of contentment was short-lived, as she knew it would be. She half turned as Sinclair came out of the bedroom. He was already dressed in slacks and a sports shirt and was rubbing an exploratory hand over his night's growth of dark stubble. He smiled faintly when he saw her.

'It might have been more prudent to sleep the night away,' he said drily. 'I'm shattered.'

'But much less fun.'

'Kate,' he began hesitantly. She stood up and put a finger on his lips.

'Leave it, Alex,' she said. 'I know all about the complications and how impossible it all is. Don't you think Sam isn't a complication too? But it was good—for me anyway. So let's leave it like that, shall we?'

'I was drunk,' Sinclair said bitterly. 'If I'd been sober...'

'If you'd been sober you wouldn't have wanted to sleep with me?'

'No, I didn't mean that,' he said quickly.

'So, if you'd been sober you'd have been more inhibited about asking? You'd have slept on the sofa and burned, like St Augustine, I suppose? Come on, Alex, we're both too old for those sorts of games.'

Sinclair turned away and looked out of the window at the almost deserted streets of the estate for a moment in silence.

'It's a complication I could do without right now,' he said at last. Kate went to stand behind him and put her arms around his waist, revelling again in the warmth and solidity of his body.

'I'm sorry,' she said quietly. 'But we can't undo what's done, and for myself I'm glad. It's part of the equation, now.'

He turned towards her and smiled faintly.

'No promises?'

'I'm not asking for any. But I'll come and visit you in gaol if it comes to that.' She kissed him lightly on the lips before turning away to hide the tears in her eyes.

'Coffee and toast all right? And then a council of war?'

ELEVEN

ALEX SINCLAIR SAT in an alcove at the back of the saloon bar of the Fox, an empty whisky glass in front of him. He had been in the pub, crowded and noisy with lunch-time drinkers, for almost an hour already and was beginning to think he was wasting his time when he saw Detective-Sergeant Wilson shoulder his way through the door and look around the smoke-filled room with his usual deliberation.

Sinclair raised his empty glass in greeting and the sergeant nodded an unsmiling acknowledgement and made his way to the bar. He was well known to many of those drinking and more than one of those who greeted him, with more or less enthusiasm according to their precise current status at police headquarters, glanced in Sinclair's direction before they spoke. It was obvious that some inkling of what had happened the previous day had already reached Highcliffe, and Sinclair gritted his teeth as he met covert glances which mixed curiosity and triumph, without a hint of sympathy, from the pub's regulars.

He had not expected the news of his suspension to become public so quickly or he would have elected to meet Wilson somewhere they were less well-known. Wilson put a double Scotch in front of Sinclair and sat down at the opposite side of the ersatz Elizabethan oak table. He took a deep draught from his pint of bitter, giving himself time to take in the signs of strain and tiredness around the younger man's eyes and the slight tremor of his hand as he picked up his drink.

'All right?' he asked.

Sinclair nodded. 'As well as can be expected,' he said, with a lightness he did not feel. 'So what's new?'

'Not a great deal,' the sergeant said after another moment's silent thought. 'The super's turned your memo down flat. Told me to concentrate on the other cases we've got on the books and leave the Carter case to the inquest. No cause for further inquiries, were his exact words.'

'I'm not sure this was a good place to meet,' Sinclair said, looking around the crowded bar again and taking in the occasionally hostile glances they were getting. 'The news is evidently out.'

'Aye, well, it would be. The press office put out a statement this morning and it were on t'local radio. Didn't you hear it?'

Sinclair shook his head bleakly.

'What did it say exactly?' he asked, staring into his glass.

'Just that there was to be an inquiry into corruption and that a detective-inspector had been suspended from duty. Didn't even name you, but I dare say there's plenty that have. No one up here seems to be in much doubt that it's you, any road.'

Sinclair picked up his drink, using every ounce of self-control at his command to stop his hand shaking, and took a slow draught of Scotch. Wilson looked at the glass and then at Sinclair.

'How much of that have you had?' he asked.

Sinclair shrugged. 'Too much, if that's what you're getting at. But it's not every day that your career and your marriage go down the tubes together, is it?'

'I can't comment on your wife, boss, but if it were my career I'd put up a bit of a fight for it, I reckon,' Wilson said slowly. He hesitated, avoiding Sinclair's eyes. 'Unless ...'

The two men sat for a long moment in a pregnant pool of silence, while the hubbub of the bar swirled around them.

'I've not been on the take, Dave,' Sinclair said at last, his grip on his glass white-knuckled. 'If that's what you want to hear.'

Wilson nodded. 'No, I didn't reckon you had,' he said, his rare smile breaking the tension finally. 'So which sods have set you up, then?'

'That's what I thought you might like to help me find out,' Sinclair said. 'I'd no right to ask you to meet me today. It won't do your career any good if it gets back. But I thought you might like to help me work out what the hell's going on.'

'You reckon it's all tied up with the Macready case, then, do you? It could be someone you sent down getting their own back.'

'It could be. You can do some digging in the files, if you like, to see who's come out recently who might bear a grudge. But somehow I don't think that's the answer. Someone used the force to warn Kate Weston off. At least, that's what Kate believes, and she's a level-headed woman. That's not the work of any old villain. It takes connections, and connections at a fairly high level.' Sinclair had already told Wilson about Kate and Sam's experience with the uniformed branch.

'And now me,' he continued. 'I *know* that bank account's a fake. In which case, someone opened it in my name and then made sure it was brought to Eddie Greaves's attention. The question then is why? Why Kate Weston? Why me? The only common factor is the Carter murder, and the fact that neither Kate nor I are happy with the case against Joey Macready.'

'I'll keep my ears open, but it'll not be easy,' Wilson said. 'There'll not be a lot I can do officially with the super in his present mood. He's tearing around looking for dirt under every CID fingernail at the present. He's taken your suspension practically as a personal insult.'

'He would,' Sinclair said. 'He's backed every promotion I've had—and the next one. You know I was his blue-eyed boy.'

'That's as maybe. Right now I'd not rate your chances of staying out of gaol as better than middling if Greaves has his way. He'll be bringing you in for questioning sooner rather than later and if he charges you, you'll not get bail in your position.'

Wilson's assessment was brutal but Sinclair knew it was accurate enough. The legal process offered little mercy to corrupt coppers.

Wilson drained his glass and shook his head to Sinclair's offer of another drink. They were about to go when they were interrupted by the arrival of a newcomer at the table, a large ruddy-complexioned man in dirty overalls with a speckling of light-coloured dust in his dark curly hair, clutching a full pint of beer which slopped perilously close to Sinclair and Wilson as he lurched to a halt beside them.

'Effing pigs,' the newcomer enunciated with painstaking clarity. Wilson stood up with surprising speed for one of his bulk and edged his way between the drunk and the unstable pub table.

'Now then, Reilly,' he said. 'That's enough.' But Reilly had clearly drunk enough to remain unperturbed by a verbal warning, and had by now attracted a small group of interested spectators from among the previously neutral crowd.

'Effing pigs,' Reilly said again more loudly, waving his glass and this time spilling beer down Wilson's mac, leaving a thin trickle of foaming bubbles from lapel to belt. 'And effing bent with it,' he concluded triumphantly, to a murmur of approval from the onlookers.

In a moment Sergeant Wilson had seized Reilly firmly by the overalls with one hand and had his other clenched into a formidable fist. Reilly's pint glass tilted far too far this time, letting beer pour to the floor within inches of Wilson, where it soaked quickly into the well-trodden carpet, to general hilarity. But before Wilson could plant the full weight of his heavyweight fist where it was obviously itching to go, Sinclair had extricated himself from behind the table and taken a firm hold on Wilson's free arm.

'Leave it, Sergeant,' he said in a tone which brooked no argument. 'Leave it alone.' Wilson glanced at him for a second, his face flushed with anger, before he relaxed and let Reilly go.

'Sir,' he said, and with Sinclair close behind him he shouldered his way through the muttering crowd of drinkers and out of the pub into the fresh air of the car park. He stood for a moment by his car, breathing heavily and looking mutinous.

'That would have been a disaster—for both of us,' Sinclair said.

'Aye,' Wilson said at last. 'Happen you're right.'

'You know I am.'

'I'll be getting back, then,' Wilson said. 'Where can I contact you? At home still, are you?'

He did not look surprised when Sinclair shook his head, nor even when Sinclair told him to make contact through Kate Weston.

'She's a level-headed woman,' he said, straight-faced, as he drove off.

SINCLAIR COULD FEEL the whisky progressively muddying his judgement as he drove to his father-in-law's house, and knew that he should not be behind the wheel of a car. The Booths lived in a solid double-fronted stone mansion with spectacular views over the moorland countryside on the edge of the old village of Broadley, a straggle of stone agricultural cottages now mainly occupied by retired couples who had installed double glazing and central heating to keep the sharp moorland winds at bay.

The house was a mile and a half from the more suburban part of the village where Alex and Margaret had set up home in the house Ted Booth had bought them. Sinclair parked on the drive behind his wife's Golf and Ted's dark blue Rolls-Royce, switched off the engine and sat for a moment with the window down to let the cool moorland breeze blow through the car in an effort to clear his head.

He had rung Margaret at home that morning after Kate had gone to work, leaving him alone in the flat. The conversation had been brief: tentative on his side, icily polite on hers. She clearly knew in some detail what had happened the day before, and she had told rather than asked him to meet her at her father's house at 2:30 that afternoon. Sinclair suspected, in the absence of the histrionics he had expected, that either Ted himself or the family solicitor had briefed her on how to behave and what to say.

The Booths' housekeeper answered the front door, took his coat and showed him immediately into the drawing-room without, he noticed, her usual warm smile. It was a room which Sinclair had always liked. Margaret's mother had had the good sense to employ a decorator with a natural eye for colour which had reached its full fruition in the large Edwardian room on the corner of the house with windows facing south and west, a sunny room made restful by beige carpet and upholstery of powder blue. But today the atmosphere was far from restful as Sinclair went in.

Ted Booth rose grim-faced from his chair by the fire to meet his son-in-law with an outstretched hand of rigid formality. Margaret herself remained seated in another armchair near the natural stone fireplace where a couple of logs smouldered smokily. She hardly bothered to look up as her husband walked in. Standing behind her was another man of more than middle age in a dark formal suit, a tie of impeccable wine-red conservatism and a small white rose in his button-hole, his iron grey hair dressed with brilliantine in the manner of the 1950s.

'My solicitor, Wayland Waterman.' Booth made the introduction almost perfunctorily. Sinclair nodded, recognizing the name of one of the partners of a large Bradford firm which occasionally represented clients in the Milford courts.

'How are you, Margaret?' Sinclair asked quietly. She was wearing a dark green fitted wool dress which emphasized the curves of breast and hip, and although she looked pale, her blonde beauty still had the power to move him. She did not answer, turning away as he took the chair his father-in-law indicated, a little away from the family group around the fireplace. How could the grand passion of their youth have turned to dust and ashes so totally, thought Sinclair bitterly. It was not just the apathy of middle life which had overtaken them, but a positive and on her side, it seemed to him sometimes, a malevolent dislike. There would be no going back.

Waterman moved from his position behind Margaret and took up an almost Victorian stance in front of the fire, his hands behind his back, swaying slightly from heel to toe as he spoke.

'Mrs Sinclair has asked me to speak on her behalf in this matter, Detective-Inspector,' he said in that curiously impersonal tone professionals adopt for dealing with the most highly charged emotional situations. Sinclair nodded his assent, his eyes still on Margaret whose hands were twisting nervously on her lap but who still steadfastly refused to look in his direction.

'My client, after some discussion this morning with her father and myself, has intimated her intention of commencing divorce proceedings immediately,' Waterman said. 'In normal circumstances, it would be my duty to recommend some attempt at reconciliation, but my client assures me that the marriage had already reached a stage of, what shall we call it, terminal difficulty before these latest events. In the circumstances, in your somewhat unusual circumstances, Detective-Inspector, my client feels that there is no alternative but to go ahead as expeditiously as possible. Can I take it you have no objection?'

'I have no objection to a divorce,' Sinclair said. 'I'll want to discuss custody of my daughters with my own solicitor in due course. In the meantime I want to make some interim arrangements for access to the girls. I want to see them as soon as it can be arranged.'

There was a sharp and unexpected hissing sound from Margaret at this and Ted Booth put a restraining hand on her arm.

'Leave it to Wayland, dear,' he murmured. Margaret flashed a look at Sinclair of such pure hatred that he drew his breath sharply. Wayland Waterman continued smoothly before he could speak, so smoothly that even in his slightly fuddled state Sinclair realized that his reaction must have been anticipated and the corporate Booth response rehearsed, in spite of Margaret's less premeditated reaction.

'My client feels that in the circumstances—your circumstances, that is—with your future status and—er—whereabouts so, shall we say, problematic, that it would be less unsettling for the girls if access were denied for the time being. We are, of course, making the welfare of the children our first consideration. However, my client does feel strongly enough on this point to be prepared to go to a judge in chambers for an injunction should you not feel able to accede to her quite reasonable request that you should keep away from the family home, which I understand is her unencumbered property, and from your daughters, for the time being.'

'And you think you'd get an injunction, I suppose,' Sinclair said thickly.

'Oh, I think so, in the circumstances, don't you, Detective-Inspector?' Waterman rocked slightly further back on his heels than usual, the faintest smile of satisfaction on his face as Sinclair struggled to find arguments to challenge his certainty.

'I have committed no crime, Mr Waterman,' Sinclair said, slightly surprised at the clarity of his voice. 'I have been charged with no crime, still less been convicted. But the punishment starts here, does it, here with my own family?' Sinclair had maintained his calm, though with increasing difficulty. He still spoke quietly, his speech only slightly slurred, but what he said was sufficient to break the dam of pent-up emotion which filled the serene drawing-room and hung in the air like clouds of some noxious gas. Ted Booth and Margaret turned on him together.

'My family, I think you mean, lad, don't you? My family? And a damned disgrace you've turned out to be to my family. After all I've done for you over the years, with the house, with an allowance for Margaret, now with the school fees. And more than one good word I've put in for you where and when it's mattered. I've made you in this town, lad! And all the thanks we get is a divorce and quite likely a criminal scandal as well. You can leave my granddaughters alone from now on, and that's final.'

Margaret stood up and, Sinclair thought, would have attacked him physically if Waterman had not restrained her by putting an arm around her and holding her back.

'You're a hypocritical bastard, Alex, and I've had enough of it. What sort of a father do you think you are, anyway? There are weeks when you never see the girls from Monday till Sunday. Days when you're so obsessed with your bloody job even when you are at home that we can't get a civil word out of you. And now it all turns out to be a pretence, a fraud. You've had your hand in the bloody till all the time.

'Do you really think the girls will care if you're not there? Do you really think it'll matter to them? If you're in gaol even? It won't make a blind bit of difference. You're never there anyway! And I'd no more bring them to see you in prison than I'd take them to the moon.'

Alex Sinclair was never completely sure what happened next. He knew he struck Margaret hard across the face, because he heard the blow, rather than felt it. Beyond that he could recall only being bundled out of the room by unidentifiable and not very gentle hands, and stumbling across the hall, past his horrified mother-in-law who appeared to make some ineffectual attempt to detain him. Out of the house in the sharp fresh air he staggered into the shrubbery on the far side of the gravel drive and was violently sick into the rhododendrons.

For five minutes at least he sat in the car with the window down, shivering and taking in great gulps of cold air. When his head finally cleared he found himself possessed of a despairing certainty that he had just, through his own fault, lost Jennifer and Sally as irrevocably as he had lost Margaret.

It was after five o'clock when Kate Weston got home from the advice centre and as soon as she let herself in through the front door of the flats she was aware that all was not well on the top floor. She hurried up the stairs, cursing the weight of her bag of groceries as she struggled up the last flight, to find her own front door open and Sam in the living-room apparently arguing loudly with Annie Macready, and with Tracey dancing urgently from one foot to the other in excitement.

'Mum, Mum,' Sam shouted as soon as he saw her. 'That policeman's on your bed and won't move!'

Kate glanced inquiringly at Annie.

'I don't know how the hell he got in, but he's asleep in there. Sam found him when he came in from school and he and Tracey have been carrying on about it ever since I came home myself.' Annie looked almost as angry as Sam, her blue eyes hard as she clipped the over-excited Tracey round the ear.

'Just shut up, can't you?' she said to her daughter. 'It's nowt to do with you.'

Kate put her shopping down on the kitchen table while she frantically worked out strategies in her mind. She had known that at some time Sam and her friends in Highcliffe would have to be told about her relationship with Alex Sinclair, but she had hoped to pick the time and place to explain to those who needed to know. This sudden confrontation was not what she had planned.

'Sam and Tracey, go and watch television next door while I talk to Annie,' she said eventually. Sam made to argue but she pushed him firmly across the landing towards the Macreadys' flat.

'Come on,' she said impatiently. 'You're missing *Grange Hill.*'

'I want to know what's going on,' the boy said, but he allowed himself to be propelled through the Macreadys' front door.

Kate closed her own front door behind the two children and motioned Annie to sit down.

'What the hell's going on?' the woman asked angrily. 'What the hell's he doing here?' She bristled with suspicion and resentment as Kate explained what had happened the previous day.

'So he's your effing fancy man now, is he? The effing copper that arrested our Joey?' Annie's eyes filled, as they so often did now, and a single huge tear crept down her face, carrying with it a grimy trail of mascara through the imperfectly applied foundation. Annie Macready's careful public façade was much cracked these days.

'It's not like that,' Kate said, helpless in the face of her own guilt and Annie's sense of betrayal. 'He doesn't believe Joey is guilty any more. Look after the kids for half an hour, Annie, and I'll get him to explain to you.' Annie got up heavily and went to the door.

'It'd better be bloody good,' she said, before she slammed the door behind her.

Kate sighed heavily and went into her bedroom. Sinclair was spreadeagled across the bed fully dressed and half opened his eyes as she sat down on the edge of the bed beside him.

'Are you drunk?' she asked coldly, her anger getting the better of the other emotions which threatened to overwhelm her. He did not answer immediately, struggling up into a half-sitting position and running a tentative hand across his face as if to check that he was still all there.

'No,' he said at last. 'I'm not drunk. Not now.'

'Sam came in and found you here. You left the door open.'

'Ah,' Sinclair nodded, understanding the implications at once. 'I'm sorry. I'd nowhere else to go. I'd forgotten he would come in from school first. That was stupid of me.'

Kate sat looking at him silently for a moment, taking in the signs of strain and the scarcely concealed despair in his eyes which he tried to prevent her seeing.

'You saw Margaret?'

'I blew it,' he said. 'Had too much to drink and lost my cool. They'll move heaven and earth now to keep me away from the girls. Money's no object.'

'I'm sorry,' she said quietly. Her anger drained away and she took him in her arms rather as she would have done an overgrown child and gradually she felt some of the tension ease out of him as she stroked the back of his neck. She had no idea how long they remained locked together, but at last it was Alex Sinclair who pulled away, ran his hands through his hair and stood up.

'It's past mending, Kate,' he said. 'So let's see if we can keep me out of gaol, shall we, at least long enough to find out who really killed Tom Carter?'

TWELVE

'WE NEED TO BE saddled with a bent copper like we need a hole in the head,' Derek Stevenson said harshly. The Joey Macready Action Committee—renamed since Joey's death and rededicated to clearing the boy's name—shuffled its collective feet uncomfortably under the advice centre table. Kate looked round at her colleagues in increasing desperation. Annie Macready stared implacably past her at the overloaded notice-board behind Derek's chair. Father O'Leary fidgeted uncomfortably with his papers. Even Bill Bairstow, whom Kate had expected to be sympathetic to her request to allow Alex Sinclair to join the meeting, was shaking his head ponderously as he filled his pipe. Stevenson's look of satisfaction increased as the silence lengthened.

'If he comes in here, I'm going,' Annie Macready said suddenly. 'He was the pig who arrested Joey in the first place. He'd no right to do that without me being there. That's where it all began.'

'It's not on, Kate,' Stevenson broke in more quietly. 'He may have changed his mind about Joey, and he may be suspended, but he's still a police officer. We can't get involved with him when we have at least three outstanding complaints against the police, all of which involve Sinclair himself in one way or another. As Annie says, the arrest itself was out of order, then the interview and the so-called confession, and then the police handling of the kids on the estate after the meeting the other night. The fact that the police themselves now think Sinclair's corrupt just strengthens our case against the bastard.'

'He asked for the case to be re-opened,' Kate said.

'Says he!' Annie said scornfully. 'I reckon he's just trying to ingratiate himself up here to find out what's going on.'

Kate made as if to argue but then shook her head, suddenly afraid of how far Annie might pursue that line of argument. She had persuaded her not to mention the incident at the flat the previous afternoon, but was not sure whether that promise would hold if Annie became really angry.

'All right,' she said. 'Forget it. I'll keep in touch with him in case he can be useful.' Annie snorted at that but said no more.

'I don't reckon there's owt in these allegations of corruption,' Bill Bairstow broke in. 'I've known the family for years and I'd be surprised to find Andrew Sinclair's son was on the take. But Derek's right. Best we steer clear for t'time being. It's a complication we can do without.'

Kate acquiesced at that, and the meeting turned its attention to its major concern: what evidence it could offer at the forthcoming inquest into Joey Macready's death which could help to clear him posthumously of the charge of murder he had faced.

'It's not necessarily going to be easy,' Derek Stevenson said. 'Coroners can more or less please themselves what witnesses they call. It's not like a trial where we'd have the right to present a defence. All the court has to do is decide on the cause of death, so with a suicide like this all he needs to do is establish what Joey's state of mind was, what sort of stress he was under, that sort of thing. Whether the stress was caused by guilt or by being locked up when he was innocent may not be a question he wants to explore.'

'Aye, and he won't want a succession of witnesses saying Joey couldn't have done it because he were such a nice lad, either,' Bill Bairstow added. 'If we want to get into that argument at all, we need some hard facts to offer. In fact our best chance of clearing Joey is likely to be at Tom Carter's inquest, not his own. That's when we can challenge the police case against Joey, and try to prove that someone else was involved. But that's adjourned indefinitely and again it's facts we need, not rumours, and not opinions, Annie love.'

'And it's facts we don't have,' Kate said. 'Not even Alex Sinclair has anything to go on that you might call a fact.'

THE MEETING BROKE UP inconclusively, with each member of the committee committed to following up a different line of inquiry. Kate Weston walked slowly back to the flats with Annie Macready.

'He's stopping, then, is he, your inspector friend?' Annie asked suspiciously as they climbed the stairs. Kate shook her head tiredly.

'I don't know,' she said. 'He's left his wife.'

'She's thrown him out, more like,' Annie suggested. 'They say coppers' marriages never last. I reckon bent coppers' marriages are shorter than most.'

'He's got nowhere else to go.' Kate knew that sounded like a feeble excuse, and Annie shrugged her disbelief.

'Till he goes to gaol, and that's t'best place for him, as far as I'm concerned. But there'll be no telling you, that's obvious.'

Kate collected Sam from Annie's flat, where he had been watching television with Tracey, and unlocked her own front door. Sinclair was sitting at the table in the living-room and the boy stood for a moment staring at him, stoney-faced, before marching stiffly into his bedroom and closing the door behind him with a bang.

'I'm sorry,' Kate said, and followed her son into his room. Sam was lying face down on the bed, with his face hidden.

'How long's he staying?' Sam asked, not looking up, his voice muffled by the pillow. Kate sat on the edge of the bed and stroked the back of the boy's head gently.

'Until he has somewhere else to go,' Kate said. 'He can't go home just at the moment. Do you mind very much?'

'Where will he sleep?'

Kate hesitated for a second before deciding how to answer.

'I think he can sleep on the sofa for a few nights, don't you?' she said. 'He won't disturb us there.' Sam turned towards her and she saw that he was fighting back tears.

'He's not to sleep in your bed,' he said defiantly.

'Is no one ever allowed to sleep in my bed?' she asked, smiling faintly. It was not so long since Sam had ceased creeping in beside her in the night when he had had a bad dream or had woken earlier than usual. Sam hesitated, giving the question some thought. She knew he understood the implications of what he was saying.

'Only if I like him,' he said at last.

'One day I might want to get married again, Sam,' she said gently. 'Your father wouldn't mind, you know. He'd want me to do what made me happy.'

'Only if I like him,' the boy said again, obstinately. 'If I don't like him, Daddy wouldn't either.'

'Perhaps you'll learn to like Alex,' Kate said, but Sam shook his head and turned away again, his face cold and closed to her.

'He's a pig, and he arrested Joey, and Tracey says her mum says that he's a crook anyway, that he's been stealing money.'

'That's not proved, Sam,' Kate said quickly. 'What's happened to him is the same as what happened to you and Gary in town: some policemen are saying things which may not necessarily be true.'

The boy rolled over on to his back again and looked at her silently for a moment with the eyes which reminded her so forcibly of Richard sometimes that it hurt. For a moment she wondered if she might have been misled by what she had taken to be Alex Sinclair's fierce honesty. It paled beside Sam's.

'Why are people telling so many lies about things?' the boy asked.

Kate kissed him gently on the forehead, something which he did not allow her to do in public any more.

'That's what we want to find out, love,' she said. 'Just be patient, and we'll sort it all out. Get ready for bed now, and I'll bring you some cocoa.'

Sinclair was still sitting at the table in the next room when Kate went back, gazing out of the window as lights came on across the estate outside.

'Does Sam want me out?' he asked.

'That's what he'd like,' she admitted. 'But he'll accept you as a guest on the sofa for a while, I think.'

'Don't blame him,' Sinclair said. 'I'd like to think Jennifer and Sally would resent it if Margaret brought someone else home.'

'There's a world of a difference,' Kate protested. 'Richard won't be coming back.'

'Do you think I'd go back, then?'

Kate did not answer for a moment.

'To be with your girls? I think you'd be tempted, if Margaret made you an offer,' she said slowly, at last.

'It's academic,' Sinclair said flatly. 'There'll be no offers. So what happened at your meeting? I gather, as you didn't phone, that they didn't want me on their team?'

'Not really. Even Bill seemed to regard you as a bit of a liability, I'm afraid.'

'Right,' he said bitterly. 'I suppose that about sums it up. The only thing we don't know is how long Eddie Greaves is going to leave me on the hook before he hauls me in and charges me.'

'Do you think he'll do that?'

'I think he's got very little choice. Whoever set me up didn't just waft a vague suspicion under Eddie's nose: they provided him with cast-iron evidence of an inexplicable bank account. They don't just want me suspended, they want me destroyed. Out of the police force certainly, out of Milford probably, and quite possibly in gaol.'

Kate shivered.

'Who?' she said, but Sinclair just shrugged.

'You could go away,' she said tentatively. 'To London or somewhere.'

'And get dragged back to ''assist with enquiries'' when the Met trip over me in six months' time? There's no future in that. We've got to fight this thing now, if we're to stand any chance of winning. But...'

'But?' she prompted.

'But, just... that I don't hold out very high hopes of winning,' he said bleakly. 'I think I've been stitched up very tight and very professionally by people who have to be prepared to lie on oath in court to get me put away. And if they've gone as far as they have, they must be prepared to do that. And they could easily make it stick.'

THIRTEEN

'I WANT TO OPEN AN ACCOUNT,' Kate Weston said to the young man at the inquiry desk at the main branch of the County Bank in Kirkgate in the centre of Milford. The clerk smiled pleasantly and rummaged in a drawer beneath the counter for a moment.

'Certainly, madam,' he said pleasantly. 'There's a simple form to fill in.'

'I have a son,' Kate said, glancing at the application form with only passing interest. 'He wants to open a similar account but he's away at the moment. Can I open it on his behalf?' The young man hesitated for no more than a fraction of a second, and then shook his head.

'We would have to see him to take specimen signatures and so on,' he said smoothly. 'We do have branches in most areas, of course...'

'Never mind,' Kate said. 'Let's just go ahead with my application, then, for the moment, shall we? Do I need to see the manager?'

'Oh no, that's not necessary. If you fill in the form, and give us a referee—look, in this section here—then I can deal with the whole transaction, and you'll be able to pay money in within a few days. The cheque-book and card and so on will take a little longer.'

'A referee?' Kate asked. 'What sort of person do you want for that?'

'Oh, someone of good standing, a clergyman, a doctor, or just someone who knows you well.'

'Would a police inspector do?' Kate asked.

'Certainly, Mrs—er—Weston,' the clerk said, glancing at her half-completed form. 'That would be ideal.'

'A police officer who has an account here? Detective-Inspector Sinclair, for instance?'

The clerk smiled again, and turned to the computer terminal at his side and typed in a few words. He looked puzzled as the screen did not apparently tell him what he wanted to know, and he repeated his keyboard query, still without satisfaction.

'You say the inspector has an account here?' he asked. 'Not that it matters at all, Mrs Weston. Just give us his name and address and we'll contact him. It's just a formality, really.'

'I'm sure he has an account here,' Kate said firmly. 'He recommended this bank particularly.'

'Well, I can't get him up on the screen, but it's probably just a computer blip. As I say, we'll contact him anyway if you give us the details.'

Kate completed the formalities and left the form with the clerk, who promised that she would be hearing about her new account within a few days. When the heavy swing doors closed behind her, the young man, still looking slightly puzzled, crossed to the manager's office, rang the security bell and, after identifying himself, was admitted to the thickly carpeted inner sanctum where the manager sat behind an enormous mahogany desk.

'Sir, I just tried to get details of an account on the computer—a police inspector, an Alexander Sinclair, and it told me to refer all queries to you,' the clerk said, a faint note of puzzlement in his voice.

A slight frown crossed the manager's face.

'Why did you need those details, Jones?' he asked.

'A prospective customer, sir, wanting to open an account. She gave Inspector Sinclair as a referee. A Mrs Kate Weston?'

'Ah yes, Jones, leave Mrs Weston to me, will you. There are some complications there. Just leave Mrs Weston's application form here, and I'll deal with it, don't worry.'

The clerk did as he was instructed and when the door had closed after him, the manager flipped briefly through the application form before picking up the telephone and dialling an outside number on his private line.

ALEX SINCLAIR SAT on one of the wooden benches in
Highcliffe Park overlooking the Beck. The stream was
channelled between steep man-made banks here as it slid
quickly downhill towards the river. Iron railings separated
it from the tussocky grass of the park and prevented children from approaching what could, in winter, be a dangerously fast-moving waterway. The Beck was a dark stream,
more coal-coloured than peaty, and carrying a copious
supply of litter down towards the river in the town centre.
As far as Sinclair knew, the local boys caught no fish there.
It was a stream which had taken on the industrial character of the town almost before it needed to, he thought, a
stream which spent very little time wandering untram-
melled on the moors where it rose from several boggy
springs little more than three miles away and some thousand feet or so above the Highcliffe estate on Broadley
Moor.

Sinclair had just walked the length of the Beck and could
feel his calf and thigh muscles still protesting at this unaccustomed exercise. He had spent much of the morning with
his solicitor, discussing the handling of his divorce and arranging for him to be contacted when Superintendent
Greaves called him back to headquarters for questioning.

It had been a grim meeting and as Kate Weston was
committed to taking a client to the small claims court and
the afternoon had started clear and bright, he had decided
that the climb to Broadley Top, a favourite local vantage-
point, would refresh him mentally as well as physically.
Three-quarters of an hour's brisk climb had found him
alone on the highest plateau above Milford, an undulating
summit of heather, gorse and bracken just beginning to
show bright green shoots among its tangle of russet winter
debris, and giving a view clear across the town and beyond
to the bluish Pennine moors to the west.

Sitting on a convenient outcrop of gritty stone, he had
watched grey rain-laden clouds roll in across the valley,
whipped by the rising wind. The air was damp and cooler
than it had been for weeks as the unseasonably early sum-

mer heat was blown away and he watched showers of rain approaching in isolated patches of silvery spume across the villages on the distant hills.

Immediately below him, shielded from the town by a spur of moorland country, he could see Broadley village and actually make out his parents-in-law's house, and the primary school where he knew his daughters would be hard at work. He wondered briefly if they were missing him and then dismissed the speculation impatiently as fruitless as well as demoralizing.

The moor fell away steeply towards Broadley, ending in a rocky escarpment at the foot of which he had had to deal with his first death as a young policeman on the beat. He could even see the jumble of rocks where a couple of children had found the body of a young woman lying apparently peacefully asleep on her back on the short springy turf. Only when he had felt how cold she was and eased her over, did he discover that the back of her skull had smashed against the stone and was a mass of blood and splintered bone. She had jumped the two hundred feet from the plateau from almost exactly where he was sitting now.

He lost track of time as he sat in his isolated vantage-point trying to come to terms with the events of the last two days. The final rupture with Margaret he accepted as inevitable. It had only been a matter of time before some irredeemable quarrel had torn them apart for good. He had resented this diagnosis from his father, when it was regularly offered, but he knew it was true none the less.

Which made it no easier to accept the fact that the break with Margaret also meant a loss of contact with his daughters, and he brooded on that near-certainty more bitterly than he thought about his suspension from duty. A battle over evidence in a court of law he could cope with, he thought. The accusation of corruption angered him, but in a way which fuelled his inner determination to unravel the conspiracy which must be behind it. The threatened loss of his daughters' company filled him with a physical ache which bordered on despair. There are times when it must be easy to take that jump, he thought, looking down again at the jagged, tumbled black rocks below.

He was driven from his viewpoint by one of the blustery showers which had been scudding across the valley towards him, and he strode back down the moorland path with his anorak collar turned up. Some hundred feet below the top of the moor he stopped briefly beside a few derelict stone buildings on a level shelf in the hillside, the point at which the rocky footpath he had been following downwards turned into a broader track up which a vehicle could climb. This was the entrance to the abandoned drifts which had once brought scores of miners up from Milford every day, until their thin seams of coal eventually gave out. Gorse and heather and scrubby brown grass had done their best to disguise the workings, but it was still possible to make out what had been two entrances into the hillside, blocked now by mounds of rubble and rock apparently firmly cemented into place. It would take heavy mechanical diggers to get the tunnels open again, he thought. It was not a spade and pickaxe job.

The streams which higher up had bubbled and rustled through boggy ground and tussocks of spiky moorland grasses came together here and had been channelled into a culvert which ran under the track and continued down the hill towards Highcliffe as a broad stream with stone banks on either side. Sinclair stood above the culvert for a moment looking at the dark moorland water which was running sluggishly after more than a week without rain. Clumps of bright yellow kingcups lined the banks and followed the boggy margins of the Beck in both directions. Sinclair shrugged. It was far too innocent a waterway to sustain his recent speculation about contamination. There was no sign of anything untowards up here.

Half an hour later the shower had passed over and he was waiting in the park for Sergeant Wilson, who came stumping across the grass with a look of some disgust on his face.

'Ruddy dogs,' he said, wiping his shoes on the grass before sitting down beside Sinclair. 'The place is filthy. So
how's it going?'

Sinclair shrugged and dug his hands deeper into his anorak pockets.

'Not good, according to my solicitor,' he said. 'All he
held out was months of hassle on both fronts, with bail
unlikely and no guarantee on either result. So what's
Greaves up to?'

'Not a lot, yet, as far as I know,' the sergeant said. 'The
brass were up from county this morning and closeted with
him for more than an hour, but no one's saying owt. Tight-
lipped isn't in it.'

'He must feel very sure I won't do a runner.'

'You won't do a runner, boss,' Wilson said somberly.
'But maybe he hopes you will.'

'It'd certainly save him some embarrassment,' Sinclair
conceded. 'I've just been up to Broadley Top, but I decided on balance not to jump. That would have been a bit
convenient, too, wouldn't it?'

'Aye, well, you'd best mind you're not pushed, then,'
Wilson said dourly. 'As to the other business, have you seen
this?' He pulled a copy of the local evening paper out of his
inside pocket and passed it to Sinclair. The front page
boasted a photograph of James Agarth shaking hands with
another prosperous-looking man Sinclair did not recognize. The accompanying story identified him as the repre-
sentative of a major national construction company visiting
Milford to discuss the possibility of taking over Agarth and
Bradley, a transaction which the paper speculated could put
a personal fortune in the region of £30 million into James
Agarth's pocket. Sinclair gave a low whistle.

'I'd no idea he was worth that sort of money,' he said.

'Well, he's not—yet, which gives him a pretty powerful
incentive to protect the firm's reputation right now, doesn't
it?'

'I think I'd like to take a closer look at Mr Agarth's affairs,' Sinclair said slowly.

'I'll ask the commercial boys if there's ever been any bad smells in that quarter,' Wilson said. 'But if I were you, I'd keep a low profile. If they catch you doing any freelance work in the present circumstances they'll find another book to throw at you. Leave it to me, will you?'

KATE WESTON DROVE BACK from town in an abstracted mood. After her visit to the County Bank she had met a client from the advice centre and taken him to the small claims court, and had then done some shopping before setting off home. She sat in the city centre traffic trying to sort out a jumble of anxieties about Alex Sinclair, about Sam, and the Joey Macready case. Her spur-of-the-moment foray to the bank should encourage Alex, she thought. Her experience of opening an account there did not tie up with the supposed evidence upon which his suspension had been based, of that she was convinced. It confirmed that someone was lying.

Once out of the worst of the early evening rush hour, she accelerated the little Citroën up the steep hill towards Highcliffe. The road to the estate followed the contours of the hillside. On the left, a low stone wall gave a clear view down an almost sheer cliff and over the long grassy strip of Highcliffe Park which ran along the side of Highcliffe Beck where it sank, safely channelled, into the valley below. Kate knew the route well, and changed down a gear as she took the steepest part of the road which curved to the right before flattening out on the final approach to the estate.

She was not aware of the overtaking car until it was level with her and she heard the roar of its engine. She glanced to her right in surprise which turned quickly to horror as she realized that the car was not simply overtaking but was cutting in on her and forcing her over to the pavement on her near-side and towards the wall and the sheer drop beyond. She wrestled with the wheel, trying desperately to keep the Citroën on the road, but the other car was a much heavier saloon, and the driver determined. He hit the Cit-

roën a glancing sideways blow on the off-side wing and that
was enough. The smaller car mounted the pavement, demolished a section of wall and somersaulted into the park
below. Kate heard her own despairing scream with a sort of
detachment as she realized that she was about to die.

SINCLAIR AND WILSON heard the sound of the impact on
the road above them, and had turned in time to watch in
horror as the car fell to the ground.

'It looks like Kate,' Sinclair yelled, already running to
where the Citroën lay on its roof, its wheels still spinning,
and its rear end, which had apparently hit the ground first,
a crumpled wreck. Wilson followed, cursing as he ran. Both
men had dealt with enough traffic accidents to know that
speed was essential and they took in the situation at a
glance.

'Turn her upright,' Sinclair said, and with a concerted
heave they toppled the little car back on to its three remaining wheels, where it sagged, lop-sided, on the grass, its
soft roof and perspex windows flattened almost to the level
of the window sills.

'Get her out. There's fuel leaking,' Wilson said urgently. They took a door each, but it was Sinclair who
managed to wrench his way inside first. With his heart
thudding, he squeezed his head and shoulders through the
misshapen passenger doorway, shoving the crumpled
roofing upwards to make a narrow passageway. Kate lay
awkwardly across the two front seats, still held roughly
upright by her seatbelt which had not broken under the
impact of the crash. He could see no sign of injury, but her
eyes were closed and she was deathly pale and he knew that
she could well be dead.

With trembling fingers he struggled to unfasten her
safety-belt, aware of the increasingly strong, acrid fumes
which were filling the confined space. He was aware too
that Wilson had failed to pull open the driver's door, and
that he had to get her out unaided. Hampered by the
crumpled roof, he found at first that he could not gain a
firm enough grip on her shoulders to move her across the
passenger seat towards the open door. He gritted his teeth

and tried again, thanking whatever gods there were when quite suddenly the inert body slid towards him and he realized that his immediate fear, that her feet or legs were trapped beneath the steering-wheel, was unfounded.

Wilson helped take the weight as Sinclair at last succeeded in sliding Kate free of the wreck, and together they carried her a safe distance away and laid her down on the grass. Neither spoke as Sinclair gently undid her coat and shirt and felt for a pulse on her neck.

'She's alive,' he whispered. Wilson nodded, his face impassive.

'I'll fetch an ambulance,' he said. 'Hang on.' He ran across the park, past the several curious passers-by who were hurrying to see if they could help.

With the help of the small crowd that had gathered, Sinclair busied himself making Kate comfortable in a rough bed of donated coats, straightening her limbs gently and trying to discover where she was hurt. He could find no obvious injuries apart from a large red bruise on her forehead which, he assumed, was what had knocked her unconscious.

Before the ambulance came, she opened her eyes and her look of puzzled recognition filled him with almost unbearable relief.

'He tried to kill me,' she said, so quietly that Sinclair had to lean right over her to hear her clearly.

'It's all right. You're all right. The ambulance is coming,' he said, taking her hand under the bundled coats and squeezing it gently.

'Don't leave me,' she said.

He shook his head with feeling.

'I won't leave you, Kate,' he said.

FOURTEEN

KATE WOKE UP to find herself in a high hospital bed in a room lit only by a shaded light to one side of the room. It took her a moment to realize where she was, and even longer to tense each limb gingerly and discover that, although her muscles felt as though she had been stretched on a rack, she was not in anything which could be described as agony. Her head ached dully, though, and her mouth was dry. She felt only the vaguest curiosity about how she came to be in a hospital bed. She wanted above anything, she thought, a cool drink and she wondered how to attract the attention of a nurse.

Before her tired brain could solve that problem another thought struck her and she was seized with panic.

'Sam,' she said sharply. 'Oh God. Sam.' A sudden movement in the darkest corner of the room told her that she was not alone. With infinite care she eased her head to one side, wincing as unexpected daggers of pain hit home in neck and shoulders, and made out a shape sitting in a chair in the corner of the room. The figure stood up slowly and even in the dim light she recognized Alex Sinclair.

'Where's Sam?' she asked huskily. Speech proved surprisingly difficult, and her eyes filled with tears in spite of herself.

'It's all right. Annie's looking after him,' Sinclair said quietly, moving over to a chair beside the bed. 'How are you feeling?'

'Dreadful. I'm aching all over. And I need a drink.' He handed her a glass of water from the bedside locker and she drank gratefully.

'Nothing's broken,' he said. 'They've done every X-ray they could think of. You were very lucky. But they want to keep you in overnight because of the concussion.' She digested this information slowly. She felt an infinite sense of relief that Sinclair was there and an uncharacteristic willingness to let someone else shoulder her problems.

'Does Sam know that's all it is? Are you sure he believes that's all it is? He'll be terrified...after Richard...for it to happen again...' The panic seized her again and made her almost incoherent.

'It's all right, I promise. I went back to see him and told him exactly how you were, and that you'd be home tomorrow.'

Sinclair did not tell her of the half-hour it had taken him to calm the hysterical boy who had instantly convinced himself that Sinclair was lying and that his mother was dying if not already dead, nor of the hour he had sat with him until he fell into a tear-stained, exhausted sleep on a camp bed in Tracey Macready's room.

'He's asleep now. If they discharge you in the morning you can be home almost before he's awake.'

'I'm always so careful when I'm driving,' she whispered, as she began to recall some of the details of what had happened. 'I couldn't bear to think of it happening to him twice.'

'It didn't happen twice, Kate. You're fine and he's fine, too.'

He took her hand and held it against his cheek for a moment, wondering if he dare question her further.

'Can you remember what happened?' he asked at last. She frowned and turned uneasily underneath the hospital blankets.

'It's all so confused.'

'Do you remember being pulled from the car?'

'No. The last thing I remember is driving up Highcliffe Lane, then someone overtook me...' Her voice trailed away helplessly and Sinclair could just see the gleam of a tear on her cheek in the dim light.

'Never mind, now,' he said, feeling a sort of helpless exhaustion dulling his own mind. A nurse bustled into the room, attracted by the sound of voices, and not pleased.

'Mrs Weston is supposed to be resting,' she said sharply, checking Kate's pulse and shining a torch briefly across her eyes. 'You're not really supposed to be here at all, you know, Inspector. It's most irregular.'

Kate fell asleep again almost at once, and after extracting a promise from the nurse that she would let no one into her room during the night, Sinclair left the hospital. He drove back to Highcliffe and let himself into the empty flat, and fell exhausted across Kate's bed. He was convinced that the accident had been an attempted murder, but if Kate could no longer remember how it had happened that might be impossible to prove. Kate herself obviously had no idea yet how lucky she had been to survive, or how close Sam had come in reality to being orphaned. Sinclair had indignantly rejected the idea of leaving Milford the previous night. Now, seized with a desperate fear for the safety of Kate and Sam as well as his own, he was not so sure. With the question still unresolved, he too fell into a troubled and restless sleep.

'NO, KATE. It's too dangerous.' Alex Sinclair did not hide his anger as he faced Kate Weston across the kitchen table. She had come home at half past eight that morning, still stiff and sore, ashen-faced, the bruise on her temple purple now. She had discharged herself from hospital and taken a taxi back to the estate. A tearful Sam had been dispatched to school, in spite of his protests, and the argument about what she should do next had raged ever since.

'They tried to kill you,' Alex said, not for the first time. 'They nearly succeeded. Next time, perhaps they will. Or it could be Sam. You must go away for a while, somewhere they can't trace you.'

'I'll send Sam to my mother's,' Kate conceded. 'But I can't leave. Annie needs me, there's the centre, the action committee, all that. I can't run out on them.' She clutched her empty coffee mug like a lifeline, her knuckles showing white, her face distraught.

'You can't protect Sam by himself,' Sinclair said harshly. 'You have to protect yourself *for* Sam. You said as much yourself last night. You're all he's got. You have to go with him.'

A single tear trickled down her cheek and she brushed it away angrily.

'I can't,' she said again. 'I can't leave Highcliffe.' She hesitated, then faced him squarely, meeting his anxious eyes. 'I can't leave you,' she said. 'Not to face all this alone.'

He took her two hands across the table and held them tightly.

'I can't offer you anything just now but trouble,' he said. 'I may well be in gaol next week and there's no knowing how it will all end. Go, if only because it's one less thing for me to worry about.'

'I love you,' she said softly.

'I know.' They sat for a moment in silence before he looked away.

'There's no future in it, Kate,' he said at last, trying to keep the despair he felt out of his voice but only partly succeeding. 'Take Sam to your mother's and wait there. I promise I'll keep in touch.'

She shook her head angrily and then gasped, swaying across the table, her face white. Sinclair moved quickly to her side, supporting her shoulders, afraid she would fall.

'What is it?' he said anxiously. She brushed a hand across her eyes and then leaned back in her chair, breathing heavily.

'It's all right,' she said. 'I just felt dizzy for a moment. It's all right now.' She closed her eyes briefly and then gasped again and turned excitedly to Sinclair.

'I can remember what happened,' she said. 'The other car. I can remember now. It's almost like a slow motion film. It was bigger, dark-coloured—black or dark green perhaps, and I saw the driver's face. He looked straight at me as he hit me.'

'Can you describe him?'

'Yes, I think I can. He was dark-haired, a big, square face, quite ruddy-coloured.'

'Would you know him again? Could you identify him?' Sinclair asked with the first glimmer of hope he had felt for days that he might be able to penetrate the conspiracy that seemed to have enveloped them.

'Yes, I think so,' Kate said. 'In fact, I'm sure I'd know him again. It's not a face I'd forget in a hurry.'

At that moment the doorbell rang. Sinclair cursed quietly and, pushing Kate gently back into her chair, went to the answer-phone. After listening for a moment he pressed the button to open the street door.

'It's Councillor Bairstow,' he said. 'Says it's urgent. Can you cope?'

She nodded. 'I'm all right,' she said. 'You don't have to worry about me.'

'You make that difficult,' he said drily.

Sinclair opened the front door to admit not only Bill Bairstow but Derek Stevenson, whose face darkened with anger when he saw the policeman.

'You pop up everywhere, Inspector,' he said curtly. 'I thought they'd have locked you up by now.'

'I wouldn't put money on my being inside before you,' Sinclair said, and the other man flushed.

'Leave it, Derek,' Bairstow said angrily. The older man looked tired and dishevelled, unusually so for someone Sinclair had never seen less than sprucely turned out. His coat was crumpled and there was a dark smudge of dirt down one side of his face.

'What's the matter, Bill?' Kate asked, taking in his state of suppressed agitation at a glance. 'What's wrong?'

'You may well ask, lass,' Bairstow said, taking off his coat and scarf and sinking wearily into an armchair. 'You've not heard about the fire, then?'

'There was a fire last night at Amalgamated's offices in Turnbull Street,' Stevenson said. 'Quite bad. Could have been much worse, but for the young chap who's computerizing the records and was working late. He raised the alarm before it really took hold.'

'Your records?' Kate asked anxiously. 'You were going to look through the records for Betty Smith's case? Were the files damaged?'

'Aye. Well, there's some water damage down in t'basement, some of them are soaked through, but the fire didn't get that far. Once they're dried out they should be all right.'

'What started the fire?' Sinclair asked sharply.

Bairstow looked at him and nodded grimly. 'Oh, there's no doubt it were arson,' he said. 'No doubt at all, according to the chief fire officer. They found traces of paraffin. If it hadn't been for the fact that young David were still on t'premises the whole shoot would have gone up in smoke.'

There was a long silence while they all took in the implications of what Bairstow had said. Stevenson cursed under his breath, but it was Sinclair who asked the question.

'How did anyone find out you wanted to go through those records? Who knew about it?'

'Only the people on the action committee, as far as I know,' Bairstow said. 'That's the three of us, and Annie Macready and Father O'Leary. I certainly told no one else.' He looked at Stevenson and Kate Weston in turn, and then at Sinclair.

'Did Kate tell you?' he asked bluntly.

'Yes, she did,' Sinclair admitted. 'But I told no one else.'

'So you say,' Stevenson cut in sharply.

'I think,' Kate said in exasperation, 'I think you're just going to have to trust Alex, whether you like it or not, Derek. It wasn't only arson yesterday. Someone tried to kill me.'

Bairstow and Stevenson looked at her in a horrified astonishment which Sinclair found hard to believe was not genuine. 'I heard you'd had a bump in your car. Are you all right . . .' Bairstow began.

'It was more than a bump,' Sinclair said harshly. 'Someone deliberately ran her off the road. She's lucky to be alive. And the only reason we can think of is that she has

been doing a little freelance investigation herself into alleged police corruption. It seems to me now that there's
someone at the bottom of all this who is prepared to stop
at nothing to deter anyone who wants to investigate Tom
Carter's murder any further. I've been pretty comprehen-
sively removed from the scene myself, and at least two attempts have been made to frighten Kate off. This last one
was nearly fatal.'

'And the fire?' Bairstow asked.

'It has to be connected. But what's really worrying is that
whoever is behind it seems to know what we are planning
almost before we do ourselves.' Sinclair paused and faced
the two men squarely.

'I know a lot of people out there don't trust me any
longer. As far as Highcliffe's concerned, my being a bent
copper is what they want to believe because it makes it easier to blame the police for what happened the other night,
instead of their own young people who ran out of control.'

Stevenson made to interrupt but Bairstow waved him
down impatiently.

'Let him finish, Derek,' he said.

'As far as the estate's concerned, I'm guilty, and there's
not much I can do to make them believe anything different
just now. But you know better. You don't have the excuse
of ignorance. You know that there's a pattern to what's
been happening, and the fact that I've been set up fits into
that pattern. It's too convenient to be a coincidence.

'So what I'm saying is simply, trust me, at least for the
time I've got before they take me in for questioning—which
may not be long. We'll only get anywhere with this thing if
we work together.' There was a silence after Sinclair finished speaking and Kate braced herself for what seemed like
the inevitable rejection of his appeal.

'Trust you?' said Stevenson, the sneering incredulity
back in his tone. 'That's a bit rich, isn't it?'

But Bill Bairstow waved him down again impatiently.

'I reckon we've got no choice,' Bairstow said firmly.
'We're getting nowhere with t'police through t'regular

channels. They won't re-open the Carter murder case. They don't want to know about Joey Macready. So we'll just have to continue with our own inquiries. And for that we need all the help we can get.'

It was a grudging acceptance but Sinclair knew it was probably the best he would get in the circumstances. Stevenson shrugged his unwilling compliance, and Kate breathed again.

'Before you came I was trying to persuade Kate to take Sam away for a while. If they've made one attempt on her life, they may try again,' Sinclair said.

'I'm not going to be frightened off,' Kate said angrily.

'Aye, but there's your lad to think of,' Bairstow said. 'They might try to harm him.'

The three men sat in silence watching Kate while she struggled visibly with the dilemma. At last Bairstow spoke again.

'Why don't you just move off the estate for a bit? You don't need to go far. In fact, if you want a safe place to hide you can go up to my caravan in t'Glen. There'll be no one up there at this time of year and it's fully equipped, got a gas heater, bedding, the lot. You could stay there and use it as a base for doing whatever it is you want to do during t'day.'

Kate glanced at Sinclair questioningly, and he nodded.

'It's a good idea, Kate,' he said. 'I'll stay with you overnight if you like. And you can come in each day with Sam so that he can go to school and you can go to the centre, if that's what you want. You'll be safe enough if you're with other people in the office, and we can ask the staff to keep a close eye on Sam at school.'

Kate nodded wearily at last and Sinclair looked at the other two men.

'There are just you two who know about this, about where we're going. If anyone else finds out, I'll know who to blame.' The implication was clear and Stevenson scowled again but said nothing. The dislike between the two men was palpable and Bill Bairstow moved quickly to dissipate the tension.

'Trust works both ways, lad. No one else will know, I'll see to that,' he said. 'Now, I'll tell you summat you don't know. If t'union records had gone up in smoke last night it wouldn't have done anyone any good. David and I spent t'whole afternoon in that basement yesterday and we found what we were looking for, an' all. The file on Douglas Smith.'

He felt inside his jacket and drew out a foolscap envelope from which he took several photocopied sheets of paper.

'On this one we're one jump ahead,' he said. 'She gave up her claim against Agarth and Bradley just as I thought she did. At least, she asked t'union to stop acting for her. But she kept in touch for a while and let us know when she left Milford. The last address we have was in Eckersley. It's dated twenty years ago but it gives us a start, at least. And it gives her new married name. She became Mrs Betty Ainsley in nineteen-sixty.'

FIFTEEN

ECKERSLEY LAY some ten miles to the north of Milford, a small stone town straggling along the valley of the Maze, with most of its original mills idle now and its solid, work-manlike terraces taken over by young couples who commuted to work in Milford or even further away in Bradford. Sinclair drove slowly down the bustling main street, where the odd bistro jostled for trade with an old-fashioned iron-monger's and gift shops selling 'traditional' crafts and foods, past the open-air market with its new, brightly coloured plastic awnings, and into the road to which Betty Smith had moved more than twenty years before. He did not have high hopes that he would find her, or even anyone who knew her, but it was a lead they had to follow up.

The house was solidly built, with stone-framed bay windows fronting a steep strip of front garden where aubretia and golden alyssum tumbled down dark rocks between dwarf conifers and the last spring bulbs. The garden was well tended, and the wooden-framed windows looked freshly painted. It was a house upon which much love and care had been lavished. Sinclair rang the front doorbell and the door was opened quickly by a woman younger than he was himself in a smart Paisley wool dress with an energetic black and white sheepdog at her heels. She held the dog's collar and looked inquiringly at Sinclair.

'I'm looking for a Mrs Ainsley, Mrs Betty Ainsley, who used to live here...'

'Yes,' the woman said, unfazed, her blue eyes sharp but neither friendly nor unfriendly. 'Still does live here, as far as I know. I'm her daughter. Can I help you?'

'Well, I think it's your mother I need to talk to,' Sinclair prevaricated, still surprised at how straightforward his inquiries had turned out to be. This had to be the daughter of the second marriage: the woman was too young to be Douggie Smith's child.

'I'm making some inquiries about a friend of hers from way back, when she lived in Milford, before she became Mrs Ainsley in fact.'

For a second Sinclair thought he saw an expression of worry pass over the young woman's face, but it was gone as quickly as it had appeared.

'I'm sorry,' she said. 'You can't see my mother just now. She's in the General Hospital. She's just had an operation. That's why I'm here at the moment, to keep an eye on things and let the dog out—you know.'

'I'm sorry,' Sinclair said. 'Is she very seriously ill? Perhaps I could see her when she's recovered?'

The woman hesitated again, weighing Sinclair up. She kept one hand on the edge of the front door as if trying to decide whether or not to close it on him. Sinclair took a quick decision.

'I'm a police officer, Miss . . . ?'

'Mrs,' the woman said automatically. 'Mrs Jackson. Brenda Jackson.'

'I'm a police officer, but I have to admit that I'm not here officially. But I do have reason to think your mother might be able to help with some inquiries into something that happened a long time ago, something that concerned her first husband, Douglas Smith.'

'You'd better come in,' Mrs Jackson said at last, after subjecting Sinclair to another searching look.

She showed him into the front sitting-room of the house, and after telling the dog to sit, which he did, with his tail still wagging furiously, took a seat on the other side of the empty fireplace from Sinclair. The room was comfortably furnished, but had the tidiness of a house which was not much lived in. Her father was at his work, she said, at the headquarters of a major building society which was based in the town. Since her mother went into hospital she had been coming in each day to tidy up and see to the dog.

'My mother has cancer, Inspector,' she said, without any show of emotion. 'I think it's very unlikely that she'll be coming home again.'

'I'm sorry,' Sinclair said. 'But is there any chance she could answer questions? It could have a bearing on a murder inquiry.'

Mrs Jackson stared thoughtfully at the empty fireplace for a moment before answering.

'You're the second person this week who has been here asking about Douglas Smith,' she said suddenly. 'A man came the other day wanting my mother to sign some forms, something to do with the pension she gets from her first husband's firm.'

'Pension?' Sinclair asked sharply.

'Oh yes, she's always had quite a generous pension from them. Agarth and Bradley have been very good to her.'

'Did you tell your visitor where your mother was?' Sinclair asked, seized by a sudden anxiety. The woman nodded.

'It's hardly a secret,' she said drily. 'Almost anyone in the street will tell you if you ask. She's been poorly a long time.'

'I think we'd better go and see her,' Sinclair said, his voice strained. 'Do you mind?' Mrs Jackson looked at him sharply, the look of faint worry returning to her eyes. She nodded.

'I'll get my coat,' she said.

SINCLAIR DROVE as fast as he dared the two miles from the Ainsleys' house to the local hospital, and followed his companion quickly down the long corridor to the surgical wards. As they passed through a final set of swing doors a passing nurse looked at them in surprise.

'Mrs Jackson,' she said. 'Sister was trying to contact you. Could you come into the office for a minute?'

'I'll just go and say hello to my mother first . . .'

'No, Mrs Jackson,' the nurse broke in, taking the woman's arm. She was pale and very young, her blonde hair scraped back unfashionably beneath the uniform cap and her eyes wide with what looked to Sinclair uncommonly like fear. She attempted to steer the visitors towards the sister's office. 'Please, Mrs Jackson . . . You must see sister first.'

Sinclair took the young nurse's arm equally firmly.

'Which is Mrs Ainsley's bed?' he asked. 'I'm a police officer and I need to speak to her urgently.'

The young nurse looked wildly from one to the other, apparently on the verge of tears.

'But Mrs Ainsley has died,' she said desperately. 'I'm so sorry, but she's died. About an hour ago. We were trying to contact Mrs Jackson or her father . . .'

Sinclair cursed softly under his breath and his shoulders slumped. Whichever way he turned, he thought bitterly, someone was there before him. Even death, it seemed, was on someone else's side. He glanced through the swing doors into the ward. Every bed was occupied by a patient, either lying asleep or sitting against the pillows, but at the far end one cubicle had its flowered curtains drawn and he could see movement as several figures busied themselves behind them.

He followed Brenda Jackson into the ward sister's office where they were quickly joined by an efficient-looking woman in a senior nurse's uniform who took a seat at the single desk.

'I'm so sorry,' she said to Mrs Jackson. 'I've managed to contact your father and he's on his way. There'll be arrangements to make, but perhaps you'd like to wait until Mr Ainsley arrives. Do please accept my sympathy, and our apologies that we didn't contact you or your father in time to be here. But we had no warning that it would be so sudden. No warning at all. She was talking to a visitor just half an hour before. It happens like that sometimes, you know. It must be distressing for you.'

'A visitor?' Sinclair said sharply. 'Do you know who it was?' The sister hesitated.

'Well, no, I don't, I'm afraid,' she said. 'We have a very open policy on visiting, no set times. I just assumed it was a friend... Don't you know who it could have been, Mrs Jackson?'

Betty Smith's daughter shook her head silently. She looked stunned by what had happened, and took a hand-kerchief from her handbag which she twisted between her hands in some agitation.

'It was a man?' Sinclair asked the nurse. 'Could you de-scribe him?'

'Well, really, I don't know.' The sister looked slightly flustered. 'I dare say someone might be able to, Mr...?'

'Inspector,' Sinclair said. 'I'm a police officer, and I have reason to believe that someone might have wished Mrs Ainsley some harm. It's just a possibility, but it might be wise if you asked the hospital authorities to make sure that Mrs Ainsley died from natural causes.'

The two women drew in sharp breaths, and Brenda Jackson turned very pale.

'Are you saying that my mother might have been mur-dered?' she whispered.

'Are you suggesting that someone might have been mur-dered on my ward?' the sister said sharply.

Sinclair weighed his words carefully, aware of the hostil-ity he had aroused.

'It's no more than a remote possibility,' he said slowly. 'But it is a possibility, and I'm going to alert the local police to it. It's out of my immediate jurisdiction. I'm based in Milford. But I'll talk to the local CID.'

'I'll get the student nurse who was on duty when the vis-itor arrived,' the sister said, sweeping out of the office bristling with an outrage which Sinclair felt was more to do with the apparent slur on her professionalism than with the possibly untimely death which had taken place.

'I knew she was dying,' Brenda Jackson said, giving way to tears now. 'But it's still a shock. I didn't expect it so soon. Do you seriously think this visitor could have killed her?'

Before Sinclair could answer the sister returned with the young nurse, who had clearly also been crying.

'She's on her first ward,' the sister explained unsympathetically. 'It's the first time she's lost a patient.'

The girl looked confused when Sinclair asked her to describe the man who had visited Mrs Ainsley shortly before she had been found dead but Sinclair was not surprised when the nurse gave him a description which, though fairly vague, tallied with the one that Kate Weston had given of the man in a dark car who had tried to kill her the previous day.

'It's the man who came to the house,' Brenda Jackson said through dry lips. 'It's the same man. I think you'd better come home with me. There's something I want to show you.'

THE AFTERNOON had gone slowly and it was more than two hours before Alex Sinclair had set off back to Milford. Harry Ainsley had arrived at the hospital almost immediately and he and Mrs Jackson had spent time with the sister making all the arrangements necessary for a possible post-mortem examination and the removal of Mrs Ainsley's body by a funeral director. Sinclair had rung the local detective-inspector, whom he knew slightly, only to be met with a hostility which had shaken him. Reluctantly his colleague had come up to the hospital, where Sinclair repeated his suspicions about Betty Ainsley's death.

'What I don't understand is what the hell you're doing here anyway,' Detective-Inspector Peter Chapman said fiercely when they had shut themselves into the sister's office briefly for privacy. 'I thought you were suspended.'

'I am suspended,' Sinclair conceded wearily. 'I'm not on duty, I'm not even pretending to be on duty, it's just a coincidence that I'm here at all. But I think there's a chance that she didn't die of natural causes. She had a visitor and her daughter has no idea who he could be, but he sounds very much like a man who was involved in a violent incident in Milford yesterday. Call it a hunch if you like, but it's worth checking, Peter, that's all I'm saying.'

'That's all?' Chapman said angrily. 'You seem to have blundered on to my patch, devastated some perfectly innocent family and infuriated a ward sister, and probably the whole hospital hierarchy for all I know, all on the strength of a hunch that a dying old woman might have been murdered, although the nurses say there's no sign of violence on the body. What I want to know is what this so-called hunch is based on. You must have some evidence? Or are you barmy as well as bent?'

'Neither,' Sinclair said bleakly. 'Though I'm up to my neck in trouble. I just think that a post-mortem of Betty Ainsley now might save us having to dig her up to do one later.'

'You're serious, aren't you?' Chapman said, still incredulous.

'Never more so.'

Chapman looked hard at the man whose name had flashed around the police canteens and rest-rooms two days ago as news of his suspension had leaked out. The signs of the strain Sinclair was under showed around his eyes and mouth, but the face retained an obstinate openness that Chapman found difficult to reconcile with the allegations against him. Like many of his colleagues, he had been shocked by the accusations, which had lost nothing in the telling, but meeting the man face to face undermined his preconceptions, and his manner softened slightly.

'I'll mention it to the coroner. No more than that. And don't be surprised if he tells me to bugger off and stop wasting his time. And if the family aren't happy, they can take it up with the hospital. That's up to them,' he conceded at last, grudging every word.

'Thanks, Peter,' Sinclair said. 'I may have got it all wrong. I've almost got to the stage where I don't know what's real and what I'm imagining any more. But I think something odd happened here today. It's worth checking out.'

'I'll have to report that you were here,' Chapman said flatly.

'Sure. It'll give Eddie Greaves something else to think about,' Sinclair said, with a slightly helpless shrug.

'Yes, what's happening about that ... ?' Chapman hesitated, embarrassed.

'I don't know. I'm waiting to hear,' Sinclair said evenly. 'If I've any friends left and they're asking, you can tell them I've not been on the take but I'm going to have the devil's own job proving it. And if I can't I'm finished.' He shrugged slightly again and lit a cigarette to avoid Chapman's gaze, but his colleague looked at him hard for a long time before seeming to make up his mind.

'I'm sorry,' he said awkwardly at last.

'Not half as sorry as I am. But thanks, anyway.'

There had been a knock on the door then, and the tiny office filled up with ward staff and the Ainsley family. At last Sinclair escaped from the clinical smell and clammy warmth of the hospital with Brenda Jackson.

'I've got to pick up my little girl from school at three,' she said. 'I'll go round to my father's then. But if you take me home, I'll give you something my mother left with me. It's a letter addressed to a Tom Carter. She said I wasn't to bother my dad with it, but to post it to this chap when she died. But he's the man who was murdered in Milford, isn't he? I saw it in the paper. I think you'd better have the letter now.'

SINCLAIR WAS DRIVING as fast as he could back to Milford on the duel-carriageway valley road in the heavy Friday afternoon traffic. His mind was still on the astonishing letter which Brenda Jackson had given him. He did not see the patrol car until it sounded its klaxon right behind him and the driver waved him in to the side of the road. He waited for the patrol man to approach with a sense of foreboding.

'Good afternoon, sir,' the young officer said. 'Pushing it a bit, weren't we?'

'Was I over the limit?'

'Not really, sir. Just taking a few chances, I thought. I'd have noticed you even if I hadn't been looking for you.'

'Looking?'

'An all cars call, Inspector Sinclair. A message from Chief Superintendent Greaves at Milford HQ. He couldn't contact you, as you're in your own car. Would you please report to his office on Monday morning at nine? That's it, I think. Take it easy, sir.'

The patrol man went back to his car without a backward glance. He must be the only man in the force not to realize the significance of that message, Sinclair thought grimly. It left him two and a half days to prepare his defence, try to clear Joey Macready and trace the man who had attempted one murder and quite possibly accomplished another in the last two days. He might as well book his cell in gaol now, he thought bitterly. He drove back to Highcliffe more circumspectly, very near despair.

KATE AND SAM were waiting for him at the flat with a couple of bags packed. They had agreed that they would go up to Bill Bairstow's caravan in daylight, and with Kate's car written off, they needed him to provide transport. It was a gloomy and introspective trio who drove out of Highcliffe and along the moorland road to Broadley Glen where a dozen or so caravans were parked unobtrusively in a fold below the moor overlooking the steep wooded valley which bisected the hillside to the north of the village. In the summer it was a favourite beauty spot, a place Sinclair had come to often with his daughters when it was busy with walkers and the groups of climbers who regularly tackled the rock face above the village, but at this time of the year on a wet and windy Friday night, the road and caravan site were deserted, and Sinclair was convinced that they had left the estate and arrived at the Glen unobserved.

Sam was not happy with the arrangement. He inspected the caravan and its facilities with a sulky expression when Kate unlocked the door, before dumping his sports bag on one of the bunks.

'Where are you sleeping, then?' he asked Sinclair.

'I don't mind, Sam,' he said. 'We won't be here for long, so I should think you can have first pick of the beds, if your mother doesn't mind.'

'There's no telly,' Sam said, scowling.

'No, but you've brought plenty of books to read, and look at this clever little kitchen,' Kate said, trying to cheer him up as she opened up the compact galley area. 'We can cook quite nicely here.'

It was already getting dusk and Sinclair lit one of the gas lights above the table, while Kate unpacked the supplies of food that they had brought with them. The caravan, as Bill Bairstow had promised, was well equipped, crockery and cutlery neatly stowed away, bunks with blankets and sheets folded ready for use. Even so, the boy's unremitting displeasure cast a shadow over the meal which Kate quickly prepared, and neither of the adults was sorry when he announced that he was going to read in bed, and climbed determinedly into the double bunk at the far end of the caravan and opened a battered copy of a Roald Dahl.

Sinclair opened the door of the caravan and stepped outside. It was completely dark now, and although the earlier rain had stopped, the night was cloudy and the darkness beyond the pool of yellow cast by the caravan's lights, impenetrable. He took a deep breath of the cool, damp, peaty air and wondered how much longer he would be free to enjoy such simple pleasures. He felt rather than heard Kate follow him out of the caravan and, turning, he took her into his arms with a feeling of desperation rather than pleasure. For a moment they clung to each other wordlessly.

'I'm sorry Sam's being so difficult,' she said. 'I feel torn in two between the pair of you.'

'He'll probably have you to himself again sooner than he thinks,' Sinclair said, and told her about his summons to police headquarters.

'They'll keep you there, you think?' she asked quietly.

'I don't think there's much doubt if they decide to charge me. There'll be a court hearing and then a remand. It's too serious a charge for them to give me bail.'

'The bank clerk was puzzled about your account.'

'I'll tell my solicitor,' Sinclair said. 'It might help, but it'll all take time. Meanwhile I'll be banged up...' He shrugged and she felt herself infected by his mood of helplessness.

'There's so little time,' he said. 'And I want to be sure that you're safe. If the worst comes to the worst next week, Kate, will you promise me you'll go away from Highcliffe for a while, until it all blows over? Please?'

'I don't suppose I've got much choice,' she said dully. 'I wouldn't like to stay up here by myself. It's too isolated.'

'Will you be all right if I go into town for an hour or so? I arranged to meet Dave Wilson to compare notes.'

'Yes, of course,' she said. 'You must do that. He may have come up with something. We can't give up yet, Alex. There's still time.'

WILSON WAS WAITING for him as arranged in a town centre bar packed with Friday night revellers.

'Let's get out of here,' Sinclair said, refusing an offer of a drink, to the sergeant's evident, though unspoken, surprise. They returned to his car parked in a quiet alleyway, and for a moment they sat in heavy silence, while Sinclair lit a cigarette.

'You got the message from Greaves, I take it?' Wilson asked at last.

Sinclair nodded. 'What's the word?' he asked.

'The word is you'd better bring your toothbrush. You'll be stopping.'

'They're not wasting much time, are they? Talk to the young clerk at the bank for me, would you?' Sinclair said. 'Kate said his name was Jones, and he was puzzled by something on his computer. It's a long shot but it looks like the only one I've got.'

'I know the manager there,' Wilson said slowly. 'Chap called Simmons. He's on t'square: same lodge as Greaves and Agarth and your father-in-law.'

'Same lodge?' Sinclair asked incredulously. 'Is there anyone involved in this thing who isn't a member of that bloody lodge?'

'There's nowt so strange about that. It's common enough with that generation. It was expected when I joined the force. It's different now. The sharp youngsters aren't joining the way they used to, in the force or out of it. No time for charity, p'raps.'

Sinclair snorted.

'Come on, Dave. Self-help, more like.'

'Happen,' Wilson replied non-committally. 'But it's not a crime, any road.'

'No, but it's a connection, and we don't ignore connections, right, even if it does tread on a few worshipful toes?'

'I've got the mugshots you asked for,' Wilson said, changing the subject and pulling a folder from inside his coat. 'I tried to correlate Mrs Weston's description with information on cars. A big, dark saloon. But without a registration number it's hit and miss.' There had been no witnesses to the actual collision which had almost killed Kate Weston, so all they had to go on was her own sketchy impression of what had happened.

'I'll get her to go through these tomorrow,' Sinclair said. 'In the meantime I may have come across our car-driving friend again, doing some extremely dubious hospital visiting.'

He told Wilson what had happened in Eckersley that afternoon.

'It's no wonder Betty Smith, as she then was, gave up her claim through the union,' he said. 'Agarth and Bradley offered her an extremely generous deal on the quiet. She's lived very comfortably ever since. And what seems to have clinched it was a medical report on her husband's health from a specialist in London. He may have died of pneumonia, as the death certificate said, but what the London hospital concluded a month or so before he died was that he had some sort of leukaemia, and that it could have been industrially induced.'

'So the firm shut her up?'

'That's more or less what she wrote to Tom Carter in this letter she left with her daughter. She writes to Carter as if he was some sort of shop-steward for their collective interests—which maybe he was. And maybe that's why he was taken out when even he got alarmed about whatever Agarth and Bradley have to do with the pollution. At least that gives us what we haven't had so far—a coherent motive for Tom Carter's murder.'

'I can't see James Agarth bumping old men on the head in back alleys just because there's a bit of pollution in t'river,' Wilson said flatly. 'And the fraud lads say they've got nowt on him.'

'Not personally, perhaps, but he's a ruthless bastard. If the old boy was being a nuisance, threatening to talk, even after all these years, it could have been embarrassing just when Agarth is trying to sell out. Just now the pollution might cost him real money if it came out.'

'Aye, I read what it said in t'paper about the big deal going ahead.'

'But if Betty Ainsley was hastened on her way to her maker as well, the question then is, how they knew Bill Bairstow had traced her for me. I didn't tell you...'

'That puts me in the clear, then, does it?' Wilson asked sarcastically. 'Thanks.'

Sinclair looked at the sergeant and shrugged.

'I'm learning the hard way not to trust anyone, Dave. Someone's driving a bloody coach and horses through security in that action committee in Highcliffe,' Sinclair said apologetically. 'It could be one of our own as well as anyone else, and with some justification. I'd want to know what was going on up there if I...' He hesitated for a moment and stared bleakly out at the narrow alley where the heavy rain was making what must be the town's only surviving strip of cobblestones gleam in the street-lighting, wondering if he would ever need to know what was going on on his patch again. He fought to turn his thoughts back to the matter in hand.

'It's not the leaks that bother me so much. Organizations like that are always as leaky as a sieve. It's the speed with which it's getting back to the other side. They've been one jump ahead so often it can't be a coincidence. And the way things look, it can be fatal.'

'What about that trouble-maker, Stevenson?' Wilson asked. 'He's no friend of yours.'

'Nor of Agarth's, I'd guess. Unless he's taken up fairly brutal capitalism in his spare time, which would be a bit of a turn-up. But you're right in one sense. He certainly knew I was going to look for Betty Ainsley.'

Sinclair leaned back in the driving seat and closed his eyes. It was all a question of trust, he thought, and he now had to decide whether he trusted Wilson, if not with his life, at least with his freedom. They had worked together in Highcliffe for almost four years, but in no sense did he feel he really knew the other man who came, as he admitted himself, from an older and different tradition of policing, a tradition deeply suspicious of university educated coppers seeking—and often getting—quick promotion. With time so short, he had, in the end, he thought, little choice but to rely on Wilson's loyalty.

'I need to take a look at Agarth and Bradley's book,' he said.

Wilson whistled in surprise.

'We've got nowt to go on,' he said.

'I wasn't thinking of asking you to get a warrant. Right?'

Wilson said nothing for a moment and Sinclair thought he was about to get out of the car. But he stayed, sunk in thought, staring at the rain running down the windscreen.

'How'll you get in?' he asked at last. 'There'll be an alarm.'

'What I'd like you to do,' Sinclair began slowly, 'is to create a diversion. I know I'm asking you to put your job on the line, Dave, so say no if that's what you want to say.

But if you could create some sort of a crisis somewhere well away from the industrial estate, I'd bank on no one hearing the alarm.'

'And if it's wired to headquarters?'

'Then I'll go down for burglary as well as the other thing,' Sinclair said bleakly. 'I've got two days, Dave, that's all. Eddie Greaves clearly isn't going to waste any time on this one. Unless we crack this over the weekend, I've had it.'

Wilson sat in silence again until the suspense became too much for Sinclair.

'Forget it,' he said harshly, starting the car and revving the engine impatiently. 'I shouldn't have asked. I'll see you around, Sergeant.'

'Calm down, boss,' Wilson said mildly. 'I were just thinking. I reckon if you wait until t'pubs turn out, around eleven say, then we could get some sort of an alert up at Highcliffe without too much trouble after what happened t'other night. What if I'd had a call from a snout warning me about petrol bombs up there? That should shift every copper in Milford up t'hill, and a few from beyond.'

'It sounds good,' Sinclair said. 'Are you sure you want to take the chance?'

'What chance? If I take this alleged call at home, there's nowt to it. It won't do community relations much good, mind.'

'Sod community relations. It just might do me a bit of good,' Sinclair said, the relief evident in his tone. 'I owe you one, Dave.'

FOR A COMPANY now reputedly worth millions, Agarth and Bradley did not spend much on inessentials, Sinclair thought as he gently eased the venetian blinds closed on their general office windows. He had gained entrance to the premises, a single-storey office block lying to one side of the firm's well-stocked yard, surprisingly easily, he thought. If there was an alarm system at all it was well concealed and it was certainly not one which had set off an audible bell as he had shinned over the six-foot mesh gates and forced the lock on the main door, although he was uneasily aware that lights might even now be flashing on some control panel elsewhere.

The main office housed three untidy desks, piled high with invoices and receipts and order forms, which he riffled through quickly and without great interest. What he wanted to know would not be contained in everyday orders for extensions and conservatories or even, in one buff folder, extensive plans for a new housing development in Broadley of which he, as a resident, had surprisingly never heard. An adjoining door, unlocked, led into James Agarth's own sanctum, where a single, extremely tidy desk dominated the small but comfortably furnished room. It was, Sinclair thought, still very much the family firm, in spite of its alleged prosperity: the boss and a small group of administrators to control what had become the best known and the biggest building contractor in the county.

Agarth's desk was dominated by a computer keyboard and screen, identical to two machines in the outer office. Sinclair sat down in the comfortable leather swivel chair and switched the machine on. It was a model he was familiar with and he easily found the file menu. He was surprised that the machine did not ask him for a password. Agarth must feel very confident that there was nothing incriminating here, he thought anxiously.

But it did not take him long to discover that Agarth's confidence might be misplaced. He called up a file entitled Pensions and began to scroll through a list of names which filled him with excitement. The list of pensioners was alphabetical and among the first to appear was that of Betty Ainsley, her address, a generous annual sum of money, and then in the final column, with that day's date, the single word Deceased. It had taken a suspiciously short time to get that information on file, Sinclair thought angrily. Scrolling down, he came to Tom Carter, similarly curtly written off, but with his wife's name and half the previous pension listed to commence on the day of Tom's murder. Running quickly through the list, Sinclair was surprised to find a

cluster of Irish surnames, all with Irish addresses and almost without exception mark Deceased. Some pensions
had been terminated and others had passed to women of
the same name, presumably the widows of former workers
with the firm. Flaherty, Flanagan and Flynn were clus-
tered together, all Kerrymen. O'Donnell, O'Neill and
O'Rourke who had come from Dublin, and were now all
dead. Further on came Ryan and Riordan, both deceased
in Ireland, and Reilly, Martin Joseph, an oddity in still being apparently alive in an old people's home in Torquay.
Sinclair switched on the printer which stood next to the
keyboard and gave the instruction to print. The clatter of
the machine worried him, but the risk seemed unavoid-
able.

Impatiently he went back to the menu and scanned the
other files. Most seemed to contain only the normal everyday transactions of a busy firm, accounts, orders, invoices, employment records. With the noise of the printer
jangling his taut nerves he picked several at random and
sent them to the printer as well. He would study them in
detail later, he thought.

He glanced at his watch. It was 11:45. He had been on
the premises for a little over twenty minutes, and if there
was an alarm linked to police HQ that was far longer than
he, as a professional, would expect it to take a patrol car to
investigate a possible break-in. But if Wilson had success-
fully diverted most cars to Highcliffe, then he still could not
be sure the break-in had not been noticed. If there was a
crisis elsewhere, it might take longer than that to get a car
back to the industrial estate which lay on the far side of the
town from Highcliffe.

He eased open the slats of the blind and looked out at the
yard, with its stacks of breeze blocks and bricks and tim-
ber. Nothing moved. He watched intently as the printer
continued with its chattering task and sheet after sheet of
printout concertina-ed into the receiving basket at the far
side of James Agarth's desk. As the machine subsided into

silence he noticed the faint blue flashing of a light in the far corner of the yard, beyond the double gates.

Breathlessly he scooped up the pile of paper from the basket, switched off the machines and the desk light by which he had been working, and hurried into the outer office. There one window opened on the side of the building away from the gates. He slid it open soundlessly and slipped over the sill into the open air. Keeping close to the building he stood in a dark pool of shadow, trying to control his breathing as he listened for sounds of movement by the gates. There was a rattle as someone tested them, but they remained firmly closed.

Some idiot's come down without getting hold of the keys, Sinclair thought grimly. I'd have his guts for garters if he was one of mine. He waited, and eventually the blue flashing light was turned off and he heard the car drive away. For once he blessed the incompetence of some junior officers as he shinned back over the wall of the yard, ran to his own car, parked in deep shadow several buildings away, and drove safely away.

SIXTEEN

'IT'S NOT THAT SURPRISING they're dead,' Bill Bairstow said lugubriously. 'They were all in their twenties or thirties when old Agarth brought them over to do that job. And pretty unpopular he made himself, importing cheap labour like that. But they'll all be near seventy now, three score and ten, like me. You don't have a high life-expectancy when you've grafted away on building sites or down t'pits all your life. Ask your dad. He knows as well as I do.'

Bairstow and Sinclair had spent the morning sitting at the caravan's cramped table going through the computer records which the inspector had taken from James Agarth's office the previous night. Kate had taken Sam for a walk to keep him out of their way while they worked, although a fine drizzle of rain was still drifting over the moors, blotting out any visibility beyond the enclosed glen itself. The higher slopes of Broadley Top above them had disappeared into the mist.

'So all the men who closed off those drift mines will be dying off now: if they didn't die years ago like poor old Douglas Smith. But how many smallish firms like Agarth and Bradley pay out those sorts of pensions to their ex-workers?'

'Aye, that's what's odd. You're right. I've never seen owt as generous as that in all the time I've worked for t'union. Especially not in construction. It's not as though those Irish lads stayed long. Old Agarth shipped them in and shipped them out again pretty quickly, as far as I can recall. The only one who stopped was old Martin Reilly.'

Bairstow scanned the list again and pointed to Reilly's name.

'Here he is, still alive in Torquay in some old folks' home. He married a local lass and lived on t'estate for years. There's a son still around, name of Terry or Gerry. Big, dark-haired fellow, about your age, ruddy-faced. He works for Agarth and Bradley, an' all, I think. But they're not union men. None of those Irish workers joined t'union, as far as I can remember.'

'A home in Torquay'll be costing Reilly a pretty penny, won't it?'

'It will that,' Bairstow said. 'There's nowt private round here for less than £200 a week that I knows of. It'll be more down there, I reckon.'

'And Terry Reilly? Is he an aggressive character? Drinks in the Fox?' Sinclair asked, recalling the brush he and Wilson had had in the pub two days earlier. Bairstow nodded.

'That's right. Lives down t'hill in Overdale Close.'

'Any form?'

'Nowt I know of,' Bairstow said. 'Though he's a heavy drinker, I've heard. Catholics. Father O'Leary will know him.'

'Is there anything you don't know on that estate?' Sinclair asked.

'Not a lot, lad,' Bairstow said. 'It's my thirty-fifth anniversary as their councillor next month. I was elected when t'ward was created, when t'first houses were finished. I've watched them move in, and t'kids grow up, and now I'm watching them die.'

Sinclair turned over the computer pages again thoughtfully.

'What about this list of land holdings?' he asked. 'Did you know Agarth and Bradley owned all this property?'

'I knew they owned property. That's common knowledge. They bought up all t'land at Highcliffe right up to t'moor edge just after t'war, when it were dirt cheap. We had to compulsory purchase the land for housing, but they seem to have hung on to a lot o' t'rest ever since, including t'drift mines. Higher up than that it's common land.'

'There's one odd thing there, though,' Bairstow said suddenly, stopping Sinclair from turning a page. 'It's not actually Agarth and Bradley which owns Highcliffe drifts, look. It's some other company: Bradley Disposals Ltd. They must be connected, but I can't say I've ever heard of them.'

'If they're a limited company we can easily check them out,' Sinclair said. 'Though not over a weekend.' He was constantly aware of time pressing at his shoulder, time running out for him to make any impression on the mystery which had embroiled him.

'The companies' register,' he said urgently. 'If I'm not around on Monday, will you check it out?'

Bairstow looked at the younger man shrewdly, recognizing how fragile his self-control was becoming.

'You know if they arrest you, you've got friends outside, don't you, lad?' he said. 'Never mind Derek Stevenson and his poison. There's plenty know better than that.'

'Thanks, Bill,' Sinclair said.

KATE SPENT AN HOUR that afternoon leafing through the pages of photographs which Wilson had given Sinclair the previous night. But in the end she shook her head in despair.

'No. He's not among that lot,' she said. 'I'm sorry, Alex.'

'Not to worry,' Sinclair said, far more cheerfully than he felt. He closed the file and ran a hand tiredly through his hair.

'Let's get out of here,' Kate said, picking up his mood and glancing round the cramped caravan. Sam was curled up on his bunk again with his book.

'We're just going for a stroll, love,' she said. The boy looked up stormily but said nothing.

'Do you want to come, Sam?' Sinclair asked.

'No,' the boy said, turning away from them with deliberation. Kate sighed, and buttoned up her anorak before following Sinclair down the caravan steps into the rain.

'We need to talk,' she said, falling into step beside him on the narrow footpath beside the road. Sinclair set a cracking pace, as if trying to burn up some of his frustration.

'Slow down,' Kate said, laughing as she tried to keep pace on the muddy track. 'You'll frighten the sheep.'

He took no notice, and strode on with Kate half running to keep up until at last he turned away from the road up a narrower, climbing footpath which ended abruptly as a steep wall of rock loomed up out of the mist ahead of them. Sinclair turned suddenly and stood with his back to the cliff confronting Kate, only half of whose face was visible, damp with the rain and pink with exertion, under the hood of her anorak. For a moment they faced each other in silence.

'I don't deserve you, but dear God I need you,' Sinclair said at last.

She leaned forward and kissed him gently.

'It's too wet for this,' she said, laughing. He shook his head.

'Down here,' he said. 'I used to come this way when I was a lad.' He led her under the overhang of the cliff for a hundred yards to a point where the rock had been worn away by some prehistoric torrent into a shallow cave floored with coarse sand. A tattered ewe which had been sheltering there fled at their approach, bleating loudly in protest, as Sinclair pulled Kate out of the rain and pushed her hood away from her face.

'There's so little time,' he said. 'And with Sam in that bloody caravan it's impossible even to talk. But I need to say this before the whole thing gets out of hand next week. We may never get the chance to be alone then . . .'

Kate took his hand and felt the tension in him.

'Tell me,' she said.

'I feel as though I'm in a shipwreck,' he said. 'Drowning in a rough sea and going down for the third time, and somewhere far up above there's just a gleam of sunlight, and I know if I can only get back up through the water to that patch of light, I'll be all right. You're that sunlight, Kate, but you're so far away I don't think I'll be able to reach you. Do you understand what I'm saying?'

Kate did not answer immediately. She unzipped her anorak and reached out to kiss him gently again.

'I love you,' she said. 'I'll wait for you, however long it takes and however bad it turns out to be.'

Sinclair groaned and pulled her down on to the sandy floor of the cave beside him.

'There's not enough time,' he said again.

'There's time,' she said, unbuttoning her shirt. They made love with fierce intensity, as if there would indeed be no tomorrow. And from just outside the cave, in the drifting rain, Sam Weston watched them with tears streaming down his face, before he turned and ran down the hill into the ravine below.

WHEN THEY RETURNED to the caravan, Sam was not there. The door was wide open and his book lay face down on his bunk, and Kate was seized with an icy terror which paralysed her. She sank on to a bench seat, white-faced.

'He'll get lost in this rain and mist,' she said. 'He could go over the cliff edge. You know how dangerous it is.' A vision of that first body, lying at the foot of Broadley Edge, flashed across Sinclair's mind. He knew exactly how dangerous it was.

'He can't have gone far,' he said, with more confidence than he felt. He went back outside and shouted for Sam, but there was no reply. If anything, the rain had intensified and it was difficult to see more than fifty yards in any direction.

They left a note for Sam on the caravan table and set off together again, calling the boy's name every few minutes, but for more than an hour they got no response except an occasional flurry of flustered sheep, indignantly protesting when they disturbed the scant shelter they had found on the hillside. After working their way downhill almost to the edge of Broadley village itself, they returned dispiritedly to the caravan site ready to start another pass up the hill towards the Top.

As they approached the caravan in the gathering dusk they were surprised to see a light on. Kate ran the last hundred yards, to find Sam standing on the top of the steps apparently unperturbed.

'I made some tea, Mum,' he said, ignoring Sinclair as usual. 'Where have you been?'

'Where have you been, more like?' Sinclair said, unable to restrain his anger any longer. 'Your mother thought you'd gone missing out there, young man. What the hell are you playing at?'

Sam turned away without a word and climbed back on to his bunk. Sinclair would have pursued it, but Kate put a hand on his arm and shook her head.

'Leave it for now,' she said quietly. 'I'll talk to him later. He has to work this out for himself.'

SINCLAIR OPENED HIS EYES and lay rigid on his narrow bunk, trying to penetrate the absolute blackness of the caravan's interior and distinguish the sound which he was sure had woken him from the steady, all-enveloping thud of rain on the roof. For several minutes he heard nothing, and then it came again. The slightest metallic chink coming from underneath the van. He swung himself to the floor and slipped on his shoes. The chink of mental had been followed this time by a faint hissing and he suddenly knew with horrible certainty what the noise was. He crept across the van to Kate's bunk and woke her, putting a hand over her mouth firmly to stop her crying out.

'There's someone under the van, fiddling with the gas cylinder,' he breathed into her ear, feeling her stiffen with alarm as the message went home. 'Get out of bed, put something on, and I'll get Sam.'

He repeated the procedure with the boy, who did not seem to have bothered getting undressed, half-lifting him from the bunk in his anxiety to get him out of the van. Within minutes the three of them were standing holding each other close to the door of the caravan, still in total darkness, but all intensely aware of furtive movement beneath their feet.

'Think about the ground outside,' Sinclair breathed. 'If you run straight ahead from the door you'll get to the trees in less than a minute. When you get there, lie flat on the ground and don't move. I'll be just behind you.' Very gently he unlocked the door and eased it open. The light outside was just faintly greyer than the dark interior of the van, and Sinclair sent first the boy, and then Kate on their way with a slight push. He followed close behind, taking huge, blind strides across what he knew was open ground. As the first low branch of a tree caught him across the face he flung himself to the ground at the same instant as the blinding flash of an explosion, and a hot gust of burning air passed over the three of them.

Sinclair eased himself round to face the caravan park. The whole area was lit up now by an incandescent light. There was little to see of the caravan in which they had been sleeping: only its outline and a faint indication of its door and window frames could be seen at the heart of the inferno where it had been. Above the sound of the flames they heard a car drive away recklessly. Their visitor had gone.

Sinclair rested his head for a moment on the peaty earth and breathed deeply, trying to calm his thudding heart and trembling limbs. He turned to Kate, who had Sam held tightly in her arms as they watched the fire in mute horror. She was visibly shaking with shock.

Sinclair got stiffly to his feet. He rubbed his temple and felt the stickiness of blood there.

'Come on,' he said harshly. 'Into the car, quickly. We've got to get away from here.'

SINCLAIR DROVE DOWN into Milford through the darkened streets, consumed by a deep anger. Whoever they were fighting was implacable, he had already realized, but quite how murderous that enemy's intentions had now become towards him personally, and incidentally, he supposed, towards Kate and Sam, had not been truly borne in on him until this night's attack. Much that had happened so far had been merely an attempt to deter them, he realized. Even Kate's car accident could conceivably have been intended to frighten rather than to kill. But this latest attack was attempted murder, vicious and unequivocal. All three of them were lucky to be alive. There should have been no survivors. Their only brief advantage now was that, until the smouldering wreckage of the caravan was raked over in the morning, the people who mattered would be assuming they were dead.

It was 2:30 in the morning when Sinclair knocked on the door of his father's house. The old man demanded querulously to know who was there before he unbolted and unlocked and let them in.

'Dad, this is Kate and this is Sam,' Sinclair said. 'We're in trouble and I need your help.'

Andrew Sinclair took one look at the ashen faces of his visitors and went straight into the kitchen to put the kettle on for tea. Kate sank into a chair by the fireplace, where a few coals still smouldered red. Sam clung to his mother like a child years younger, dark smudges under his eyes. Sinclair ran up the narrow staircase and came back with blankets, which he put round their shoulders.

In the kitchen he told his father briefly what had happened. The old man looked at him in concern.

'Ye've cut your head, lad,' he said. 'Here.' He handed his son a cloth and pointed him towards the mirror over the sink. Sinclair dabbed at his temple and winced.

'I hit a tree,' he said. 'Better that than what was planned for all three of us tonight.' The image of the blazing caravan was still seared on his brain, driving out coherent thought.

'Is this to do with your trouble at work, then?' Sinclair's father asked.

The younger man nodded. 'I've stumbled on something very nasty, something that goes back a long way, before I was born, I think. Fortunately Bill Bairstow's got the evidence I got hold of on Friday night, so that's safe. But time's running out. Superintendent Greaves wants to see me on Monday, and once he's got me back at HQ I don't think he's going to let me go again.'

Andrew Sinclair's face was shadowed briefly as he looked at his son.

'Ye've not been near me since all this began, lad,' he said softly, so that the others in the next room could not overhear them. 'I've heard it all at second hand, and no doubt much embroidered. I didnae know what to think.'

'You should know me better than that,' Sinclair said, looking away to hide the hurt in his eyes.

The old man nodded slowly.

'Aye, I think I know ye well enough,' he said. 'Ye're your mother's son. If she found a farthing in the gutter she'd spend half a day asking after its owner. So what can I do to help?'

EARLY THE NEXT MORNING Sinclair looked into his father's spare bedroom. Kate and Sam were sleeping peacefully side by side in the double bed and did not stir. He stood for a moment looking at Kate's pale face, half veiled by her hair but with the terrors of the night washed away by sleep. He wanted to spend the rest of his life with this woman, he thought, but fear of what might come between them before that became possible made him draw breath against an almost physical pain. He closed the door softly and went downstairs to finish dressing by the sofa where he had slept restlessly under a blanket, before going into the kitchen to find his father with tea already on the kitchen table and slices of toast under the grill.

They sat down together and Sinclair thought with a sense of sadness that it must be a year since he shared a meal in this house. The older Sinclair sipped his mug of dark tea and watched his son in silence as he buttered toast and ate it slowly. He could see the change in him and was angered by it. He was thinner and paler than a week ago and the lines of anxiety had deepened around his eyes.

'I'm only asking, ye understand,' he began tentatively, 'but this young woman? She'll be married as well, will she?' Alex Sinclair smiled faintly at the echoes of generations of puritanical Scots who would put the question much more bluntly.

'She's a widow. Mother would approve,' he said.

'And Margaret?'

'That's finished. You knew that would happen, even better than I did.'

'Aye, well, I canna say I'm surprised. But does Kate feel the same way ye obviously do?' the old man persisted.

Sinclair shrugged slightly. 'I can't ask her for anything in my present situation.'

'No, I can see that. But is she in trouble now because of you? Is that why she's been threatened?'

'No, she was involved before... before me... She was involved in the action committee up at Highcliffe, anyway.' Sinclair stopped speaking suddenly as if a new thought had struck him.

'Dear God,' he said in horror. 'The girls.' His father looked at him uncomprehendingly.

'They might try to get at me through the girls,' he said harshly. 'They tried to warn Kate off by harassing Sam, and they've moved on now from harassment to murder. Sally and Jenny could be at risk too.'

He gulped down the rest of his tea.

'I'll go up to see them. It's early yet and they won't be awake, and in any case, with luck, whoever's behind all this still thinks we're dead. Then there are some other people I need to see today. There's so little time left. You'll keep Kate and Sam here with you? Keep them safe?'

'I'll get help to keep an eye on them, don't ye fret,' the older man said firmly. 'No one shall harm a hair of their heads.'

'If anyone from the force comes looking for me, you don't know where I am,' Sinclair reminded him. 'I don't know who I can trust there any more than anywhere else.'

'Aye, I'll not forget. But take care, lad. And not just for my sake. That lassie upstairs is worth six of Margaret Booth.'

Kate Weston heard the front door slam as Alex Sinclair left the house, and lay in bed, stock still so as not to disturb Sam, trying to assimilate the events of the last two days. She was, she realized, very frightened, not just for Sam or for herself, but for Sinclair as well. She looked at the child sleeping beside her and felt the familiar guilt. Had she failed him at last, she wondered, after all those years of carefully containing her emotions in the hope that one day she would find a substitute father for him, a father he would like and respect. Fat chance of that now, she thought. Alex and Sam would have to work out their own accommodation. She needed them both desperately.

SEVENTEEN

SINCLAIR LET HIMSELF into his own house with his front-door key, thankful that Margaret had not got around to changing the locks to keep him out. He realized as he stood in the silent hall for the second time in a week that his family were not there. The curtains were undrawn and the kitchen unnaturally tidy, far tidier than it would ever have been left on a Saturday night by Margaret and his daughters. He went upstairs and found all the beds neatly made, and Sally's favourite teddy-bear absent from his usual perch at the end of the bed beside the pillow. Wherever Sally went, teddy went too. They had probably gone to spend the weekend with Margaret's parents, he thought.

He stood for a moment looking round his daughter's pretty primrose and white room, the rose-sprigged quilt, the white shelves piled high with toys and books, a discarded pair of pyjamas flung into a corner, and a reading book left open on the small desk which he had helped her choose when she started school.

He wandered round the room for a minute, touching Sally's things, picking up her pyjamas and folding them carefully and placing them under her pillow before the aching sense of loss which he felt for the children overwhelmed him and he slumped on to his daughter's bed and buried his face in his hands. Still shaken by the events of the previous night, he was ever more aware that the little freedom left to him would not be enough. Time was slipping away too quickly. The few days he had been away from home could quickly turn into months or even years without contact with the girls, and the prospect filled him with utter despair.

Slowly he pulled himself together. He had to keep on fighting to the end, he told himself, for the girls and now for Kate as well. Almost absent-mindedly he collected some clean shirts and underwear from where they were still neatly stowed in his dressing-chest drawer and dropped them into a Laura Ashley carrier bag from Margaret's wardrobe. All the belongings he had taken with him last week had been reduced to ashes in the caravan fire. Grimly he put in a pair of pyjamas. If what Wilson said was true, he would be needing those at police HQ tomorrow.

Ten minutes later he drove up his father-in-law's drive and parked again behind his wife's car. The front door was flung open almost before he had locked the car and a small whirlwind flung itself at him excitedly.

'Daddy, Daddy,' Sally cried. 'Mummy said you weren't coming, but I knew you would.' Sinclair picked his daughter up and kissed her and carried her up the steps to the house.

'I'll always try to come and see you, love,' he said. 'But sometimes it's difficult, you know.'

Margaret was in the hall, in a navy silk kimono, her face unmade-up and icily angry.

'How dare you come here,' she said. 'You know what my solicitor said.'

Sinclair put Sally down gently.

'Go and finish your breakfast, love,' he said, kissing her again. With a puzzled glance at her mother, she did as she was told.

'I need to see Ted,' Sinclair said. 'It's very urgent. It couldn't wait.'

'I don't believe you. It's just an excuse. I meant what I said about getting an injunction, you know.'

'Margaret,' Sinclair said wearily. 'By tomorrow night the chances are I'll be in gaol and you won't have to worry about me seeing the girls any more. Now where's Ted? Whatever you believe, it's him I came to see.'

'He's out with his precious orchids,' she said coldly. 'You know the way.'

The glasshouse where Ted Booth grew orchids was on the north side of the house, gently heated in winter, but shaded from the direct sunlight which the plants hated. Sinclair found his father-in-law carefully tying a spike of heavy flower buds to a cane with raffia. Booth glanced up as he came into the glasshouse, closing the door carefully behind him as he had been taught many years before, but the older man carried on with his task.

'I'm surprised to see you here,' he said eventually, cutting off his raffia with a sharp click of his scissors. 'What do you think of this one? Four flower spikes, and I've only had it a year.'

'I came to give you some information, Ted,' Sinclair said. 'Something you need to know. And I hoped you'd be able to help me with some.'

'In return, you mean, lad?' Booth asked. 'You want to do a deal?'

'No, not exactly,' Sinclair said. 'I'd tell you about Margaret and the girls whatever.'

Booth looked at him sharply and waved him into one of the cane chairs in which he was commonly to be found relaxing and admiring his horticultural handiwork.

'Trouble?' he asked, and Sinclair told him what had happened to Kate Weston and Sam over the previous week, and then to all three of them the previous night. When he had finished Booth nodded. He did not appear surprised and for one hideous moment Sinclair wondered if he either knew who their attacker was or could actually be involved himself. Booth must have recognized the sudden suspicion in his eyes.

'I've known for a long while that there are people in this town who would, let's say, bend the law to suit their purposes. We've all done it at one time or another, lad: an expense exaggerated, a payment made in case and no question asked, a VAT return massaged. You're a policeman so I don't expect you to condone it. I'm not even sure I condone it myself. But I recognize it and have never let it interfere with a business relationship, or a friendship come to that. It's not love and war that all's fair in, in my book, but trade and war.'

'This is more than bending the rules,' Sinclair said urgently, thinking that his father-in-law had failed to understand what he said.

'Yes, I hear what you're saying,' Booth said. 'I'm just filling in the background, seeing as you are a police officer, and the more I've thought about it the more I've been convinced you're an honest one, in spite of everything.'

'Thanks,' Sinclair interjected ironically, but he relaxed again.

'When you join a masonic lodge, you know, you expect to aid and assist your brethren,' Booth said, ignoring the interruption. 'It's not part of the secret oaths, or anything daft like that. It's just expected, and I see nothing wrong with that. Nothing at all. It's an honourable notion, within reason. But what you're now telling me is that some of my brethren have begun to aid and assist each other beyond all reason. Isn't that what you're suggesting?'

'I'd say attempted murder is beyond reason,' Sinclair said quietly. 'And I'm afraid that in their anxiety to get at me, they might threaten the girls. I want you to look after them, Ted, until this thing is resolved. Take them away somewhere, if necessary. Anything you think fit. I can't do it myself. You know that.'

Booth was silent for a moment, clearly considering the options before coming to a decision. At length, he nodded to himself, apparently satisfied.

'They can go down to the villa in Sardinia with Mother,' he said. 'I'll book the flights myself tomorrow. A holiday will do them good. In the meantime, Mother and I won't let them out of our sight.'

'I'm grateful,' Sinclair said formally.

'And you want to know now which of my brethren might be involved in some sort of conspiracy, I suppose. You seem pretty sure about James Agarth. Have you got proof?'

Sinclair shook his head wearily.

'Nothing that will stand up in court,' he said. 'Just suspicions and coincidences. But time and again it comes back to members of your lodge. A list of members would be a help. There's no one else I can trust who I can ask.'

'I'm flattered, but what about your boss, Eddie Greaves?' Booth asked. 'Can't you trust him?'

'I don't know,' Sinclair said flatly.

Booth nodded, his face grim. 'Yes, well, I don't know either, lad, so it's no good looking to me for evidence against any of them. If I had any, I'd give it you. As you say, all this has gone way beyond bending the rules to put a bit of jam on the bread and butter. I know nothing that would help you. But I'll do what I can. Have you got your little notebook handy? Let's make you a list.'

SINCLAIR DROVE BACK from Broadley to Highcliffe in a sober mood. Ted Booth had insisted on taking him back into the house to see his daughters, in spite of Margaret's obvious displeasure, and he had told them about the planned holiday, to wild excitement from Sally and a more sober response from Jennifer who was worried about missing school. Even Margaret, though, had acquiesced, and Sinclair had driven away reassured at least that his family would be safe from any malevolent interference for a couple of weeks.

Sinclair had telephoned ahead to ask Bill Bairstow and the other members of the action committee to meet him at the advice centre at Highcliffe. The list Ted Booth had given him had, he thought, possibly shed light on the mystery of how the action committee's every move had been made known to its enemies, but his suspicions could only be confirmed by a direct confrontation at Highcliffe.

It was eleven o'clock when he arrived at the centre, to find Councillor Bairstow and Annie Macready making coffee in the general office.

'Is Stevenson coming?' Sinclair asked. Mrs Macready looked at him without warmth and nodded.

'Where's Kate, though?' she asked. 'We thought you'd bring her down. Father O'Leary's at mass, but will come in later, he said.'

'Kate won't be coming,' Sinclair said, and told them briefly what had happened during the night. Surprisingly, no one had yet contacted Bill Bairstow to tell him about the destruction of his caravan and he sat heavily in one of the hard-backed chairs, his face grey with shock. Annie Macready too had paled and stood looking at Sinclair in puzzlement.

'Someone tried to kill you all,' she said, more as if to confirm that she had heard Sinclair aright than as a question. 'Who'd do that, in the name of God?'

'I think I've got a good idea now who it might be,' Sinclair said. 'But I'm still a long way off proving it. But if I'm right, it's the same person who was responsible for Tom Carter's death, and for the trouble I'm in down at the nick. And if that's right, we all have an interest in pinning this down to the right person.'

Annie pushed her hair away from her face tiredly. The last week and a half had aged her: she had lost the resilience with which she had previously faced life, and with it had gone her attempts to disguise what damage fate and time had done her. She was wearing a pair of jeans which had seen better days and a baggy sweater, an outfit which Sinclair knew she would not have stepped out of her flat in before Joey's arrest. But Annie Macready's public face had disintegrated now, and the pale blue eyes which gazed at him held for the first time a flicker of sympathy.

'Jesus, what a mess,' she said.

Derek Stevenson arrived noisily, as always, with the air of a man who had got out of bed too early and dressed too quickly. He greeted Sinclair with his usual hostility, but even he looked visibly shaken when told what had happened overnight. Sinclair took up a position across the table from Stevenson and Bairstow and looked at them both silently for a moment.

'Who did you tell? You were the only people who knew where we were going last night. I trusted you.' His voice was cracked with fatigue and suppressed anger.

Bill Bairstow met Sinclair's gaze squarely and shook his head.

'I said nowt,' he said flatly. Sinclair looked at the older man for a long moment. He no longer fully trusted his own ability to judge but he could not bring himself to believe that Bill had betrayed them. He turned to Derek Stevenson and the younger man also met his gaze defiantly.

'Come on, Stevenson,' Sinclair said, impatience adding an edge to his voice. 'Who did you tell? Was it Rangely? Or do you report straight back to Agarth? I've just discovered they're both in the same bloody Masonic brotherhood.'

'I don't know what you're talking about,' Stevenson blustered. 'I talk to Gordon Rangely all the time. It's my job. I'm supposed to be getting publicity for this action group. You know that. He's done us proud in the *Echo*.'

'So you spoke to him yesterday?' Sinclair persisted.

'Well, yes, as a matter of fact I did. I had a drink with him at lunch-time.'

'And you told him where Kate and I had gone.' It was a statement rather than a question.

'Of course not,' Stevenson said. 'I wouldn't do that after what you'd said, would I?'

'You bloody would,' Annie Macready said suddenly. 'You said after t'trouble t'other night you'd like to see Inspector Sinclair rot in hell.'

There was silence as all four of them absorbed the implications of what Annie had said. At last Stevenson pushed his chair away from the table noisily. There was no disguising the hatred in his eyes now as he turned on Sinclair.

'So what if I did tell Rangely?' he almost snarled. 'He needs to know what's going on. It's his job. What are you saying? That he went up to the Glen and set the effing caravan on fire? That's bloody nonsense. If you want to know what I think, I think you're getting bloody paranoid. Like the rest of the effing police force, you're up to your neck in corruption yourself and now it's catching up with you, you don't know which way to turn. Well, you can count me out of your conspiracy theories. I might have let slip to Gordon where you were last night. I can't remember. And so what if I did? It proves nothing. Nothing at all.'

'That's enough, Derek,' Bairstow broke in coldly, with an authority which took Sinclair by surprise. 'If there's been loose talk, then we know who to blame, don't we? So if I were you, I'd keep quiet now.'

Stevenson flung an angry look at the older man and went to the door.

'Yes, well, I came here to help clear young Joey's name, not set up a benevolent society for bent coppers,' he said. 'So I'll leave you to get on with it. But just you remember one thing, Annie. It was the effing police who locked Joey up and threw away the key. It was the police who refused to look at the case again. And it was this policeman here who arrested the lad in the first place. And then think who got the protest movement started. Who organized petitions and meetings for you, and got all that publicity in the Press. Just you think about who your real friends are, Annie. And when you've decided, get in touch.' With that he slammed the door behind him.

Annie Macready sat down at the table beside Sinclair with a heavy sigh.

'He really hates you,' she said.

'But that's not just politics, is it?' Sinclair asked, shaken by Stevenson's vehemence. 'It's personal.'

'Of course it's personal,' Annie said. 'He's crazy about Kate Weston. Has been for years. Didn't you know?'

EIGHTEEN

ALEX SINCLAIR woke suddenly, uncomfortable and stiff on the back seat of his car, to find the sun coming up in full magnificence over the immense sweep of Lyme Bay. He had parked in the small hours of the morning in a public car park high on the cliffs of Babbacombe, on the eastern side of Torquay and quite close to the residential home where Martin Reilly now lived. The drive down the M6 and M5 had been a long one and, uncomfortable as the car had been, he had slept fitfully for the rest of the night. He rubbed his unshaven chin speculatively, and wondered if he would be looking respectable enough by nine o'clock to gain access to the old man he had come to see.

He opened the car door and climbed out, stretching his cramped limbs. Beyond the car park the land dropped away sharply and he could see a solitary figure apparently beachcombing with a dog along the frothy edge of the sea where it lapped the reddish sands of the beach. Beyond the edge of the town, the undulating coastline, a far deeper green than he was used to on the northern hills, swept away to the east in a morning light so clear that he could make out buildings which must, he guessed, be beyond Exeter on the far blue arm of the bay. He had left Milford in the rain which seemed to have been falling now for days, but this soft, southern morning promised a warm spring day. There was a gentle breeze off the sea and he breathed the salty air appreciatively and realized that he was hungry.

An hour later he had breakfasted on a couple of buns from a local bakery, where he had been the first customer through the newly unlocked door. He had decided against trying to shave in cold water in the car park lavatory and had contented himself with swilling his face and trying to straighten out his crumpled jacket and tie. At nine o'clock on the dot he presented himself at the front door of the Seaview Nursing Home and asked to see Martin Reilly. The uniformed assistant who opened the door looked surprised, and commented on the early hour. Mr Reilly, she offered, did not get many visitors, and she looked blank when Sinclair asked whether his son ever visited.

'I didn't know he had a son,' she said, but without surprise. 'I expect Matron has him down as next of kin.' That, she implied, was all that really mattered. She led Sinclair upstairs, where she knocked on a door neatly inscribed with Reilly's name.

The old man came to the door himself. He was obviously an early riser, no doubt from long habit, and was already dressed in grey flannel trousers and an old-fashioned blue and white striped shirt without a collar. He was a big man. Age might have brought a stoop to his shoulders but they were still the shoulders of a bull, broad and powerful, and something of a belly hung over the belt which held his trousers up with some apparent strain. The hair was iron grey, but had been dark, and the eyes were still a bright piercing blue and they stared suspiciously at his visitor from a face which, for all the creases and wrinkles of age and a yellowish, unhealthy tinge, was a carbon copy of his son's.

The attendant left them alone and when Sinclair identified himself Reilly grudgingly allowed him into his room and waved him into one of the two armchairs.

'You've come from Milford, then, have you?' he asked. His accent was still broadly Irish, but it had allied itself to the phrasing of the north of England.

'Didn't you think someone would, in the end?' Sinclair asked.

'Why would I think that, then, Inspector?' Reilly challenged back, apparently unruffled.

'I suppose because most secrets come out finally.'

The old man nodded almost absent-mindedly.

'Aye, well, it doesn't matter one way or t'other to me now. Did they tell you about my liver? A whisky liver, the good doctor called it, and it'll not last me much longer, they say.'

Sinclair shook his head: nothing he could say would be an adequate response to Reilly's fatalistic acceptance of his condition. It was not a moment to press him and for a minute Reilly said nothing more, staring with those blue eyes out of the window at the distant sea.

'I should have gone home, you know,' he said quietly, at last. 'I mean home to the old country. But Terry said this would suit me as well.'

'Terry?' Sinclair prompted.

'My lad, Terry. He and Mr Agarth fixed this place up when my Mollie died. Said I'd be comfortable here.'

'And aren't you?'

'Oh, aye, I'm comfortable enough,' Reilly said. 'Any road, it's too late now, with the liver. I'll not be here much longer, but I'd like to have seen Kerry again.'

'There were a few Kerrymen with you on that job in Milford, weren't there?' Sinclair prompted. 'They're all dead now.'

Reilly looked at him then, without emotion, and Sinclair realized that the whites of his eyes were also tinged with an unhealthy yellow.

'Aye,' he said. 'I'm not surprised. It were a mucky job, as they say up there. Mucky and dangerous. The wonder is Agarth's got away with it so long.'

'Tell me,' Sinclair said very quietly, and equally quietly, the old man did.

IT WAS MID-AFTERNOON when Sinclair turned wearily off the motorway spur on to the main road into Milford from the south. The sense of elation with which he had left Torquay, a signed and witnessed statement from Martin Reilly in his pocket, had been dissipated on the long drive back, and he faced the next few hours with more foreboding than exhilaration at having at last pinned James Agarth down. He was already hours late for his appointment with Superintendent Greaves and he was not altogether surprised when a patrol car flagged him down on the outskirts of the town.

'Are you arresting me, Graham?' he asked the patrolman when he asked him to accompany him to police headquarters.

'No, sir, we're to ask you to come voluntarily to help with inquiries,' the young constable said, obviously embarrassed by his task. He had worked with Sinclair for six months as a beat officer in Highcliffe.

Sinclair nodded. 'All right, Graham, I'll follow you down there in my own car,' he said. 'Don't worry. I was on my way in anyway.'

The officer looked relieved and allowed Sinclair to tail him into the headquarters car park where he hovered anxiously while Sinclair locked his car and pocketed the keys.

'Come on,' Sinclair said. 'You'd better come in with me as you were the lucky lad to track me down.' The constable grinned, pleased that Sinclair was making an unpleasant task easier, and they went through the swing doors together. The desk sergeant looked at Sinclair with some relief.

'I'm glad to see you, Alex,' he said. 'Eddie Greaves is doing his nut.'

'I was unavoidably detained,' Sinclair said drily. 'I'm here voluntarily, right?' The distinction was more than semantic: while he remained a 'volunteer' at the police station, he would not be asked to surrender his personal possessions and he would retain, at least nominally, some freedom of decision.

The sergeant nodded and waved Sinclair through to the rear corridor behind the reception desk.

'If you'll come through you can wait for the superintendent in interview room three.'

When the door slammed shut behind the sergeant, leaving him alone in the bleak interview room with its table screwed to the floor, its couple of hard chairs and a frosted glass window deliberately placed so high that it could not be reached by hand, Sinclair felt a moment of blind panic.

He could feel Reilly's statement in his breast pocket giving off an almost physical heat and he knew that his ability to extricate himself from this room, and an endless series of others as grim, rested on his capacity to use that statement effectively in the next couple of hours and above all to avoid letting it fall into the hands of any friend of James Agarth. He had hoped to hand the document to Bill before reporting to the police station. Now inside, the problem lay in knowing just who Agarth's friends were.

The door opened quietly and Sinclair was surprised to see not Superintendent Greaves, but Dave Wilson, looking anxiously behind him down the corridor before closing the door behind him.

'I heard you'd been brought in,' he said, by way of explanation. 'Greaves is out for your blood. What kept you?'

'He'll be out for yours if he catches you here.'

'Aye, well, his latest theory is that I must have known you were on t'take and why didn't I report it,' Wilson said bitterly.

Sinclair clenched his fist angrily. 'Listen, Dave, I've cracked it, but I don't trust Greaves. He's too close to Agarth and if he's protecting him, he might get away with it now he's got me back here. I left Bill Bairstow collating all the evidence we'd got together by yesterday, and with this statement I got in Torquay, I think we can nail Agarth. But there's only one copy of this, and I'll be damned if I'll let Greaves have it. You take it and photocopy it and put the original somewhere safe—and I mean really safe—until it's needed.

Wilson took the document Sinclair handed him and put it in his inside pocket somberly.

'I'll bring you a copy if I can,' he said. 'Old Nick himself won't get the original.'

He left Sinclair alone again, and it was a good ten minutes before Superintendent Greaves eventually came into the interview room, tight-lipped, carrying a buff file which he placed deliberately on the table, before motioning Sinclair into a chair and taking the one opposite.

He was, as usual, impeccably dressed, his striped shirt starched to Victorian crispness and his silk tie knotted at exactly the right tension. But his face was paler than when Sinclair had last seen him, and there were dark rings of tiredness beneath his eyes, and an edginess in his manner which was unusual. This business is getting to him, Sinclair thought, and felt obscurely pleased at the idea. He wondered why Greaves had not brought a uniformed officer with him, as normal practice demanded. The superintendent sat looking at him for a moment, his eyes unfriendly and a nerve twitching at his temple.

'This is unofficial, Alex,' he said at last. 'You've not been cautioned yet, so it's just you and me, right?'

Sinclair shrugged slightly. That explained why Greaves had come alone but made him no less eager to confide in his superior.

'I want my solicitor here, sir, before I talk about anything,' he said formally.

'Your bloody solicitor was here earlier, at the proper time,' Greaves retorted tetchily. 'I've got someone giving him a call now to let him know we've brought you in. What the hell kept you?'

'I needed to talk to someone before I came in,' Sinclair said non-committally.

'And I don't suppose you're going to tell me who,' Greaves came back, angrier now. 'That's what I want to ask you about—just you and me—off the record, no notes, no formalities. Do you mind telling me just what the hell you've been doing, carrying on some sort of freelance investigation of your own this week? I've got a whole sheaf of reports on my desk, from Eckersley Hospital, from DI Chapman, something about a car smash that no one bothered to report, a fire in a caravan you were supposed to be staying in but clearly weren't—it took the fire brigade half a day to be sure there was no one in that bloody van burnt to a crisp, so now the chief fire officer's doing his nut too. Just what the hell have you been playing at?'

Sinclair ran a hand through his hair wearily. His eyes were gritty from lack of sleep and for a moment he felt an overwhelming desire to tell Greaves everything, and leave the rest to the man who, ever since he had joined the CID, had been his ever irascible guide and mentor. He could not honestly say he had ever liked Eddie Greaves, but he had, until ten days ago, trusted him and it was a difficult habit to break.

'I'll make a statement,' Sinclair said, 'but I'll make it to a senior officer from another division.'

Greaves looked at him in silence again, his eyes like chips of ice, fury very near the surface now.

'You will not,' he said. 'You'll make a statement to me, and like it. Who the hell do you think you are, Sinclair? You're here on suspicion of corrupt dealings, remember? What gives you the right to lay down conditions about who you'll talk to? You'll bloody well talk to who I say, when I say, and you'll not leave this station until you do.'

'Superintendent Swallow would do,' Sinclair said. 'I'll give him a full statement when my solicitor arrives.'

'I came in here to try and help you, lad,' Greaves said, his voice tight. 'I came to say to you—just between the two of us—that if you came clean about the bank account I'd do my best for you when it came to court, put in a word as to character, an aberration while you were under a lot of domestic stress, that sort of thing, see if we couldn't swing a suspended sentence. But there's no helping you, Sinclair, is there? You're an arrogant young bastard, always have been. Always sure you're right, just like your bloody father.'

'I don't need your help, Eddie,' Sinclair broke in, his own irritation uncontrollable now. 'I'm not one of your bloody freemasons looking for favours.'

'So sod you, then,' Greaves said, getting to his feet and going to the door. 'I'll see you formally when your brief gets here, but if you think you're going whining to Swallow or anyone else with some fairy story about the Carter murder, you've got another think coming. You're on the

line for corruption, lad, and I can make it stick. And I will.'
With that Greaves left the room, slamming the door angrily behind him.

Sinclair sat alone in the empty interview room for what seemed like hours. The fatigue of the long drive to Devon and back kept forcing his eyelids closed and eventually he put his head on his arms and slumped across the table and slept fitfully. He woke to find the uniformed custody sergeant shaking him by the shoulder, and Superintendent Greaves in the room with him.

'We haven't been able to contact your solicitor yet, sir,' the sergeant said.

Sinclair realized that darkness had fallen while he had been asleep and guessed that he would face a night in the cells if the lawyer did not turn up soon.

'Will a duty solicitor do, sir?' the sergeant asked.

Sinclair shook his head. 'I want my own solicitor,' he said.

'I'm not letting you off these premises again,' Greaves broke in angrily. 'You either stay here voluntarily or I'll caution you and go through the procedures and keep you in a cell overnight.'

Sinclair shrugged. 'Hobson's choice,' he said with a lightness he did not feel. 'I'm at your service, Superintendent, an unwilling volunteer.'

The door opened again and Sergeant Wilson came into the room, looking agitated. He spoke in Greaves's ear, and both men glanced at Sinclair and appeared to hesitate, with a look in their eyes which Sinclair could not interpret but which sent a shiver down his spine.

'What is it?' he appealed to Wilson directly. 'What's gone wrong, Dave?' Wilson look at Greaves for guidance and after another moment's hesitation the superintendent nodded his assent.

'You'd better tell him.'

'It's Kate Weston's lad,' Wilson said slowly. 'He's gone missing up at Highcliffe. They think he's gone up on to t'moor. They've got search-parties out.' The cold finger of fear turned into an enormous grasping fist clutching at Sinclair's stomach and he steadied himself against the table and took a deep breath. He didn't need to be told how Kate felt at this moment. He knew.

'Let me go up there,' he said desperately. 'Send Dave with me—anything—but let me go up there to help, Eddie. Please.'

Greaves looked at the man sitting at the table, fists clenched, face ashen, and eventually he nodded grimly to Wilson.

'All right,' he said. 'But don't you let him out of your sight, Dave, or I'll have you on a charge as well.'

NINETEEN

THE POLICE CARS which had been parked outside the advice centre at Highcliffe were beginning to pull away when Sinclair and Wilson arrived in Sinclair's car. A few officers were still pulling off wellington boots wearily in the entrance lobby, while in the office a uniformed inspector and sergeant were talking to Derek Stevenson when the two detectives walked in. They looked at Sinclair in some surprise, tinged, he thought, with hostility, and he was only too aware that his appearance, unshaven, his shirt collar undone and his jacket crumpled after the best part of two days' living and sleeping in his clothes did not inspire confidence. The inspector glanced at Wilson but after a moment's hesitation decided to make no comment on their obviously unexpected arrival.

'Have you found the boy?' Sinclair asked urgently. His colleagues both shook their heads gloomily.

'We've called the search off until morning,' the inspector said. 'We've combed the park, and the moor up as far as the old drift mines. There's nothing more we can do now until first light, Alex. It's too dangerous up there. I can't risk anyone going over Broadley Edge in the dark.'

'Who saw him last?' Sinclair might be dog-tired and dishevelled but his authority had not deserted him now there was something urgent to do.

'His mother,' the sergeant said. 'She left him in the flat, she says, while she popped down here to pick up some papers from her office, and when she got back he'd gone. She wasn't away more than ten minutes, she says.'

Why had not Kate stayed safely with his father, Sinclair wondered angrily. This new crisis was a distraction they could all do without.

Kate Weston had reported Sam's absence in the late afternoon, the inspector offered, becoming more forthcoming once he had got over his surprise at Sinclair's arrival and recognized his colleagues' carefully controlled but clearly desperate anxiety. She had gone to the police less than an hour after she had found him missing from the flat, after spending some time fruitlessly looking around the immediate neighbourhood and contacting his friends to see whether the boy had gone to someone's house to play. The police would not normally have launched a full-scale search for a missing child quite so quickly, but the inspector said that she had managed to convince headquarters that this was likely to be either a serious attempt to run away—and that's probably down to me, Sinclair thought bitterly—or worse.

'You mean she thinks he might have been abducted?' Sinclair asked.

'There's absolutely no evidence for that,' the inspector said, somewhat testily. 'But his mother seems to think it's a possibility.'

'He's much more likely to have bogged off on his own initiative,' Derek Stevenson, who had stood listening to the conversation with unconcealed curiosity, broke in harshly. 'He's a sulky little sod when he chooses. A bit unstable if you ask me.'

'Nobody asked you,' Sinclair snapped, wondering whether Stevenson had suffered the same hostility from Sam that he had met himself. The idea gave him a certain grim satisfaction.

'Where's Kate Weston now?' he asked.

The uniformed inspector looked uncertain.

'I think she's gone back to Annie Macready's place,' he said. 'She's pretty distraught and there was nothing she could do here. She was just getting in the way, to be honest.'

'Come on, Dave,' Sinclair said to Wilson. With no more than a slight shrug to his colleagues the sergeant followed Sinclair back out into the open air.

'Do you seriously think he could have been snatched?' Wilson asked doubtfully as they walked the few hundred yards to the flats.

Sinclair stopped for a moment and faced the sergeant, his shoulders slumped. He ran a hand through his hair wearily. He knew he was stretching the other man's loyalty to the limit, and if the sergeant was beginning to have doubts about the conspiracy he believed enveloped him, then he did not give much for his chances of convincing anyone else.

'As far as the opposition in this affair is concerned, I'm discredited, Dave—about to be banged up in solitary on prison Rule 43 for my own protection for God knows how long, I guess. Done for, in fact...'

'I'm sorry, boss,' Wilson broke in awkwardly.

'Don't be,' Sinclair came back quickly. 'You asked a serious question and I'm trying to find a serious answer. Which is that even if I'm apparently finished, Kate Weston isn't. She's still a joker in the pack, as far as the opposition are concerned. All the attempts so far to shut her up have failed. So why shouldn't they have tried again, possibly by snatching Sam as a way to get at Kate? They've not stopped at murder, so why should they stop at kidnapping?'

'So we ask her if she's been contacted by anyone?'

'If she'll tell us,' Sinclair said. 'I'm not sure that if it were my child that had been snatched I'd be sharing many confidences with the police—and I know all the cast-iron reasons why I should.'

'She'll tell you,' Wilson said flatly. 'I'll put money on that.'

'Maybe,' Sinclair said bleakly. 'Let's go and see, shall we.'

A ring on Kate's bell brought no response, but Annie Macready unlatched the front door for them and waited for them at the top of the stairs. She had her hair tied back severely from her face, and watched them grimly as they took the last breathless flight of stairs too quickly for comfort.

'They let you out, then, did they?' she said to Sinclair, unsmiling. 'More than they did for our Joey, but I suppose that's only to be expected—coppers looking after their own.'

Sinclair did not feel able to reply. Annie's pain was etched deeply into her face now, too deeply for make-up to hide, and he knew she still blamed him as much as anyone for what had happened to Joey. He and Wilson followed her silently into her living-room, where Tracey lay on the floor watching television, and Bill Bairstow sat slumped in a chair by the gas fire, looking tired and grey but with a fat file spread out on his knee.

'Now then, lad,' he greeted Sinclair in apparent surprise. 'How did you get on, then?'

'Where's Kate?' Sinclair asked.

'She over at t'centre, isn't she, wi't'police?' Annie asked.

'No, she's not,' Sinclair said. 'They thought she was here.'

The four of them looked at each other with a growing puzzlement, and Sinclair felt a momentary loss of control as his tired brain tried to grapple with this new anxiety.

'I'll go and see if I can find, her, boss,' Wilson said finally, sensing Sinclair's sudden uncertainty. 'She won't be far away. I'll ask around.' He handed him a sheaf of papers from his inside pocket.

'Here. That's Reilly's statement and the copies. You sort that out with what Councillor Bairstow's got. I'll not be long.'

'IT'S STILL all circumstantial,' Sinclair said wearily half an hour later after going through Bill Bairstow's file. He had pushed Sam and Kate to the back of his mind with difficulty and tried to concentrate on Bill's analysis. 'There's nothing to link Agarth with the Carter murder—or with any other violence, for that matter. You could argue he's just a very generous employee who looks after his old folk—a highly commendable fellow, in fact.'

'Aye, well, maybe. But it gives you a motive, doesn't it? The last thing he wants to come out right now is some old scandal about dumping toxic waste. Just when he's about to sell out. And what it gives the council is a good reason to open up those drifts. Reilly says there's summat in there that there shouldn't be, that Bradley Disposals was carting stuff in from all over t'county at that time, acting as chemical dustbin-men, effectively. The river's running foul again, by the way, and I've asked for an independent analysis o' t'water from there, and from t'Beck. I don't think we can trust our own people, from what you say. Our man Wright in environmental health is in t'same bloody lodge, according to Ted Booth's list of members, and I'm not convinced we can believe him when he says t'Beck's clean. I'm having the tests done again by a laboratory in Leeds to be on the safe side.'

'Sure, you can get him on the pollution,' Sinclair conceded. 'But that's all a cover-up that's thirty years old. Reilly says the waste disposal firm went out of business as soon as the drifts were sealed. It was only a subsidiary to the construction business and Agarth himself can't have been more than a lad at the time. He wasn't responsible personally. The magistrates'll tut-tut and impose some nominal fine on the company, and perhaps the sale will go through, perhaps not. Who knows? Agarth will be furious if it falls through, but that will be the end of it. We've still got nothing definite on the murder, nothing, in fact, that would even clear Joey Macready.'

'Nor you, lad, nor you,' Bairstow said heavily. 'The fact that a bank manager's in t'same lodge as Agarth isn't proof of anything bar they probably know each other. But who doesn't in this town? I've known Agarth myself since he were a lad, and his father before that.'

Annie, who had been gazing unseeingly at the television while the two men had been talking, swung round angrily at that, her eyes glinting with a mixture of tears and fury.

'So what good's all this bloody investigation been, then?' she asked. 'Derek's not such a fool, is he? He reckons folk like us can never get a fair deal the way things are. If it suits them to blame a lad like our Joey they'll blame him, and there's nowt I can do to stop them. It's all wrong, you know, all wrong.'

'We've not finished yet, Annie,' Sinclair said gently. 'We can't prove anything against Agarth yet, but there's enough evidence here to at least re-open the investigation into Tom Carter's murder, and to look again at Joey's case, and a lot else besides. The next step is to get all this to a senior officer outside Milford, because I don't know who we can trust inside.'

'Aye, that's what Derek says, an'all,' Annie muttered bitterly, almost to herself. 'You can't trust anyone.' She turned back to the television and sank into a simmering silence.

Sinclair looked at Bairstow helplessly. He wondered if he would ever be able to work effectively in Highcliffe again, or indeed if he would ever be given the chance to try. Whatever happened, he thought, much of what he had worked for lay in ruins.

'Why did Kate come back up here from my father's place?' he asked Bill quietly. 'I asked her to stay away.'

'She heard you'd been arrested,' Bairstow said. 'She came storming up to t'centre to look for me. I told her there were not a lot I could do about that. Which she knew already, of course. I'm surprised they let you go.'

'I'm surprised they let me go, too,' Sinclair said grimly. 'I'm surprised they didn't arrest me. That's what I was expecting, till Eddie Greaves had a sudden and uncharacteristic change of heart. But I don't think it'll last. Dave Wilson's supposed to see me safely back again before too long. And I'll have to make sure he does, too, or his job'll be on the line as well. Where the hell is Dave anyway?' he added explosively. 'And where's Kate?'

The phone rang shrilly and Annie Macready got out of her chair to answer it.

'It's for you,' she said, handing the receiver to Sinclair with ill grace.

Sinclair listened to the voice at the other end in silence, his hand tightening on the receiver until his knuckles showed white.

'Straight away,' was all he said quietly before putting the receiver down very carefully, whatever emotion he felt tightly under control. Bairstow and Mrs Macready looked at him in astonishment as he put his coat on, grim-faced.

'I have to go out for a while,' was all the explanation he offered before leaving the flat. Outside he got quickly into his car, which Dave Wilson had left parked outside. Approaching the flats on foot a minute later, Wilson himself looked after the receding tail-lights in astonishment and fury.

'Damn and blast you, Inspector bloody Sinclair,' the sergeant said bitterly, as he watched the car head out of the estate and take the hill road towards Broadley Moor. 'I thought I could trust you not to land me in the shit.'

SINCLAIR SWUNG INTO the parking area at the caravan site on Broadley Glen and was surprised to see several cars already there, and also, well back from the road, a low-loader with a caterpillar-tracked digger on its back dimly visible in the light of his headlights under the overhanging trees. He got out of the car wearily, dogged now by a sense of utter defeat. He did not know what James Agarth was planning, but his phone call had been personal, precise and full of menace. He had Kate Weston at the Glen, he had said, and he required Sinclair there at once and alone, if he wanted to see her alive again. He had not mentioned Sam, but Sinclair assumed he must have the boy at the caravan site as well.

Several men got out of the other parked cars as he arrived and among them Sinclair recognized the tall figure of Agarth himself, in a dark overcoat, his face muffled in a pale silk scarf against the wind and driving rain.

'You are prompt, Inspector,' Agarth said smoothly. 'I have men posted on the road, so I trust you are also alone, as I requested?'

Sinclair nodded in acknowledgement.

'I did exactly as you said. Where's Kate?'

'She's quite safe in one of these very useful caravans,' Agarth said. 'But before you get together, I have a little job I want you to do for me.'

'I don't believe you,' Sinclair interrupted. 'I want to see her. And Sam.'

Agarth shrugged imperceptibly.

'Such devotion,' he said lightly, with just a hint of a sneer. 'No wonder your wife has thrown you out. Terry, take our friend over to see Mrs Weston. But I'm afraid the boy is not here, Sinclair. He is the precise problem I need your help with.'

The burly figure Sinclair now knew was Terry Reilly detached himself from the group and led Sinclair to a caravan where a dim light could be seen inside. Reilly walked with one arm held across his body and as they moved into the slanting light from the caravan window Sinclair saw, without much surprise, that he was carrying a sawn-off shotgun. Reilly waved him up the caravan steps ahead of him, and once inside Sinclair saw Kate slumped fully dressed on one of the bunks at the far end of the single compartment. He moved quickly to her side and lifted her gently upright. She moaned slightly but did not open her eyes.

'What the hell have you done to her?' Sinclair demanded furiously.

'She's quite all right, Inspector, I assure you,' said Agarth, who had followed Reilly into the van. 'I merely gave her two of these to save her unnecessary distress.' He threw Sinclair a small bottle with a chemist's label. Sinclair recognized the name of a common tranquillizer. Kate muttered again and opened her eyes sleepily. Sinclair held her close to him and kissed her.

'It's all right, Kate,' he said quietly. 'Go back to sleep.' He laid her limp body down again and pulled up the blanket which had been half covering her, and stood up to face Reilly and Agarth again. He looked at Agarth expressionlessly. The older man's face was slightly flushed and damp from the rain, but his eyes were as cold as ever and his arrogance undiminished. He had the look of a man who sees victory within his grasp, Sinclair thought, and the thought was not a comforting one.

'What do you want with me?' he asked flatly, with the resignation of someone who knows that all his options have run out.

'I want you to find the Weston boy,' Agarth said. 'Contrary to what you clearly imagined, I had nothing to do with his disappearance. He seems to have contrived that on his own. What concerns me is that his mother says he has found a way into the old drift mines up here, at the bottom of the gully just down the lane. And there's certainly a fissure in the rocks that a child could squeeze through, and as far as we can see it drops into one of the old levels. I've had my men make the entrance a little wider, wide enough for a grown man.'

'So why do you need me? If you can get in there, you can search the place yourself, can't you?'

'We could. But I think it would be far more effective if someone the boy knows goes down there first. Otherwise he might just hide, and we'd never find him. If he's in there, I want him out tonight, Sinclair. Dead or alive, I want him out. I don't want the police or anyone else to find an excuse to open the mines up in the morning.'

'You're too late, Agarth,' Sinclair said. 'They're going to open those drifts pretty soon to check out the source of the river pollution anyway, whether they go looking for Sam Weston in there or not.'

'You're a clever young man, Sinclair,' Agarth said dismissively. 'A pity you didn't take advantage of the chance you had to be on the winning side in this town when it was on offer. We could have used your brains, like we've used Eddie Greaves's over the years. Someone at police HQ is always useful.'

Agarth paused, watching Sinclair with an ironic smile as the inspector took in the full significance of what he had just said.

'You asked Greaves to let me out, then?' Sinclair asked, understanding now the superintendent's unexpected change of tack and feeling physically sick as ten years of his life lurched into a new and deeply disillusioning perspective.

'And the bank account? You and Greaves set that up...?

'As I say, you're a clever young man, Sinclair, but when it comes to the point, you've not been quite clever enough. In the end you let your heart rule your head and so here we are. And by tomorrow no one will believe there's any source of pollution to find down in the drifts, thanks to the Weston boy and the very convenient back entrance he's found to the mines. But first I want him out of there. If he's still missing in the morning, it's likely they will start tearing the hillside apart, and I think I'd rather avoid that if at all possible.'

'I wouldn't bank on the fact that Sam will come when I call,' Sinclair said grimly, thinking of the antagonism he sparked in the boy.

'And I wouldn't bank on the fact that you'll find him alive anyway, if that's where he tried to hide,' Agarth came back, coldly and without hesitation. 'There'll be gas down there. I've got you some breathing gear. You've got about an hour, which should be enough. I want you and the child out of there by, say—' he glanced at his watch—'by midnight.'

'And if I refuse?' Sinclair asked, although he knew the answer well enough.

Agarth glanced at the sleeping Kate Weston and then at Terry Reilly, who grinned and licked his lips obscenely.

'You don't need me to spell it out, Inspector, do you?' Agarth said dismissively. 'We have an obvious hostage for your good behaviour.'

THE LIGHT ON SINCLAIR'S miner's helmet cut a thin swathe through the profound darkness of the mine. The only sound he could hear was his own measured breathing inside his face-mask and the receding sound of running water from the fault where he had been lowered into the level.

The stream was running quietly under Sinclair's feet now, sometimes between the worn railway track in the centre of the tunnel, sometimes in a water-worn channel beneath one wall, but always following the slight downward incline of the mine-working which had surprised Sinclair by its breadth and height. It provided an easy highway through the hillside rather than the difficult crawl he had anticipated.

Agarth had given him a rough sketch-map of the drifts which ran from the two entrances on the Highcliffe side of the moor roughly in parallel under the hillside towards Broadley Glen. They were joined together by a single passage about half way along their length, turning the whole mine into an H-shape with the easterly upright, in which he now stood, rising slightly from its entrance, and the other limb dropping more steeply to a greater depth.

From time to time he took a deep breath, pulled off his mask and called Sam's name. There was no response, and in spite of Agarth's fears, Sinclair could see no real possibility that the boy could be hiding out of sight of the lamp's reach. The passageway was remarkably clear of debris and if, as old Martin Reilly had alleged, there was a large cache of industrial waste in the mine, it was not visible in this roadway.

Halfway down Sinclair veered left into the narrower side tunnel which led to the other main road. The narrower passageway dropped steeply and within a few minutes' walk Sinclair found that the water underfoot was becoming deeper. He stopped and directed the beam of his light as far as he could down the tunnel. Inky black water stretched ahead as far as he could see leaving progressively less and less space between its surface and the roof of the tunnel. Long before the tunnel reached the other road, he guessed, it would be completely flooded. There was no way anyone could be alive down there.

He retraced his steps uphill and rejoined the main tunnel. He shouted for Sam again, without response, before turning left towards the main entrance to the mine. He glanced at his watch. He had been underground for fifteen minutes. He came surprisingly quickly to the mine entrance, where a solid wall of boulders and concrete blocked the two arches leading to the head of the mine.

By now he was slopping about in several inches of surface water. Even so, he turned again and began to follow the other drift which headed quite steeply downhill. Before he had gone more than a couple of hundred yards the water was half way up his boots, dark and glutinous in the fitful light of his lamp, and here and there throwing off a multicoloured gleam as if someone had scattered petrol across its surface. Even as he watched a succession of bubbles burst up to the surface, disturbing its oily sheen and creating small wavelets around his ankles. He took off his mask to shout, and before he could push it back into place he took in a mouthful of the mine's atmosphere and choked and almost retched as its harsh reek hit the back of his nose and throat. He stood for a moment leaning against the wall, clutching his mask to his face and breathing his air supply deeply to rid his lungs of the choking fumes, aware now if he had not been before that he would find no one alive down here.

Wearily he began to retrace his steps. As he passed the sealed-off main entrance, twin doorways to the outside world securely blocked, he could see where the water level in the mine was draining away between boulders and presumably out into the open air beyond. As rain fell, he realized, the lower spur of the drift, where the now defunct Bradley Disposals must have concealed their dump of waste, was filling up with water from the fissure up above and eventually lapping out to find its way into the Beck, carrying with it whatever pollutants had seeped out of the dump and poisoned the water and the air around him.

When the water level fell, the pollution would be trapped again inside the mine, until the next heavy fall of rain. Intermittent pollution, the experts had reckoned, meant intermittent dumping in the river. They had been wrong. The wayward contamination of the Maze was no more than a function of the weather.

It had taken him forty minutes to complete his tour of the workings, and of Sam there had been neither sight nor sound. Sinclair tugged on the rope down which he had been lowered into the mine, and strong hands from above hauled him up to the surface again. He took his mask off and breathed the clean night air again thankfully. Agarth himself, in gumboots and with a waterproof over his overcoat now, was waiting for him. Sinclair shook his head.

'He's not in there,' he said. 'And there's no sign he ever has been.'

'Is there any fresh air down there?' Agarth asked.

'It's foul. Full of fumes of some sort. What the hell did they dump down there?'

'Never mind that,' Agarth said. 'By tomorrow there'll have been a very fortuitous roof-fall which will bury all that deeper than anyone will want to dig in a hurry.'

'You underestimate how determined some people might be to keep on digging with that filth pouring into the Beck,' Sinclair said.

Agarth laughed. 'I admit I may have underestimated how determined you would turn out to be,' he said. 'But you won't be around tomorrow to cause me any further embarrassment, and there'll be no more pollution after tonight.' He turned to Reilly, who had been listening to this exchange with an anticipatory smile on his face.

'Bring him up to the van,' Agarth said, and strode back up the hill towards the caravan site. Reilly moved behind Sinclair and prodded him viciously in the back with the muzzle of his shotgun.

'You heard what the man said,' he said. Sinclair did as he was told. On the steep climb back up to the road he passed several of Agarth's labourers carrying boxes down towards the mine entrance. He recognized some of them as explosive containers. The roof-fall Agarth pinned his hopes on would obviously very soon be a reality, he thought, and whatever was bubbling away in the witches' cauldron which must lie at the bottom of the deeper of the drifts would be buried beyond hope of easy recall.

Kate Weston was awake, sitting on her bunk in the caravan, when Sinclair and Reilly climbed back up the steps. She looked deathly pale and there were dark rings under her eyes, which filled with fear when she saw Reilly's gun pressed close against Sinclair's back. Sinclair crossed to sit beside her and put his arm round her for comfort.

Agarth was talking to a tall man in a navy donkey jacket who seemed to be some sort of foreman for the heavy work going on outside.

'It's only a matter of a few yards to divert that stream down towards Broadley,' Agarth said. 'Once the roof is down and the water source is removed, they'll have the devil's own job proving that there's anything coming out of there that shouldn't be. And I can't see anyone tunnelling half way through Broadley Moor just on the off chance.

'You'll never get away with it,' Sinclair said.

'Don't you think so?' Agarth asked, almost conversationally. 'Oh, I think with you and Mrs Weston out of the way, I have a very good chance. No one will imagine for a moment that the boy has got into the drifts once we've finished, so there'll be absolutely no reason to open them up. The chances are he'll have turned up safely in the morning anyway. Such a pity you won't be here to welcome him home.'

Kate gasped as the implication of what Agarth intended sank in. Sinclair tightened his hold on her.

'Hang on,' he said quietly.

Agarth turned to Reilly impatiently.

'Keep an eye on them for ten minutes while I just finish off down there,' he said, and left the caravan, followed by his foreman. 'Then we'll get this business finished once and for all.'

Kate Weston took hold of Sinclair's hand and gripped it tightly. Sinclair could feel her trembling. The effects of the tranquillizer Agarth had given her were obviously wearing off.

'Hang on,' he said again softly. 'It'll be all right.'

'You really think so, pig?' Reilly said at once, taking up a more menacing position facing his two prisoners with his gun at the ready. It was not Reilly's size which worried Sinclair, although he was a burly figure, but the almost manic gleam which had now crept into his blue eyes, and the nervous way he handled the shotgun. Even so, he calculated that their chances of escape were better now than they might ever be again, if only Reilly could be distracted in some way from his present wary vigilance.

But even while he was estimating his chances of jumping Reilly and avoiding the threatening muzzle of the gun, Reilly's own precarious self-control snapped.

'I hate coppers,' he said thickly. 'And coppers' tarts.'

He looked at Kate for a moment, leering, and then turned on Sinclair with a look of pure malice. The implication was obvious enough and Sinclair was already on his feet, impelled by instinct rather than coherent thought, as Reilly swung the butt end of his weapon into his stomach with sickening force. Sinclair went down gasping for air in the cramped space between the bunks and it was probably that which saved his life as Reilly's second mighty blow was deflected by the bunk and caught him glancingly on the side of the head. Stunned and still trying to drag air into his paralysed lungs, he was only dimly aware of Kate's muffled scream as Reilly turned to her and pinned her back against the bunk.

Kate fought Reilly with a desperation born of despair. She got a knee against the man's stomach and pushed with all her strength while wrenching one hand free of his initial grip and making contact with his face. She felt her nails meet flesh and Reilly shouted in alarm, but he was heavy and determined and with his full weight bearing down on her he grabbed her free hand and pinned both her wrists together against the bunk while he fumbled with his free hand at her shirt.

The nightmare ended with a single word as Reilly's name cracked out across the caravan like a whiplash. Agarth stood in the doorway, white-faced with anger, and Reilly quickly scrambled to his feet, looking almost sheepish as he picked up his gun.

Agarth looked at Reilly with distaste.

'I thought I could trust you, you fool,' he said icily. He glanced at Sinclair, who was sitting on the floor now, his head between his knees, breathing heavily, and then at Kate, who still lay on the bunk, shaking with shock, trying ineffectually to rearrange her clothes.

'I told you their deaths have to look like an accident,' Agarth said, crossing to Sinclair and helping him impatiently on to the bunk beside Kate.

'A few bruises won't notice, the way they're going,' Reilly said.

'It depends on what sort of bruises,' Agarth came back angrily. 'Have you never heard of forensic evidence?'

Sinclair turned to Kate and helped her upright. She collapsed into his arms, sobbing quietly.

'Get that animal away from us, Agarth,' Sinclair said, barely able to control the rage he felt.

'My apologies, Mrs Weston,' Agarth said unexpectedly. 'I did not intend that sort of unpleasantness.'

Sinclair looked at him with contempt.

'You prefer a nice clean sort of murder, like Tom Carter's, is that it? Well, you know what they say about people who sup with the devil?'

Agarth did not reply. He turned back to Reilly and took the shotgun off him, training it steadily on Sinclair. He was calm again now, and his eyes were cold and totally devoid of expression.

'Tie them up,' he said to Reilly. 'And make sure you do it thoroughly. I don't want any more mistakes. Then I want you outside. They're having trouble getting the digger down to the stream.'

TWENTY

KATE WESTON and Alex Sinclair sat side by side on the caravan bunk, half slumped against the wall, with their hands firmly tied behind their backs. Both appeared lost in their own thoughts, and they were not happy ones. Sinclair's head throbbed where Reilly's gun butt had grazed the temple, leaving a dark red weal, and he found it difficult to think coherently. Kate's face was pale and tear-stained, and more than once she looked at Sinclair and appeared about to speak, but then turned away again, fighting fiercely to maintain her self-control.

'What is it, Kate?' he asked at last, her suppressed emotion eventually making itself apparent through the insistent pounding of his head. 'Is it Sam? He'll be OK. He'll turn up. He'd not been down the mine.'

'Oh, Alex,' she said. 'Alex, I'm so sorry. All this is my fault.'

He looked at her helplessly.

'Don't be silly,' he said. 'You've got nothing to blame yourself for. I'm the one who got it all wrong. I underestimated Agarth all along the line. I'd no idea he'd go this far.'

'No,' she said. 'You don't understand. Sam isn't missing, he's safe at home with your father. I made the whole thing up.'

'You did what?' he asked incredulously.

'When they said you were at the police station, I thought if I could get them to start searching the moor for someone it might provoke Agarth into doing something rash, coming out into the open. I thought it might help you. So I told the police Sam had run off, and I told Gordon Rangely that he'd found a way into the drift mines. Which

he did—when he ran off on Saturday in the rain, you remember. He told me about it afterwards. You said Rangely
was the link with Agarth, so I guessed if I put the idea into
his head it would get back and provoke Agarth into doing
something careless.'

'Dear God, it certainly did that,' Sinclair said quietly,
understanding now why Agarth had apparently inexplica-
bly come out into the open just at the point when his plans
appeared to have succeeded. 'You stirred it all up very suc-
cessfully.'

'I'm sorry, Alex,' Kate said again. 'I'd no idea it would
end up like this. They just stopped me in the street as I was
walking back to the flat and bundled me into a car. They
had a gun, but no one even noticed what was going on. It
was so quick...'

Sinclair attempted a smile which turned quickly into a
wince of pain as the effort cracked open the deep graze on
his forehead again.

'You couldn't have anticipated that,' he said. 'None of
us knew quite how quick and ruthless Agarth would turn
out to be when pushed.'

'What's he going to do with us?' Kate asked soberly.

'At a guess he's going to engineer an accident up on the
moor...' Sinclair stopped, suddenly aware of exactly the
accident which would ring true if it was believed that he and
Kate had continued to search for Sam on their own in the
dark on Broadley Top. Closing his eyes for a moment, he
saw again the body of the young girl lying among the rocks
at the foot of the crag above the village as clearly as if he
had found her yesterday, and he knew with a cold certainty that that was where their two bodies would be found
in the morning. As Reilly had said, a few extra bruises
would not notice, though, as Agarth must have realized, the
signs of rape might have led to awkward questions at the
inquest. His daughters would be able to visit the spot where
he died quite easily, he thought, momentarily on the edge
of panic himself.

'What is it?' Kate asked, looking at Sinclair anxiously. He shook his head and took a deep breath to steady himself.

'Nothing,' he said. 'I was just thinking.'

'Surely killing us won't get Agarth off the hook?' Kate said desperately.

'Oh, I'm not so sure. When you think how many people are in his pocket—Greaves at police headquarters, and Rangely, and the rest. When you think that I'll be even more firmly discredited dead than I am alive. And if the Beck really does run clean from tonight...he just might get away with it.'

'They won't believe it's an accident, will they? Bill and Annie won't believe it!'

'They may not believe it, but you can guarantee Agarth will make it look like the real thing.' Sinclair stopped. Annie and Bill, for all their determination, would, he was sure, be defeated by another tragedy, but that was one conclusion too much to share with Kate. Their only chance now, he thought, was to find a slender thread of hope.

'Listen to me, Kate. There may just possibly be one opportunity for us to get out of this. I don't know when. You can't anticipate it. But if you see a chance, take it and run like hell. And if I say run, don't think about it, don't even hesitate for a second, just go.'

She shuddered slightly.

'I can't help thinking about Sam,' she said quietly.

'Don't,' he said sharply, knowing very well where that led. 'Think about nothing but the job in hand—which is to find that one chance of getting away. Everything else can wait.' She nodded, annoyed with herself for not remembering that Sinclair had children too.

It was half an hour before Agarth and Reilly came back to the caravan for them. Agarth's usually calm demeanour had deteriorated into a sort of ragged tension and there were streaks of mud on his expensive overcoat. Reilly on the other hand seemed ebullient, as if he were looking forward to whatever was to come next. With the younger man standing by warily with his gun at the ready, Agarth waved the two prisoners out of the van ahead of him. Outside they could see that the digger had been manoeuvred into the deep gully where the stream dropped down into the mine entrance, and was still busily piling earth across the dip in the land. Other men were digging further down the hill close to the road, taking the dammed stream water away into another brook which Sinclair knew joined a tributary of the Maze not far from Broadley village.

After a few days' rain and wind, he guessed, the night's work would look like little more than a natural landslip which had followed the heavy rain. It would soon be almost invisible as the fast growing spring bracken and moorland grasses sprang up to cover the scars the workmen left behind. If anyone wondered about the changed course of the stream, they would put it down to natural causes.

'Up there,' Reilly indicated, pushing Sinclair roughly with his gun barrel towards a narrow path which led to the top of the moor. Sinclair did as he was told, although climbing the rocky footpath with hands still tied behind him was not easy. On his feet, he found that he still felt dazed and dizzy from the blow to the head, and he had to concentrate hard to keep his footing on the treacherously wet slope. Kate followed close behind and Agarth brought up the rear.

The darkness was relieved only by the glimmer of a small torch which Agarth used to illuminate the way. Several times Sinclair slipped on unseen boulders and patches of mud in the still gently falling rain. Each time Reilly prodded him upright again with his gun while Agarth kept a restraining hand on Kate Weston's bound wrists. Behind him Kate made similarly uncertain progress, guided by Agarth's steadying hand.

He did not need to spell out the threat which kept her plodding steadily upwards in Reilly's wake. She knew that if she tried to escape, the gun butt, if not the gun itself, would be used on Sinclair with even less mercy than the last time. She felt the rain running down her unprotected face and she was seized with a deep despair. Only think of getting away, Alex had said urgently, but she was sure that if she took any unexpected initiative now, Alex would be dead within seconds. And that was not all that held her back. In her mind's eye her son travelled every inch of the way up the steep hillside with her and she wept inside, not for herself, but for the boy. She knew that when it came to the point, she could not make him motherless of her own free will.

At length the path levelled out as they reached the top of the moor and felt the sharper edge of the wet wind which was sweeping across the Milford valley from the northwest. The fresher air revived Sinclair a little and he felt his mind move sluggishly back into gear. It was slightly lighter here, with the moon showing fitfully between the ragged edges of clouds as the rain came across the hill in squalls. Agarth waved the party to a halt and Kate moved close to Sinclair and stood with him shoulder to shoulder, facing the other two men.

'Reilly?' Agarth said. 'You know the best place?'

'Aye,' Reilly said, his voice edged with hysteria. 'The highest spot's over there.' He nodded towards the crest of Broadley Edge, where Sinclair had stood just days ago looking down at the village two hundred feet below.

'Where are we going?' Kate asked. Sinclair did not reply. He could not bring himself to tell her what he had guessed, and Reilly pushed him on again up towards the top of the moor without giving Kate a chance to repeat her question.

From the highest point on Broadley Edge Milford and its surrounding villages lay stretched out below in a panorama of winking lights, the roads looping across the valley like strings of beads, glittering and twinkling in the wind and rain. Agarth waved the party to a halt again and Kate gasped as she took in the steepness of the drop below them.

At that moment she also realized what Agarth intended and her mind became very sharp and clear. She was still conscious of her son's presence, but he seemed to be standing well back from her now, stretching himself up to his full height as he did when he wanted to prove how close he was to out-reaching her these days, and willing her to escape. She remembered what Sinclair had said about seizing a chance when it came and realized, as Sinclair had already done, that the opportunity must come in seconds now if it was to come at all. Otherwise that glittering view from the moor's edge would be their last.

Agarth held her arm firmly and nodded to Reilly, who put his gun down and took a pocket-knife to the ropes which held Sinclair's hands behind him. It had clearly been decided already that Alex Sinclair was to go over the edge first and that their hands must be untied before the execution.

Sinclair stood very close to the lip of the cliff, looking down at the village. A car was passing along the darkened main street lighting up the neat cottages and the school which he knew so well. He thought of Jenny and Sally, thankful that they were a thousand miles away and aghast that the thought of deliberately taking that drop had ever crossed his mind.

He gritted his teeth and braced himself to resist the sudden push from behind which he knew was intended to send him out into the void but Reilly was having trouble with the ropes, and was sawing increasingly frantically with his knife. Sinclair knew that there was no choice now about when to resist. It was now or never. The last strand gave way and for a split second he was free of Reilly's grip.

In the same instant, a muffled explosion beneath them made the ground tremble, startling them all, and further down the hill, towards Highcliffe, a vivid red tongue of flame leapt out of the hillside into the night air, illuminating the main pathway down to the estate and the town beyond. Agarth cursed and Reilly let out a whistle of surprise at the force of the explosion.

The moment was enough. Sinclair spun round and caught the bigger man off balance making him stagger dangerously near the edge of the cliff and cry out in alarm. At the same moment, Kate kicked her heel viciously backwards, catching Agarth sharply on the shin. As he cried out in surprised outrage and staggered she pulled her own bound hands free from his restraining grip.

'Run, Kate, run!' Sinclair yelled and, ignoring his own advice, he waited to make sure she was ahead of him before dashing after her up the slight slope and away from the menacing edge of the cliff.

'Catch them,' Agarth screamed, and within a minute Reilly had found his balance, retrieved his gun and set off in pursuit.

They ran for their lives. With her hands still tied behind her, Kate made awkward progress over the wet and slippery grass and heather and Sinclair took her arm and half pulled, half dragged her upwards. They could hear Reilly stumbling behind them as they scrambled over boulders and barked their shins on unseen outcrops of rock, keeping just ahead of their pursuer.

They heard Agarth quite clearly when he screamed at Reilly to shoot. The first shot followed quickly but the pellets whistled harmlessly overhead. The second came as they reached the ridge at the top of the moor. Kate was thrown forward by what felt like a tremendous blow and she knew she had been hit. Alex was there at once, lifting her to her feet and taking her weight, urging her on. There was no pain, only a tremendous weariness which took away all her will to continue their headlong flight. Then all at once there were figures ahead as well as behind, looming out of the darkness in the deep shadow beyond the crest of the moor.

Kate fell forward helplessly on to the rough heather, free of Sinclair's supporting arm as he twisted desperately to dodge the outstretched hands of the men who were waiting for them. She was conscious of shouts and a flurry of fists nearby as she slumped to the ground before strong hands seized her and the first wave of pain hit her arms and back as she was pulled upright and carried helplessly away. Her last feeling as she lapsed into unconsciousness was an overwhelming sadness that they had come so close to winning, and yet had failed. Sam would be alone now, she thought, as the darkness engulfed her.

KATE WESTON LEANED against the pillows in her hospital bed with Sam close by her side reading a book. The painkillers that had kept her drifting in and out of an uneasy sleep for days after the shotgun pellets had been dug one by one from her lacerated back and arms were beginning to relinquish their hold on her mind now. But she looked deathly pale, with dark rings under her eyes and still visible bruises on her face and cuts and scratches on her hands, evidence of that desperate flight on the moor.

Every now and then Sam looked up from his reading and caught her eye. She knew he was very aware of how close he had come to losing her: there was a new insecurity in his blue eyes which grieved her. He had shown little curiosity about what had happened on Broadley Moor and although Kate had told him more than once that Alex Sinclair had saved her life, his only response had been to nod non-committally and return to his book, although she suspected that he was doing less reading than he pretended.

'Good book?' she asked softly, and he nodded and managed a wan smile.

'Do you want a grape?' he asked, pulling a stalk from the bunch on the bedside locker. She shook her head.

'You eat them,' she said.

She had seen Alex Sinclair only once since she had wakened up in Milford Infirmary's casualty department, and had been too drugged to take in much of what he had told her. All she really knew was that the men who had apparently ambushed them at the top of Broadley Moor had not been Agarth's men but a squad of police, alerted by Sergeant Wilson and hoping to rescue not to capture them.

Sinclair came again that afternoon. He came into the ward almost tentatively, holding a bunch of flowers in front of him like a peace offering. Kate's eyes lit up as he approached down the ward though she was aware that Sam was watching her stony-faced.

'You're feeling better?' Sinclair asked, taking her hand and brushing her cheek gently with a kiss. She nodded, not daring to speak for a moment. Then she looked deliberately at the boy and back to Sinclair.

'I'm so pleased to see you,' she said softly, some of the strain smoothed away from her face simply by his appearance. Sam turned away and buried his head in his book again silently. Kate shrugged slightly and motioned Sinclair into the visitor's chair by the bed and for a moment simply took in his presence. The haggard, near-desperate figure who had dragged her across the moor for her life just a few days previously had all but disappeared. In his place was the same quiet man who had first attracted her longer ago than she could now remember, a touch more tired, still bruised around the head and perhaps less quick to smile, but essentially the same. It seemed like a lifetime.

'Is it all over?' Kate asked, and Sinclair nodded.

'As good as,' he said, and told her all that had happened since they had been so unexpectedly picked up by Dave Wilson and his hastily assembled squad of officers. Agarth and Reilly had been arrested there and then on the moor, and charged with abduction and attempted murder the same night, Sinclair said. There had been enough police witnesses to that for them to be able to offer little in the way of defence.

Further arrests had followed the next day and it had not been long before some of those involved in the conspiracy, safe in the knowledge that Agarth was in custody and likely to stay there for a long time, had begun to talk to try to save their own skins. The final account would include a charge of murdering Tom Carter against Terry Reilly and conspiracy charges against Agarth, the reporter Rangely, the pollution officer Wright and the manager of the County Bank where Sinclair had allegedly opened an illicit account.

The mystery of the pollution had also been cleared up at a stroke by Agarth's own explosion. A miscalculation with the explosive had opened up the drifts and exposed the flooded tunnel for all to see. The lethal cocktail of chemicals was still being pumped out, Sinclair said, at Agarth and Bradley's expense. The records of the waste disposal company the firm had run in the 1950s had shown that industrial waste had been dumped into the mine from all over the North of England. The southern construction company which had been trying to buy Agarth out had suddenly, and only too explicably, lost interest. Even after he had served his sentence, James Agarth would not be the millionaire he had hoped to be.

'And you're back on duty?' Kate asked, knowing that that meant more to Sinclair than all the rest. He nodded, unsmiling.

'That nightmare's over too, thank God,' he said. 'My father and my father-in-law both feel, in their own way, that they've been vindicated. As for me, I'm not sure what I feel about the job any more.'

'Not everyone believed you were corrupt,' she said quietly.

'No. But some did, and I'll never be sure who did and who didn't, will I? And then there's Eddie Greaves,' he added grimly.

'He was definitely involved?'

'Oh yes. He let me go on Monday night because Agarth asked him to, basically. It's not clear yet how far he was involved in the Carter murder, how much he knew that could have let Joey off the hook. He was certainly ready to do a favour for his brother Agarth whenever he was asked, even to the extent of sending me down for corruption. I'd guess he leapt on Joey as a convenient—and helpless—scapegoat that night I arrested him and he questioned him and played it by ear from there. He must have been absolutely delighted to get that confession from poor Joey.

'But in the end that decision to let me go was so odd that when I disappeared up on to the moor, Dave Wilson went to Superintendent Swallow in the next division to get help. He didn't go back to Greaves. And thankfully Swallow believed him and didn't stand on protocol. He decided to act himself. If anything saved our lives, it was that: two old-style coppers who generally do it all by the book—and just for once didn't.'

They sat in silence for a moment as Kate absorbed what Sinclair had told her. He looked older, she thought. Neither of them would remain unmarked by what had happened, and nor would Sam.

'And your girls? How are they?' Kate asked quietly at last.

'They're fine. I spoke to them on the phone yesterday. They're coming home at the weekend and I'll see them then. I think my father-in-law has been talking to Margaret. She seems to have softened her line somewhat.' He hesitated and half smiled.

'I won't be going back, Kate,' he said. 'We're both clear about that.'

It was what she wanted to hear and she took his hand and looked across the white hospital counterpane at her son, whose head was still bent determinedly over his book, though she was sure he had been listening to every word they had been saying.

'Sam,' she said. The boy looked up, and they saw that there were unshed tears in his eyes. She took his hand too.

'Sam, do something for me, love,' Kate said. The boy nodded, watching her intently.

'When you go home will you show Alex your Hornby engine? He'd like to buy you a carriage to go with it.' For a long moment Sam did not reply but at last he looked at Alex and smiled uncertainly.

'All right,' he said.

LOVE BYTES
SALLY CHAPMAN

First Time In Paperback

A Silicon Valley Mystery

USER UNFRIENDLY

Trading her high-tech, high-stress Silicon Valley career for her own computer fraud investigations agency, Julie Blake embarks on her first case: the disappearance of Arnie Lufkin, a renegade programming genius and suspected embezzler.

Julie and her partner/lover, Vic Paoli, have barely agreed to take the case when her system is broken into and a threatening message left on her screen. Scared, but with creditors snapping at her heels, Julie decides to dig deeper.

A foray into virtual reality proves that the missing Lufkin is not only a brilliant man, but a dangerous, egocentric manipulator. Wherever he is, Lufkin is playing deadly games, making murder a reality.

"[Chapman's] books are not only *diverting,* they are lucid."
—*Oakland Tribune*

Available in April at your favorite retail stores.

WORLDWIDE LIBRARY®

BYTES

First Time in Paperback

LYNN BRADLEY
A Cole January Mystery

STRANGE BEDFELLOWS

It all began when a very hung over Cole January stepped out of a warm bed and onto a stone-cold corpse—a beautiful blonde in a slinky number that would have done his male ego proud if she'd had a pulse.

She is identified as Molly Jones-Heitkamp. That is, until the real and remarkably alive Ms. Jones-Heitkamp asks January to find out who's trying to kill her. So who's the gorgeous stiff? And who's trying to frame Cole?

The answers take him to Houston's mayorality race, as well as the dirty laundry of some prominent citizens. Cole begins to wish he'd stuck to insurance fraud, because murder was becoming bad for his health.

"Will please mystery lovers."   —*Abilene Reporter-News*

Available in April at your favorite retail stores.

WORLDWIDE LIBRARY®   STANDS

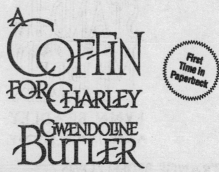

A COFFIN FOR CHARLEY

First Time in Paperback

GWENDOLINE BUTLER

An Inspector John Coffin Mystery

IT'S HOT...AND GETTING HOTTER FOR COMMANDER JOHN COFFIN

His wife, actress Stella Pinero, is being stalked. Adding to his worries, London's Second City is terrified by a cunning and inventive serial killer. Coffin has cast a wide net, but the killer is elusive...and continuing to kill.

Somehow connected is a murder that occurred twenty years before. A young girl had witnessed the crime and testified. Now the killers are free and returning home, possibly for revenge. When Coffin's niece turns up missing, he fears the worst—pushing himself and his force into London's darkest underbelly to match skill and cunning with crime's cleverest own....

"Butler excels..."   —*Publishers Weekly*

Available in May at your favorite retail stores.

 WORLDWIDE LIBRARY®

CHARLEY

GRIZZLY

(First Time in Paperback)

CHRISTINE ANDREAE

A Lee Squires Mystery

FAIR GAME

English professor Lee Squires is spending Easter break in
Montana as cook for the J-E dude ranch, where friend and
owner Dave Fife is hoping that some Japanese investors—
plied with home cooking—will pour cash into the
struggling J-E.

Lee has come ready to whip up hotcakes, biscuits and
chicken fried steak—but not to wrestle her libido over Dave's
brother, Mac, a tireless bear activist...or to find a dead body
with missing parts.

Another mangled body later, officials are hunting a bear.
Lee doesn't buy the theory—but in tracking the truth, she
comes face-to-face with a human killer who is nothing
short of...grizzly.

**"Good character interaction, great sense of place, and
steady suspense."** —*Library Journal*

Available in May at your favorite retail stores.

To order your copy, please send your name, address, zip or postal code along with a
check or money order (please do not send cash) for $4.99 for each book ordered
($5.99 in Canada), plus 75¢ postage and handling ($1.00 in Canada), payable to
Worldwide Mystery, to:

In the U.S.	In Canada
Worldwide Mystery	Worldwide Mystery
3010 Walden Avenue	P.O. Box 609
P.O. Box 1325	Fort Erie, Ontario
Buffalo, NY 14269-1325	L2A 5X3

Please specify book title with your order.
Canadian residents add applicable federal and provincial taxes.

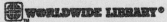 **WORLDWIDE LIBRARY®**

GRIZZLY

DARK SWAN

KATHRYN LASKY KNIGHT
A Calista Jacobs Mystery

THE RICH ARE DIFFERENT

Children's book illustrator Calista Jacobs is house-sitting in posh Beacon Hill and gets a peek into the world of wealth and privilege of the old-guard Boston Brahmins when she befriends neighbor Queenie Kingsley.

Unfortunately, Calista is also the one who discovers Queenie's lifeless body, a pair of garden shears protruding from her heart. Certain she can stand up to women called Bootsie and Titty, she enlists the aid of her teenage son, Charley, and Queenie's colorful brother-in-law, Rudy, and ventures behind the family's polished exterior.

And what she discovers are the ugly, dark secrets steeped in tradition…secrets worth killing for.

"Well-plotted…"   *—Booklist*

Available in June at your favorite retail stores.

 WORLDWIDE LIBRARY®

SWAN